Angel Cry

by Heather Spraga
edited by Michael Marcus

(c) 2009 Heather J. Spraga
Second Edition Printing

Cover Concept by Michael Marcus

All Rights Reserved.

ISBN 0-9840818-1-X

All rights reserved except for use in a review. The
reproduction or utilization of this work in whole or
in part in any form by electronic, mechanical, or other
means without prior written permission by the author
or copyright holder of this novel is forbidden by law.
If this book was purchased without a cover, you should
be aware that this book is stolen property. It was
reported "unsold and destroyed" to the publisher, and
the author received no payment for this stripped book.

Publisher's information:
Hamtramck Idea Men, P.O. Box 12097,
Hamtramck, Michigan 48212
http://idea-men.us

Angel Cry

Table of Contents

I0552922

It is said that everyone is put on this Earth for a purpose. I didn't believe that I had a reason to live. I wondered if I should exist. From a young age, others discouraged me from living. At times, it seemed as though others feared me. I never understood why, until I learned who I was.

"Hope! Come on!" I still hear my friends calling to me. Memories flood my mind of the past. I keep following my friends higher and higher up the hill, through the trees. I am so young, just ten years old. They lure me up there, pretending to be my friends. They tell me there is this cool view of the town at the drop off point. I believe they are my friends; I trust them. I stand on the ledge, seeing the colors of dusk sky, orange fading into red. It is so beautiful. As I gaze at the sight, I feel lighter. I'm not standing on solid ground anymore--someone just pushed me. As I fall, I hear laughter above and scornful words,

"Die, Witch!"

The voices started to blur together and I heard a single voice speaking. I looked up from the table. I couldn't believe it! I fell asleep in class! When I looked at the clock, it was approaching nine-thirty. Class was almost over. The professor still droned on. Would this class ever end? In the next long moment, he finally stopped babbling and class was over.

Walking outside in the cool night air, I felt better. It was so hot in that classroom. The only sounds around were the whistling wind and some college frat boys talking about getting wasted after class.

"Yeah man, I'm getting messed up tonight!" I heard one guy shout to no one in particular. Somehow, I felt lost in this world. Everyone else went to parties and got drunk. I turned twenty a few months ago so I couldn't drink legally. But that didn't stop others who were not the legal age yet. Some people have been drinking since they were fourteen. It was hard to blame them. There was nothing much to do in a town like Fallen Ridge but get drunk.

I felt tired as I walked past the rectangular fountain standing in the middle of the campus. There were a few others walking towards the same direction. The parking structure was straight ahead and I wanted to be in my warm bed. It was strange, I wanted to sleep, but there were some who were just waking up at this time. As I moved on I felt the wind pick up. I kept moving, not caring about anything but getting to my car.

"Hope!" the voice called.

I turned around, but didn't see anyone. Maybe I imagined it. I started walking.

"Hope!" the voice was more dramatic.

I jumped around at the voice. I didn't see anyone. As I turned back, I felt someone touch my shoulder. I gasped pushing the hand away. A woman stood there. Her dark red hair was half done in tiny braids; one long strain of hair covered part of her face. Other than her hair, I noticed she was really tall, much taller than me or anyone else I knew. I felt pierced by her vibrant aqua colored eyes.

"I found you finally!" she exploded.

"Do I know you?" I asked trying to recall her face.

"Not yet. I am Aria," she introduced herself. "I am so happy I found you, you have no idea how long I've been searching for you!" she went on. Her eagerness was a bit too much. I just stood there staring at her, not sure how to respond.

"I want to help you find your path," she said.

I had no idea what she meant. "I don't understand," I admitted.

"You feel different from others, like you don't belong," she kept talking.

Now she started to scare me.

"You are a timid person, unsure of yourself," she said. Now she was just staring at me. "You have very stunning eyes," she remarked. "They're silver." I didn't expect the compliment. My light colored eyes were a contrast with my dark hair. I thought I looked strange to other people.

"Uh...thank you," I responded not knowing what else to say.

"Come with me. You will understand everything," she said with a definite tone.

Go with her? I didn't know who she was. And she wasn't giving me any reason to trust her. She acted like she knew me, but I knew I'd never seen her before. I just needed to go home.

4

"I'm sorry, I have to go," I said quickly and began walking away.

"Don't make this hard, Hope!" she yelled angrily.

I didn't turn back. My feet moved faster and now I began to feel dizzy. Something flashed through my mind. The visions were so fast. I saw people in pain. They were in some desolate place with horrifying creatures everywhere. I heard terrible moans of pain and suffering. Why was I seeing this? I felt sick. My vision blurred.

"Stop!" I screamed out. I heard the echo of my own voice. Everything was still now. Aria was gone and I was left alone. The warm air was now a very chilling breeze. I thought I saw my breath. Something was wrong. The campus looked different. The whole atmosphere felt dead. The trees were covered in full leaf a moment ago, now they were bare as if it were winter. I hurried to the parking lot. I saw it up ahead. As I approached, flames suddenly shot up from the ground to the sky high above me! Was I just seeing things? There was no way around this obstacle.

"What's going on?!?" I cried out. No one was around to hear me. Would that woman know what's happening. She seemed to know enough about me. I had to find her. That woman, Aria. I felt that she was the only one that could answer my questions.

I ran towards the fountain spaced in the center of the four academic buildings of the campus. I noticed that the fountain wasn't working. The inside of the pool was cracked; a big crack split down the center of the cement.

There had to be people somewhere on this campus. I last saw people in class. I ran as fast as I could back the classroom. Through the front door of the building and up the stairs to the second floor, my book bag weighed on my shoulders. Dim light filed the hallway with flickering florescent lights. Everyone had left. The classroom door was locked and dark. I felt panic leave me a little when I saw light flowing out from my professor's office. The office floor was cluttered with papers. And folders. Not the most organized man. At first, I was relieved to see him sitting at his desk. I sighed, feeling some tension leave my body.

"Mr. Takoto, I'm glad you're still here!" There was no response. Maybe he didn't hear me. I moved towards his desk chair.

"Mr. Takoto? Are you all right?" I peered around the chair. When I saw his face, I stumbled back in horror. No. This wasn't real, it couldn't be! His face! His hands! Every part of his skin was severely burned. *What happened? This can't be real! It has to be some kind of bad dream, right?* I tried to make some sense of the situation, but I couldn't. I tried to run, but instead stumbled blindly out of the room. I felt dazed, they hallway swayed in front of me. I ran down the hall towards the bathrooms. Maybe someone was in there. Inside the ladies' room, I found the floor cluttered with paper towels. I turned the handle on one of the sinks expecting fresh water to emerge from the faucet. But nothing came out. My face felt so hot, I wanted to splash cold water on myself. At that point I looked up at the mirror. It was red, like blood. The message was scrawled out.

Where is your god now?

It was bad enough that it looked like blood, but I always thought the word God should be capitalized and in this message, it was not. There might have been a reason why the g wasn't capitalized, but right now I didn't care! I was going crazy! I felt so sick and there was no relief for this aliment.

I left the bathroom and saw the men's bathroom across the hall. Under any normal circumstances, I would not think of entering, but right now I was desperate to find a living person. I entered slowly.

"Hello?" I called out.

I was afraid to check the mirrors, but my eyes looked at them anyways. Nothing was written on these mirrors. The place was a mess just like the other bathroom. One of the stalls was closed. I knocked on the door. Maybe someone would answer. But no one did. Suddenly, I heard a clunk as if something hit the stall door. The door fell right off the hinges and would have fallen onto my feet if I didn't quickly jump back. The occupant in the stall collapsed onto the floor. From where I stood, I could see he was dead. I wanted to scream, but couldn't. Only a slight gasp came out. Who did all of this? Why? Maybe Aria?

Once again I ran down the hallway. My mind raced about the happening events. Why is everyone dead?! I was sweating now. Driven only by adrenaline, I ran down the hallway. As I ran, a shadowy figure walked through the doors to the stairwell. Who was that? I was anxious to find out and also a little afraid.

At the end of the hall was an open door that was closed the first time I passed it. A steel pipe leaned against a shelf. I may have lost my mind, but in this alternate reality things were not right. I had to defend myself from whatever killed my instructor and that other guy. Taking the pipe, I headed towards the stairs. I practically tripped, my mind working faster than my feet.

Outside, there were still no signs of life. I adjusted my book bag on my shoulders before making my way back towards the fountain. This time there was something on the border of the fountain… blood. It covered a metal plate implanted into the brick rim. It hurt my head to look at it. I felt like I was in such a daze; it felt so unreal. My muscles felt so tired and I wanted to rest, but I knew I couldn't. I moved forward and bumped something with my foot. I looked down to see someone laying prone. Instinctively, I bent down to see what was wrong. It looked like a girl; her dark hair covered her face. She was dead too. I nudged her shoulder just to make sure. She didn't respond. I pushed over her body and sighed with disheartenment. Her skin was burnt just like my professor's. How many would I find this way? At that moment, my question was answered as an eerie light showed many more bodies laying head to toe in a line. They were all the same; burnt skin. The stream of corpses circled the fountain. The girl's hair fell away from her face. Her face was burnt and scarred; her eyes stared blankly into the sky. I couldn't stand this! I didn't want to see it anymore! I tried to ignore the presence of the ugly, bloated corpse to see the gold plate stuck in the brick. The blood dripped off into the cracks of the fountain. There were words carved into the plate.

Enter a different world,
A place that reveals another reality,
God becomes the Devil;
The Devil becomes God.

Something moved. I became paralyzed, not able to take my eyes off the red substance now filling the fountain pool. It came up out of the crevice and filled all of the cracks in the fountain pool. The entire pool filled up with crimson blood. Now I felt terribly sick. Why? Why was this happening to me?!

More bodies filled the interior of the fountain. I think my mind had said, 'too much' and shut down. All I saw was blackness for a moment. Then light flashed my way. One single stream of light led from the fountain to an old castle. The campus was gone. There was nowhere to go, but to a new destination I was not ready to see.

Chapter Two:
Fallen Sanctuary

So now that I'd completely lost my mind, I headed towards the castle that just appeared out of nowhere. Up the swerving path ahead was the entrance of this forbidding fortress. It was not one of those traditional castles with a drawbridge and a moat circling it. The fortress was built in stone; the doors were decorated with Celtic décor. Looking up at the sky, there was just one big dark cloud looming over the place. Life did not exist here. No green leaves or green grass existed at all. The door had a knocker, and I might have used it if I wasn't concerned about awakening the content within this place. I still held the metal pipe I found earlier in one hand, and pulled the heavy door with the other. The weight of the door was too much for one arm. I thought that I could get away with putting the pipe on the ground for a moment, so I did. It was so quiet that the sound of the pipe hitting the pavement was loud enough to startle me. Then, I took off my backpack, giving relief to my shoulders. I looked up at the gigantic door. As I pulled on the door with two hands with all my arm strength, I heard footsteps behind me. I turned in time to see someone staggering towards me. It was a man, moaning as if in pain.

"Are you all right?" I asked as I ran up to him. He lifted his head and I saw the burnt skin on his face. He suddenly flung his arms at me. I kept moving back until I backed into the door. I had no idea what to do, but I realized I had that pipe. Picking it up, I raised it above my head ready to strike the abomination.

"wWhy?" It tried to form words. "wWhyiS thiS h-HAppenING?! Don'T UnDerSTanD! H-Help m-MeEE!" It spoke grabbing its head, still staggering about.

Was this thing a person? I had to force myself to look at this creature. I remembered seeing him before, sitting in a chair with his head hung down. I couldn't believe it. My professor from the university now stood in front of me as this undead figure.

"Mr. Takoto? You are stuck in this nightmare too!"

He came at me, his hands grabbed my neck, he started to choke me. I pulled his hands off of me. He was actually very weak. I took the pipe and just started swinging. I hit the side of his head several times. Each time, he flinched. But he kept coming at me no matter how many times I struck him. He stopped moving and I stopped swinging. His expression changed. His eyes dropped down as if he was sad. He moaned loudly and I had to cover my ears from the painful sound. I wanted to do something to end his suffering. I struck him again and again until he fell. Not only was the skin on his face burnt, but the skin on his arms too. All of his skin was burnt, I bet. Who or what burned him? Part of me wanted to know and part of me was afraid to know.

I had to get away from here. The doors were ahead of me. I put down the pipe and pulled with all my effort. The door opened just enough for me to squeeze through. There was a faint light illuminating the room from the lit torches on the walls. My eyes adjusted so that I could see. Around the atrium were statues of knights in armor. A staircase was ahead of me, red velvet carpeting covered the steps. Halfway up the stairs I realized I forgot my bag… and the pipe! I hurried back down to the front door. It wouldn't open. A large wood plank bolted the doors. How did this get here? I studied the piece of wood for a moment. I know I'm not the strongest person, but I thought I at least could move this stupid thing! It wouldn't budge. In frustration, I kicked the door, creating a thunderous 'boom' echoing through the hallway. The sound was startling. I looked around feeling nervous that someone or something might have heard me.

I finally decided that I was better off without the excess weight anyways. I returned to the stairs. To the right led nowhere so I turned left once I reached the top. I walked into an old style kitchen. The largest pot I've ever seen sat in the center of the room. It was large enough that me and several other people could fit in it. Curiosity overwhelmed me. I had to see if anything was in that pot. The smell was repulsive. It made my stomach sink. I couldn't identify what the stuff in there was. It almost looked liked cooked flesh. No! Not going to think about that!

I left that room and continued down the hallway. Another stairway stood at the end, this one was a black metal staircase that spiraled up to the next floor. Moving upwards, I soon reached the top where there was an enormous timber door. I pushed down on the brass handle. On the other side was a library, shelves upon shelves of books lined the walls. My attention was drawn to the back wall where two fancy twin swords hung on a gold plaque. I had this overwhelming urge to take them. I was not a thief, but these blades just called to me. The blades were curved in an S-shape. The silver hilts gleamed and each hilt had a decorative wing attached to it. Whether they were wings of a large bird or maybe of a mystical beast like a dragon, I couldn't say. They might even be wings from an angel. It didn't take me long to grab the swords and hold them in my hands. I felt strong just holding them. I started to walk back to the door. Suddenly, the weapons were torn away from my grip by some unknown force. They floated in front of me. My eyes became entranced by them floating there.

Suddenly, they flew at me. I had no time to react. The long blades struck the palms of my hands! I don't remember crying out in pain or anything. When I looked at my hand, the blades pierced the skin all the way through! Then I heard a crisp voice speak.

"The chosen is found."

I looked at the swords stuck in my hands. I was able to pull them out. Don't ask me how! Then the blood faded into my skin and the punctures themselves were healed! I didn't know what just happened, but I was still alive and that was good enough!

After that horrendous incident, a book fell out of the bookshelf next to me. *Now what?* I wondered. I picked it up. The book had a hard, leather bound cover. When I opened it, something fell out. I heard a clinking sound as something metal hit the floor. I looked down to see a key. Picking it up, I studied its unique shape and design. It looked like an old fashioned key used to unlock broom closets or something of that nature. The book was more of an interest to me right now. There were words scribbled out on the first page.

> *We were made beautiful. We were given great power. He made us bow to lesser beings. He will pay! God will pay! So, we stood against God. We were powerful. But God threw us down to Earth to suffer with the wretched mankind.*

That was it. There was nothing else written. Something bothered me about this passage. It sounded like the passage talked about the angels that fought against God and fell from heaven. It seemed as if one of the fallen angels did write this. That was impossible!

11

An angelic being wouldn't write this and then put it in this library. My head would start to hurt as I figured this one out. What was even stranger was that this was the only thing I was able to read in English. All the other book titles were written in a foreign language.

There was nothing else in this room. As I turned to leave, shrill laughter came from behind me. Three women appeared by the plaque. I looked down at the swords I recently stole

I knew I shouldn't have taken them!

These were some interesting women. They wore Gothic style dresses, black with red trimming. Their long white hair flowed down their backs. From a distance they might appear beautiful, but they were definitely monsters. Their mouths showed pointed teeth, and their deep reddish eyes gleamed. They reminded me of vampires. I didn't know how to use these swords, but I was going to have to learn quickly.

One of the fiends rushed at me from the side. I instinctively pushed her away, causing her to fall into the bookshelf. I suddenly became strong. I couldn't lift that piece of wood off that barred the front door, but I could suddenly fight supernatural beings. Suddenly, another one attacked with a frontal assault. She swiped with her long claws. I swung down and stabbed her with one blade. It was stuck in her arm and she screeched in pain. As I pulled the sword out of her, there wasn't any blood, the blade glowed red. By her response, I must have hurt her.

My body acted on its own as I stabbed her in the chest. In the next moment, she turned to dust. I spun around, stabbing another one turning her to dust too. Now I had one left. The last one dove at me from behind. As she grabbed me, I somehow threw her over my shoulder. She landed on the floor and I finished her with one fatal stab wound. That was so weird. I acted as though I fought with these weapons my whole life! What was even weirder was the weapons themselves disappeared.

"Hold on! I need you!" I cried out. But the swords didn't return.

Now that the women were gone, I could take a closer look at the plaque they came out of. There was a small hole in the middle of the plaque. It might be a key hole, I had a key. Inserting the key and turning it made the wall move to reveal a spiraling staircase leading downward. It seemed endless. Lanterns lined the walls, lighting the way down. I moved on until I reached the bottom. Another large door stood in front of me. Through it was a room with many odd devices. One metal device looked like it framed a body; spikes came out from all sides. I knew what it was called, an Iron Maiden, used in medieval times. From where I stood, I saw pieces of flesh handing from the spikes. There was blood too and it didn't look dry! I had to get out of here!

Hooks hung from the walls covered in blood, as were knives and other instruments on the tables. Three tables stood parallel to each other. I refused to imagine their use. The scent of death surrounded me.

On the center table was a piece of paper. The sketch marks of a pen made an effort to form words.

Fallen Angels... Offspring… Nephilim.

My head hurt too much to try and figure it out. There was no other way out except the way I came. I turned to the stairs, just as bars slammed down to block my path. The deafening sound of the bars crashing was followed by a deadly silence. I suddenly was a captive here!

Looking around the room, I noticed a hole in the far wall, under the table. I didn't think twice about using it. I ran over and starting crawling through the dark hole. I didn't know where it would lead, but it had to be better than this room. I wasn't claustrophobic so the cramped space didn't bother me. It was completely dark in this small tunnel. Finally, I climbed out into yet another room. This looked like a storage room. It was just an ordinary room; nothing looked out of the ordinary here. There were many large chests, but I couldn't open any of them. After trying a few, I gave up and turned towards a door.

I was in another long hallway. I didn't get too far down it when I heard more high pitched laughter. More of those vampire women were charging at me from the other end of the hall. As I wished for those swords, my hands held them again. I wasn't going to complain. These things felt attached to me somehow. One strike after another, each opponent became dust. The sound of the screeches these inhuman beings made were embedded into my mind.

I struck down the last one and silence returned. The air was so thick that I started having problems breathing. The environment was getting more intense. I hurried down the end of the hallway where a gigantic room stood before me. I've never seen anything like this before. The door was open a sliver just wide enough for me to pass. This room was hideous. The interior was stone; there were no windows. Actually there weren't any windows in this whole place. The room was so big that I couldn't see to the other side, it looked dreary like a dungeon or something. These enormous tables were spread throughout the room. When I took a closer look, they appeared to be beds, huge metal beds. Reason I knew that was because an outside frame went around the perimeter and a tarp covered it. The legs were metal spikes stuck in the concrete floor. These beds were so large, who slept in them? I didn't want to see those creatures.

Continuing on, I came to a room with big chandeliers hanging on the ceiling in a straight line. Jewels were encrusted into the gold chains. The chandelier glistened even though there wasn't any light coming into the room. I guess they glistened off the light of the torches. This room was a complete contrast to the rest of this place. The white marble floor was so elegant and the silver and gold statues of angels lining the walls gave the place a peaceful feeling. I came to another stairway. How many floors did this place have? These steps were covered in blue velvet carpeting.

Yet another door stood before me. This one had to be the easiest door I opened. Its weight seemed like a feather compared to the heavy doors I pulled open. Now I stood in a small circular room. Nothing was in here. Did I do this for nothing? I was so tired, and annoyed by all of this! I turned back to the door just in time for it to shut and lock me inside! I pulled on the wooden knob, making no headway in opening it.

Suddenly, I felt a presence behind me. A voice spoke, sounding as if it came from my own mind.

"All will pay for their sins!"

I turned to see someone covered in a long white cloak. A radiant glow emanated from the figure. I couldn't see his face. He held a long staff. The ceiling opened showing the thick clouds. I heard thunder, and lightning struck the top of the staff. It glowed now as he held it above his head. Then, I heard the words repeated from my dream.

"Die, Witch!" I heard the voices combined. There was another ear piercing sound. Something struck the cloaked figure. The lightning shot past me, hitting the wall. The cloak fell to the floor empty and lifeless.

"What happened?" I asked aloud.

A figure dropped down to the floor. Someone else now stood in front of me. I stared at a young man, tall and somewhat muscular. His white hair fell into his bluish-green eyes. He wore common clothes, a black t-shirt with jeans. His hand held a pair of smoking hand guns. He eyed me suspiciously. Finally he spoke,

"Having problems?" he asked as casually as you would say 'hi' to a friend.

"Where did you come from?" I looked down at the empty cloak. "Did you do that?" I asked even though the answer was blatantly obvious.

"Yeah," he answered, proudly showing his weapons of mass destruction. "Don't ask me how I know how to use these things; they just sort of came alive," he said.

"You dropped down from the ceiling?" I asked. He nodded.

"How did you get up there?" I asked even if it sounded like a dumb question.

"I climbed up to the ceiling's support beams from some boxes on the floor. After running into some weird creatures, I thought I should give myself a better advantage by watching from up there. I guess you never know what you're going to find in a place like this," he said with a slight smile.

"What boxes?" I asked. There was nothing in this room. He turned to look and then back a time. His lips pressed together in an expression of being puzzled.

"Well, they were in here earlier. Um…oh, I'm Damon by the way," he introduced himself.

"Uh, hi… my name is Hope," I said feeling awkward. Being in this place didn't help with good introductions. "So, how do we get out of here?" I asked.

He went to open the door, ignoring my question. I thought the door was still locked, but it obviously wasn't. He started walking and I raced to keep up with him. I followed him down the stairs, wondering if he was intentionally ignoring me. Suddenly, the place shook like an earthquake. We both fell off balance and I had an embarrassing encounter as I fell on top of him!

"Oh, are you all right?" Damon asked.

"Uh, yeah," I answered standing back up, regaining my composure.

"Don't know what that was," he admitted.

He began walking again and I followed closely. Did he know where was he going? We walked through the room of chandeliers, and continued down the hallway. He walked so fast.

"Hey! Hold on!" I shouted after him. He didn't seem to hear me. I started running to keep up. As I ran, I saw a light shining ahead where Damon was. It grew, engulfing him and soon, me.

"Damon, where are you?" I called. He didn't respond.

No! I don't want to be alone again!

"Damon!" I yelled as loud as I could.

The light faded. I saw the night sky above and trees covered with their usual green leaves, and a fountain with running water. Did I black out? The trees and grass were filled with life, and the fountain was running again like usual, reflecting multiple colors from the lights in the pool. I found myself on the ground. Getting up, I quickly looked around. Now I was really confused. I was back on campus; everything looked normal. Maybe I dreamed everything? Even stranger, my book bag was on the ground beside me. I just needed to go home, I decided. I ran to the parking structure where my car was parked. My car sat alone in the corner, on the third floor. I took the keys out of the front pocket of my bag. Unlocking the car, I quickly got in and started it. The clock read 11:55; class got out at approximately 9:30. I slept for over two hours!

What caused me to fall asleep on the ground? I thought about that woman I met after class. Was that real or part of the dream? What about the other things I saw? I was too tired to contemplate everything right now. I drove out of the parking structure and away from campus. I headed home with the windows down to keep me awake with the moving wind.

Chapter Three:
Dogma

I felt so exhausted when I awoke. I was glad that I woke up in my bed. As I got up, my head felt heavy. I waited a moment for the feeling to pass. Dragging myself out of bed, I searched my closet for an outfit to wear.

"Knock. Knock," I heard a familiar voice. My mother stood in the doorway.

"Do you mind? At least let me get dressed first!" I reprimanded.

"Oh, okay," she said timidly. "I'll be downstairs."

Where did that come from? That wasn't how I usually greeted my mother. Maybe I should apologize to her. But first, I threw on a light blue tank top and black shorts, a nice summer outfit.

I walked into the kitchen to see my mom sitting at the table drinking tea, not coffee. The teas bag sat next to her cup on a napkin. Odd, she usually drank coffee. My sister was the one who drank tea.

"Hi, um, I'm sorry about being rude," I said. "I had a strange night…"

I wondered if I should tell her what happened.

"It's all right. You have a right to want privacy. You are a grown woman," she replied

I nodded. It was weird when she referred to me as a grown woman. I didn't feel like one.

"So, what was so strange about last night?" she asked.

She had to ask.

"Um, the class... was strange. Strange discussion," I told her.

"Really?" she asked.

At that moment, my sister Charsi entered the room. For once, I was happy she interrupted a conversation with our mom. She bounced in with her cute pink tank top and matching shorts. Part of her blond hair was put up in tiny ponytails held back by white butterfly barrettes. She appeared like a young school girl, but somehow carried of this look with maturity.

"Mom! I need to go clothes shopping! School starts in a week and I have nothing to wear!" she cried out overdramatically.

Thank you Miss Drama Queen.

"Charsi, you have a bunch of cute outfits," Mom reminded her.

18

Charsi rolled eyes, "Those were from last year. I can't wear the same clothes I did last year," she said in a pushy manner.

"Fine, we can go this afternoon," Mom agreed.

Charsi let out a sigh, "Thank you!" She said the words, but she didn't sound thankful.

After some breakfast I returned to my room. I lifted my book bag on the bed. It felt really heavy. It sounded like something in there was metal clanking together. Unzipping the bag I saw the cause. To my absolute shock, I found two swords! My mind flashed back these same blades piercing my skin when I stood in that castle's library. But that was just a dream, right? And I never put these things in my bag in the first place! I took them out. As I looked at the blades, I noticed something. The blades were much longer in the other world. The blades were shorter now, like short swords. I thought of showing them to my mom, but something told me not to. Telling others that I got transported into a different world sounded preposterous, but, what about the people I found dead on campus? If the news reported that many people died at the university, that would prove it happened.

I ran to the stairs, practically tripping down the steps and stumbled into the kitchen.

"Mom! Do we have a newspaper? Anything about my campus closing?" I asked desperately.

She still sat at the table with Charsi.

"What? Why do you need to know that? You don't have class today," Mom replied with some irritation in her voice.

"Yes, I know, but I thought I heard about something happening and I just wanted to check," I said.

"I already read the newspaper," Charsi stated crudely. "There's nothing in there about your college."

Her emphasis on the words 'your college' sounded as if she mocked it. Well, we can't all be destined to go to the big named universities.

"Thank you Charsi," I answered, not hiding the sarcasm in my voice.

"Hope? You look flushed. Is something wrong?" My mom asked.

I wished I could talk to her about this, but I didn't want Charsi around.

"Oh, no. Nothing at all." I don't believe it was a lie, I just wasn't telling her anything right now.

Tuesday came around again. I was the first student in the class to arrive. My eyes widened when I saw my instructor, unharmed, sitting at his desk.

"Mr. Takoto?" I asked.

He looked up at me. "Oh, hello, um…" he trailed off.

"Hope Eden," I said, helping him remember my name.

"Right. Do you need something?" he asked.

I stayed quiet for a moment, thinking about how I could ask him about last week? Before I said anything he asked a question.

"Have you picked a topic for your term paper?"

I kept thinking about that dream. I couldn't get the dark cultic images out of my head. Maybe if I researched a topic like Satanism and the Occult, I could learn about the things I saw in that dream.

"Well, I am interested in the uh…darker religions, like the Occult. How it came to be? I thought about researching if for my term paper." I said this as if I was unsure.

His expression of interest told me I came up with something good.

"Do you think you can find enough information on the topic? I want real facts," he explained.

"Yes, of course." I wondered if the library had books on the subject matter.

"Have you written out a thesis yet?" he inquired.

"No, I haven't…?" I raised my voice at the end like a question.

He gave me a dubious look. "Have you at least written a thesis statement?" he asked more crudely.

He already told the class the difference between a thesis statement and a written out thesis. Now I had to quickly come up with a sentence that clearly defined the objective of my essay.

"Um, Satanism and the Occult have had a dramatic effect on the beliefs of the American population throughout history," I squeezed out.

"Okay, that is not specific enough, too general. Anyone can come up with that," he put down my attempt to conjure up a well put together sentence. "You can come by my office during my hours to discuss it further. Right now, I need to start class," he said.

I gave a light nod before turning to find a seat. I usually sat in the second row.

"Oh, and no falling asleep in my class tonight. It's going to be a good discussion," he said without looking at me.

I can't believe he remembered that! I wanted to talk to him about what happened last week, but I knew I couldn't. For some reason I saw all of those things, and somehow, this world was separate from the other world I saw.

My thoughts drifted throughout class. Professor Takoto lectured on about Pagan beliefs, focusing on the role of women in the faith. The pagans worshipped many different gods and goddesses. The topic shifted from the Pagan to the Roman Catholic Church.

"So, on that note, I'm going to be shifting gears to the next part of the discussion. What do we think about when we speak of the Roman Catholic Church?" 'Shifting gears' is what our instructor called it.

"It represents power," the guy next to me answered. "No one wanted to question its integrity. I read about it trying to assimilate everyone into its beliefs, especially Christian," he added.

There was a deadly silence in the room after he spoke.

"So, you're saying that the Roman Catholic Church, who are Christians themselves, hunted other Christians?" Professor Takoto asked.

There were some rude snickers from the rest of the class.

"I'm sorry to disrupt your theory, but the church led the Crusades to hunt down the Pagans. This is how Christianity spread to other lands," the professor explained.

"Wait, I don't understand," the young man next to me continued. He pushed a strand of his auburn hair away from his face. "You're saying that these Pagans were the only target of the church, but I heard a different story."

"Oh really? What is the story you know?" Professor Takoto questioned.

"There was a book I read that explained that the Roman Catholics went after everyone, including Christians," my classmate explained.

"Uh, I have not heard that. What is the name of this book you read from?" The professor asked him.

The young man looked a little downtrodden.

21

"I don't remember its name. But the Romans were the ones who crucified Jesus, so because he was Christian, I thought…"

"Actually, Jesus was a Jew," Takoto corrected.

"But didn't Christianity begin with Jesus?" he asked.

The instructor pulled his thoughts together for a moment. "Jesus himself was a Jew. Christianity was not really formed until years after his death. It is really up to one's beliefs to say if he was more than a Jew."

"But he wasn't. He was proclaimed as god by his disciples. He died on the cross for humanity's sins, right?" My classmate struggled with the question.

"Hold on!" Someone from the back yelled. "You can't just claim Jesus was God and that he died on a cross for humanity's sins!"

The whole class turned to a girl with bright red hair, looked dyed, wearing a low cut tight fitting black top.

"Care to explain, Cheryl?" Takoto asked her.

"In the first place, most of the Jews did not see Jesus as God. They had their own beliefs. The ones who might have followed a prophet like Jesus were looking for other beliefs to suit them better. Whether or not they saw Jesus as god was their choice. People saw a man who supposedly healed people? Well doctors heal people, why aren't they referred to as God?" she asked.

"So? What's your point?" the guy next to me asked, raising an eyebrow.

"My point," Cheryl answered hotly, "is that people called him God when he may have been just a man," she said bitterly.

"But Jesus did more than heal people." The voice that intervened was mine. Did I want to get into this discussion? I should have just stayed quiet, but I couldn't.

"He restored the faith of people. He showed people things they never saw before. He drove demons out of people; he miraculously healed those with leprosy, which no doctor could cure. He gave people hope and stood for peace," I tried to inform.

"You don't know what really happened. You weren't there. Besides, you're claiming the will of one man, not the will of an entire religion!" That girl Cheryl sounded so offended. She would not drop the conversation and for some reason, neither could I. I felt strong about my beliefs.

"Jesus asked for the church to represent peace and life."

Why did I keep talking?

"Well obviously the church didn't listen!" she countered. "The early Roman Catholic Church saw it fitting to break this 'rule' and kill every Pagan they found!" she exploded.

"Which brings me to ask this next question," the professor intervened. "I am interested in receiving some feedback. When did Paganism end and Christianity begin?" he asked formally.

"Paganism never ended," Cheryl spoke powerfully. "There are Pagans out there today; here in the United States. But it is so sad that they have to live in fear. And because of the beliefs I chose, people look at me like some kind of witch. If I lived in those times, I would have been burned like all of those other innocent people because I follow the Wiccan faith," she said forcefully. I couldn't believe she said all of that. I felt bad suddenly. I didn't mean to be judgmental. She didn't stop there.

"People can be prejudice if they want to, it won't stop those people from believing in something that is real to them. Not even a church can stop them," she said.

"I guess not," I shyly answered. "Some churches don't preach the real gospel. What the Roman Church did was wrong," I decided.

"It is not about who is right or wrong," Professor Takoto stated firmly. "This is a class on discussing the similarities and differences of religion and its effects on society. Let's keep that in mind before we start a war."

Tonight, class let out early. He let us out at 9:15. He told the class that we deserved to get out early because he held us over too long last week, but I really wondered if that was the real reason. I began to gather my things when Professor Takoto walked over to me.

"I think it is very interesting that a Christian such as yourself is interested in the Occult," he said offhandedly.

"Why do you say I'm a Christian?" I asked.

"Because you made a big fuss over proving your point, proclaiming Jesus as God," he said.

"Oh, it's just that I don't want others to get the wrong impression about Christians. I'm not sure about everything the church did in the past, but there are Christians who believe in loving each other," I tried to save face.

Professor Takoto tightened his expression; he was making me nervous.

"I really want to avoid the 'I believe' and 'you believe' comments. You need to understand that we are looking at religion and spirituality as a whole. It does not matter what our own beliefs are. I grew up in Japan as a Buddhist and I did not have much say in the matter. Maybe you had a similar experience growing up as a Christian. But the point of this class is to put religious differences aside and discuss as a class the effects of different religious practices in our society."

I nodded feeling defeated. There was not much else to say. When I turned to leave, the thoughts about last week came to my mind again. I just had to ask.

"Um, Mr. Takoto..." He turned to me; he always looked so stern. Maybe that was how they act in Japan. "I wondered if..." How could I phrase this without sounding crazy? "I went to your office last week after class, and I saw your office was open, but you..."

He gave me with a questionable look. "My office was open?" he asked, then shook his head. "No, no, I left the building right after class. I did not go back to my office. I had some errands to run before going home. The usual ten minutes I spend in the office after class were gone. It wasn't me that opened my office," he said with puzzlement.

His words struck me hard. Something was definitely wrong. I didn't see my professor that night. All logic in my mind told me that what I saw last week was not real. But what didn't follow the logic was the fact I still had those swords.

"But I apologize," he continued. "Usually, I don't hold class over that long," he assured me.

What else could I say? He would think it was ludicrous if I told him how I found him that night.

"Alright then, thanks for helping me with my paper," I said.

He nodded. "Have a good night," he said.

Outside, the cool air blew. I suddenly felt an awkward presence around me. I ran, holding my bag tightly. I kept running. I practically ran over a guy walking with that girl from class who argued with me.

"Watch it!" he yelled. I slightly turned to see the girl glare at me. Why didn't Mr. Takoto talk to her? She didn't have to act the way she did!

As I approached my car, someone tapped me on the shoulder. I instinctively went into a defensive mode as I twirled around. I relaxed when I saw it was the guy who sat next to me in class. He looked to be around my age.

"Hey, I'm sorry about what I said in class. I didn't mean to start anything. I was just curious," he said with an apologetic expression. I didn't expect this.

"Oh, it's fine. But I wondered why the professor didn't say anything to that girl though," I wondered.

"Probably because of the way she was acting. He was most likely afraid to say anything to her. Did you see how she acted? That was so uncalled for," the guy drastically stated.

"Well, I guess I didn't have to keep talking," I said.

"You were just standing up for your beliefs," he said.

"Are you Christian?" I asked him.

He shook his head. "No. But I am interested in the religion; I'm interested in all religions. That's why I took this class, to learn how all religions came to be and are connected. That's why I asked when Christianity began from a historical point of view. Maybe I should have made myself clearer," he said. He kept his eyes on me. I tried to focus on him while he spoke. I didn't want to be rude, but I felt so uneasy. It was this campus, I think. I may never feel safe here again!

"I should go," I said hesitantly. "Nice talking to you," I said as I opened the door to my car.

"I'm Tristan by the way," he said.

"I'm Hope," I replied. When I looked at him, I noticed that he had these bright emerald eyes.

"Nice to meet you, see ya in class," he said giving a slight wave before turning away.

"Yeah, you too,' I answered. That didn't quite make sense. Where was my mind? I watched him walk over to a red truck.

When I got into my car, I felt safer. I stared the car and drove out of the parking lot. Nothing strange happened tonight. But something strange happened last week. As I drove down the road, a thought came to me. It was that boy I met in the dream, (or whatever it was.) I remembered his name. Damon. Then that thought was replaced by a more disturbing one. I thought about the discussion in class. Why are so many people against Christians? If a person is Jewish, Muslim, Hindu, or any other religion, people are kind to them and don't want to offend them. Why is it different for Christians? No one seems to care if Christians are offended! Is our religion stranger than any other? So we believe Jesus is the son of god who died for our sins. Buddhists and Hindus pray to statues. Pagans worship the Earth. Muslims believe in Allah as their god and Jew believe in Jehovah as their God. What about worshipping Jesus as God is such a questionable belief? I wonder, am I a bad person for choosing to be Christian?

Chapter Four:
Power Within

Motivating myself to write this paper was not as hard as I thought. I guess Occult is widely discussed in literature. I worked hard to find references to the Occult. There were books on the religion Satanism. It was weird to me seeing it referred to as a religion. Apparently there actually is a Satanic Bible written and a Church of Satan constructed in the 60's. There was this man named Aleister Crowley, born in 1876 who was a well known Satanist. He received the name, 'black magician.' I found a lot of information on both Satanism and the Occult. In some ways they were connected and others they were not. Much of the literary material seemed to be people stating their opinions on the subject and about religion and spirituality in general. I still used it for my paper anyways. I asked my teacher questions during the process of writing my paper. This paper was practically half our final grade.

When I received the paper after being graded, I saw a B+ at the top. My final grade for the class was an A-. I didn't think I would get any A's in college! My other class, Creative Writing was a solid A. My sister is usually nosy about my grades, but this time I was proud to show her. However, she turned her nose up.

"So, you got two A's; you only took two classes. I always get A's in my classes and I take six every semester. Besides, one of them is an A-, not an A," she said and turned prancing away. She never could just be happy for me. Charsi intended on finishing her high school career in perfection. She planned on taking some college courses to show on her portfolio as a candidate for Harvard or whatever pristine university that will accept her.

Fall semester began, I started off with twelve credit hours. One class I took, 'The Great Arts of the Centuries,' was a class of studying great artists and their works from the twelfth through the nineteenth century. I was doubtful I could get all A's while taking twelve credit hours. All my spare time got replaced by studying. The distractions took my mind away from the adventure I had a month ago. Those weapons I found stayed in an empty shoe box under my bed.

On September 21st, the first official day of fall, I attended a trip with my art class to the Museum of Artistic History, (didn't take long to come up with that name, did it?) It wasn't that big of a place; it wasn't that impressive. I went with a small group of five people in a van. Vera was the name of the woman who owned the vehicle. Vera told us she had such a big vehicle to transport her four kids, and a Siberian Husky. Everyone in the group talked and laughed, even me.

Vera told me that she was also a Christian. We stood at the entrance of the museum when I told her about the incident from last semester during that discussion on religion. She nodded in agreement with me.

"It is hard to discuss religion when people believe differently. It was unfair for the instructor to blame the argument on you, but I believe it is what Christians need to go through, bear the cross. There are too many that feel Christians are prejudice, but the truth is many other religions are prejudiced against Christians too," she explained.

I nodded in agreement, but it didn't answer my pressing question, why are my beliefs criticized?

Inside the museum, we were instructed to look around and choose three pieces of art to compare and contrast in our essay. Nothing interested me at first. Many of these paintings looked alike, using different shapes subject matter. There was a whole section devoted to Da Vinci--one of his most famous works, the Last Supper, caught my eye. The painting showed Jesus and His Disciples sitting around the table eating bread and drinking wine. Jesus tells the Disciples to eat and drink in remembrance of Him. We discussed this painting in that religion class, no one seemed to mind talking about Jesus then.

"Oh look, Da Vinci's 'Last Supper.' A female voice chimed behind me. I turned to see a girl with black hair, blue streaks, cut short around her ears.

"Hi, my name is Angelica. We're in the same class," she said.

"I'm Hope," I said, giving her short glance.

"Are you thinking of using this painting in your essay?" she asked.

"I don't know yet. I'm still looking around," I answered while looking away.

"I think I'm going to compare oil paintings to water color, something simple. Why make it too hard?" Angelica continued.

I nodded.

"I was interested in some of the ancient artifacts. Like some of Egyptian displays," I said making a great attempt to actually look at the girl's face.

"Oh, well I guess I could check that out," she said.

I was surprised she wanted to come with me since her interests were different than me. I nodded to her and we wandered down the main hallway. We acted as wandering souls, not sure where to go. A few times we stopped to look at the map in the museum's brochure. It was not much help, all of the paths drawn on this thing made the whole building look like a big maze. We moved down a long, winding hallway, moving along until this big stone head popped out of nowhere. We both jumped back, startled. When we realized what it was, we started laughing. The statue just sat in the middle of the hallway; nothing else was around it. The hallway ended at a door.

"So what do you think we'll find in here?" I asked turning the doorknob. When I looked over at her, she was gone!

"Angelica?" I called out.

The door opened into a room filled with a variety of statues. I didn't see her anywhere. I was by myself, alone surrounded by various statues.

Where did she go? I wondered.

I felt a sudden chill. There were statues sculpted in different materials, marble, stone, clay, tin, and even wood. This room led me to another that featured medieval artifacts. This room felt colder than the others I visited. Was there a draft in here? I grew even colder as I stood there. I felt panic take over. I had to get out of here and find people! All at once, I rushed back to the hallway I was in before. No one was around...anywhere. I kept running. It was like I ran down an endless hallway.

"Hope!" Someone called me.

Someone just called me. The voice echoed, sounding as if it came from all sides of the room.

Who called me?

It sounded like a familiar voice. Was it Angelica? I ran down the rest of the hall that curved to the right until it reached a wall. A dead end? That didn't make sense! I just came from here! There was nowhere else to go. I spun around and went back the opposite way. Things passed my view, things began to look different. I felt completely wrapped up in the madness.

Now I stood still, taking in everything around me. Everything looked blurry. The colors of the paintings smeared together. Was something wrong with my vision? Suddenly, I felt a presence behind me. This time I didn't look. I ran. I ran down a hallway I was sure headed towards the exit. But when I looked ahead, I saw another dead end! Somehow, I ended up in the room with the medieval weapons and armor again. Then a voice echoed through the room It sounded hollow, inhuman, and of no specific gender.

"Ignorant girl! Do you not know your own purpose?!"

The floor shook. I lost my balance falling forward onto my knees. I regained my footing, standing and looking up at the creature that caused the shaking. In front of me was a creature taller than any person I've ever seen. The facial features looked distorted, and on its back were torn, grayish wings. This being resembled an angel, but it wasn't pretty. Its hair was a matted mess of gray locks. Before I could react, it grabbed me and threw me into the wall. I thought that should have killed me, but it felt like someone just bumped me. Looking up at his thing, I would never believe that I could defeat it. I made the feeble attempt to run down the main hall toward the exit. I heard the sound of massive wings as it chased me down the hallway. Three clay pots sat on a shelf. I took one of them and threw it at the creature. Pieces of clay spattered everywhere. My adversary was not even fazed by my attack. It gave out an ear piercing screech which shook the room, making pieces of the ceiling fall onto the beast.

While he was distracted, I quickly made my way towards the main entrance. As I approached the door, I realized that the whole place was silent suddenly. The creature was gone. Where did it go? There was daylight outside and it looked so comforting. As I went for the door, the monster jumped down from the ceiling in front of me. It grabbed me with one hand and held me in the air. It was choking me! *Would I die like this?*

From somewhere within, I felt this strength within me. My mind only triggered one thought,

I WON'T DIE! NOT NOW!

Light exploded around me, then…nothing.

When I woke up, there were all these people crowded around me.

"Is she all right?" I heard a female voice

"Just back up, give her some space," a man said.

Among these people I saw Angelica who looked very concerned. One man, who looked like he worked there, knelt down next to me.

"How do you feel? Are you dizzy or anything?" he asked.

I actually felt fine.

"No, I'm all right," I answered.

"I'll call an ambulance," he said.

"No!" I said a bit too excitedly. "I'm fine, really." He looked unsure so I crawled to my feet and stood without any problems.

"O…okay," he said. He probably was worried that I would sue him or something if he didn't tend to me, but I really felt perfectly able. The crowd began to part. Angelica came over to me.

"Wow, what happened? Did you just black out?" she asked with concern. Vera, who drove the van I rode in earlier, walked over. "Honey, are you all right?" she asked. Before I answered, she gave me some water in a bottle. "It hasn't been touched, you can have it," Vera offered. I couldn't explain what happened to me. But I knew this nightmare wasn't over.

Chapter Five:
Apocalyptic Hell

I contemplated what happened today. Lying in my bed, the thoughts overwhelmed me. It took hours before I stopped tossing about and became dead to the conscious world.

A previous dream played over in my mind. I was a child again. And once again I was in a heavily wooded area with other kids. The kids lured me to the top of the hill. I didn't want to go, but I couldn't stop myself. I stood on the edge of the cliff looking over the water. I felt hands on me; I was pushed off. I heard laughter.

"You demon! Go to Hell where you belong!" I heard the kids yell down at me.

Why did my friends do this? My internal thoughts kept asking. I landed hard on my back. I looked up at the dusk sky. The laugher above began to sound inhuman. I rolled over slowly and pushed myself to my knees. I go to my feet and brushed myself off. I fell so far. I should have died, but I didn't.

The environment around me felt unbearably hot. Looking up, I saw the outline of the Earth. I fell deep in the Earth somewhere. Hard rock walls surrounded me. I held something in my hands. They looked like the swords I found in that castle. The blades were at least twice as long as they were when I looked at them back in my room. They went back to the length when I first found them at the castle. As I tried to understand this, something came towards me. The outline of the being looked human, but they were on fire!

"Oh my God!" I gasped.

I backpedaled into the cavern wall. This thing still moved towards me; its skeletal structure engulfed in flames. If I got to close I would catch on fire too! Another being like this one moved up along the dirt floor. At once, the two creatures charged me. I started swinging the swords, trying to fend them off. I made a direct hit on the side of the head of one figure. The creature fell to the floor. It was surprisingly weak. I swung again, hitting the other at the neck and it fell instantly.

This is crazy! I thought.

The creatures I stuck down weren't dead. They both were moving slowly to their feet. They stumbled towards me, crying out as if wanting vengeance. Taking another swing, I struck at them again and they fell easily back onto the ground. They still weren't dead. I ran. My thoughts going wild.

Where am I? This place is a wasteland!

Ahead was a river of flowing magma. The heat was so intense. I couldn't understand how I was still alive. This kind of heat alone could kill a person. I wasn't even sure how I was breathing since there wasn't any air. As I ran, something grabbed my foot. A fiery hand held my leg. I felt the burn. I cried out, trying to shake it off. I got my foot loose then stomped on the creature's head. I heard a crunch and figured I killed it. But when I removed my foot, it still moved!

More fiery beings crawled up out of the river of fire. I looked behind me to see a ledge sticking out of the rock wall. It was higher than I could jump, but somehow I jumped up there anyways. I actually reached the ledge and pulled myself up. Maybe it was the adrenaline. I started climbing up the wall. The fiery fiends were climbing up after me. Those things were weak fighters, but somehow they were fast climbers. One of them caught up to me. It grabbed me and started to pull me off. I shook the leg it held on to, knocking it off. I watched as the being fell onto another fiend sending them both plummeting to the canyon floor. Continuing upwards, I didn't stop. As I climbed higher, a white light engulfed me. It felt like a blessing. When this happened I heard an eerie, yet familiar voice speak inside my head.

This is only a fragment of what your power can give you! I woke up, lying in my bed. Another dream? I rolled over to my side. The swords were there, right beside me.

Another week went by and once again I was on campus heading towards class. The green leaves of summer were changing into beautiful, vibrant colors of autumn. Crimson and gold filled the treetops giving me a feeling of tranquility. The sound of the running water of the fountain could be heard nearby. Students sat nearby the tables or on the grass. Among them I saw someone familiar sitting under a tree in the courtyard.

Damon? My thoughts questioned. I recalled us parting in that light. Was that actually him? I guess I could ask, but I would feel dumb if it wasn't him. Slowly, approached him, keeping my eyes centered away so he didn't think I was looking at him. Now I was only a few feet away and he hadn't notice me yet. He kept reading his book. From where I stood I could see the bold print of the title and music notes on a bar staff printed below it. So he was reading a music book.

"Um…," I tried. He didn't hear that. "Uh, excuse me," I tried to be louder. He looked up at me. I saw the same cool colored eyes. In this light, they looked more blue than green, like the color of the ocean. I recalled how he saved me that night. Did he remember me? His eyes widened as he focused on me.

"Hey! I know you! What's up?" He did remember me, and he was glad to see me. That was a good sign.

"Uh yeah..I'm Hope." I reintroduced myself.

"Oh good. I felt bad that I forgot your name. That saved some awkwardness. I'm…"

"Damon." I finished for him. "I remember." Maybe I should tone it down a little. I sounded too happy to see him.

"So, what have you been doing since our little adventure?" he asked sounding way too causal about it.

"Going to classes," I said. Suddenly, I felt weird.

"Uh, about the adventure, how…do you think…it happened? I mean it was an unusual thing to happen. What do you think…?" I stopped at that point. I was talking too much again.

"What do I think happened?" he finished my question. "I don't know. But I did meet this woman, Aria," he offhandedly mentioned.

Aria. The name rang in my ears.

"I met her. This whole thing happened because of her!" I gave the accusation.

"Whoa, hold on," Damon said calmly. "We don't know if she caused it. Maybe she was trying to warn us," he said.

"I don't know," I admitted. "She was overly excited to see me first of all and she asked me these weird questions. 'Have I ever felt different from others?' or 'Do you feel separated from this world?' Stuff like that," I recanted. "I thought she was crazy so I started to walk away. Then she yelled at me, 'Don't make this hard!' After that the whole campus changed. Everything looked so dead…" I remembered the horrible things I saw. I found all those people dead. But I guess everyone was fine. It couldn't be explained. Damon looked towards the ground. Was he listening to me?

"Did she have red hair?" he asked as he looked up at me.

"Yes, she did," I confirmed.

He gave a short laugh. "Yeah, she was really messed up. I think she was smokin' something. I tried to walk away from her too. She yelled something weird to me too. 'Your own sins will finish you.' I have no idea what that meant," he said and laughed quietly to himself.

"What did she mean?" I wondered.

Looking at Damon's expression, he looked as confused as me.

"The hell if I know," he said.

In the middle of our conversation, Damon took out a pack of cigarettes, pulling one out of the package.

"Sorry, I haven't had one all day. You want one?" he offered pointing the pack at me. This may sound sad, but no one has ever offered me a cigarette before.

"Uh, no, I don't smoke," I told him.

"Oh, alright, that's cool," he said. Taking his lighter, he breathed in and lit the cancer stick. He exhaled the smoke as he breathed out.

"That's better," he said looking at me. "Come on, sit down," he invited me. I knew I was going to get smoke blown into my face, and onto my clothes and hair, but I didn't want to be rude. So I sat next to him, feeling uneasy. I always feel this way when I meet someone new. Well, I guess I already met him before, but still…

It was too quiet. All of the sudden, I just asked, "So why do you think that happened to us?"

"Honestly, I have no idea," he answered taking a puff off his cigarette.

"Oh, my class starts in five minutes, "I said as I stood up. "Is there another time we could talk?" I asked.

"Yeah, after your class," he suggested.

"It's about an hour and a half," I said.

"That's fine. I'll wait here," he said with a smile, blowing out smoke.

"Really? You don't have anything else to do?" I asked

"No. I'll just sit here and watch people. That's what I do. It's fun," he said nonchalantly.

"Well, I guess I'll see you later then," I said.

"Okay," he nodded. "I'll be here."

About an hour and fifty-five minutes later I was running back to the tree to meet Damon. Class ran over again! What is it with instructors that like to talk for hours? Technically I could have left at the designated time class ended, but I needed to hear the information for the midterm. As I approached the tree, my heart sank. He was gone. He must have gotten tired waiting for me.

During the drive home, I kept thinking about Damon. Would I ever see him again? I needed to see him again! When I got back home, I walked inside the house and straight upstairs to my room. Then I threw my bag to the corner and sat on the bed with my head in my hands. What was I going to do? I always mess things up somehow. I just should have gone to meet him when I said I was going to.

"Hope?" I looked up to see Charsi standing in the doorway with one hand on the door frame. "Someone is here to see you. They're waiting downstairs," she told me.

"Who is it?" I asked

Charsi shrugged and turned away, then looked back at me.

"Why do I smell smoke?" she asked.

"Smoke?" I questioned.

"Yeah, like from cigarettes," she said snidely.

"Oh, I talked to someone on campus, he was smoking," I answered.

"Is it that boy downstairs? Was he the one smoking?" she inquired.

"It's a guy downstairs?" I asked with surprise.

"Yeah, he has this crazy white hair and…"

I didn't wait for her to finish, I rushed past her, towards the stairs.

In a moment, I was down the steps and into the living room. He stood there just looking at me.

"Hey! You missed our date," Damon said smiling at me. Charsi gave me a look of wonder formulating around the word 'date.'

"I came to see you, but you already left," I told him sounding somewhat agitated.

"I went to the bathroom," he replied. "Geez, a guy can't take a bathroom break without a girl freakin' out?" he playfully asked with a sly smile that barely turned up the edges of his mouth.

"So anyway, we need to finish our conversation," he began.

"Can we take a walk?" I hesitantly suggested, seeing Charsi standing close at the doorway between the living room and kitchen.

"We're going for a walk," I told my sister. She nodded, but gave me this weird smile.

As we walked down the front steps and down the walk that curved into the driveway. Charsi waved at us from the door.

"Have fun kids!" she yelled.

"That's your sister?" Damon asked with disbelief.

"Yes. Isn't she cute?" I asked with sarcasm.

"Blondes are always cute," he remarked.

Was he being serious? I didn't want to think so.

"So, that's interesting that you two have different hair color," he said.

That was odd.

"Well, I look more like our mom. And she looks like our dad," I told him.

It was strange how different I looked from my sister. She had blue eyes and I had these weird silver colored eyes.

I looked back to see how far we walked from my house. I couldn't see it anymore, just rows of the other homes on my street. I saw one guy ranking leaves in his yard, no one else was out in the chilled weather. I was sort of cold too. I had a sweater on, but I forgot my coat. Damon didn't wear a coat either. In fact he just wore a black t-shirt and jeans. Wasn't he cold?

"Yeah, so back to what we talked about earlier," Damon began. "What do you think about this Aria?" he asked.

"I don't know," I admitted. "Hey, how did you know where I lived?" I asked him suddenly.

"Oh, I followed you. So anyways…"

"You followed me? Why didn't you just talk to me on campus?" I questioned him.

Damon glanced slightly at me. "You already were in your car. Look, I'm not stalking you or anything," he said with a grin.

It was sort of creepy. I never noticed anyone following me home.

"Do you still think Aria was trying to warn us about what would happen?" I asked letting go of the stalking incident.

"I thought so at first, but then I thought more about it. She was so weird. How she approached us, like she already knew us. She was definitely trying to show us something," he stated.

"Show us what? All those people dying! People burning!" I let out in rage. That came out louder than I wanted. I nervously looked around hoping none was around to hear that. We seemed to be the only ones who decided to take a walk today.

"I first met her when I was at Fantasy Nights," Damon went on. I heard of that place. It was a dance club. It was a popular place to go, but I wasn't old enough to drink. "I met her while sitting at the table around the dance floor. It was so crowded there that night. She started talking to me. She was freaking me out and to think of it, I really can't explain why. I left to go to the bathroom, and I was looking for the guys I came with. When I came out of the bathroom, everything was dead...literally!" he exclaimed.

I knew exactly what he meant. "So, we both experienced that," I concluded.

"Yeah, so I've been talking to a friend, and we thought since this crap is like supernatural, we were going to summon her...like with a Ouija board," he said.

"Why use a Ouija board? What will that do?" I asked not sure of the connection.

"I'm guessing Aria is somehow connected to the spiritual realm. I'm not saying she's a ghost, but there's something about her that screams 'horrifying and mystic,'" he concluded.

I understood, but I had an issue using anything to call the dead.

"I'm not doing a séance!" I crudely protested. Then I sort of regretted being so prudish.

"Wow, you don't smoke, or summon spirits? You really live a clean life," he remarked.

"No, uh I just..." I felt trapped with words. "What else happened to you?" I asked trying to get off the topic of séances. "Has anything else happened since you were in that castle? What about those guns you used?" I kept asking.

"Oh, uh…," he abruptly stopped at the corner of the street. "Yeah, I found them in this display case hanging on the wall in this den. I broke the glass and took them. Then these demonic looking women attacked me," he said with a puzzled look.

"Women?" I asked.

"Yeah, they were like vampire chicks or something. I used those guns to blast the witches!" he exclaimed.

It sort of offended me how he said that. It seemed like he enjoyed killing things. I guess I also felt envious, I wished I found those guns instead of the swords. I could have shot the monsters, and not had to get so close to them. I've never shot a gun before, only been told about how they work.

"I wondered how the weapons we found could easily defeat those creatures," I thought out loud.

Damon's face contorted like he was in deep thought, "I think they were special weapons. You know how silver bullets kills werewolves and stuff like that?" he asked me.

I nodded even though I don't know much about that stuff.

"Well, it works the same for vampires only it's more of stabbing them with something silver, like a blade of a sword."

"Are those the only creatures you found there besides the strange cloaked being in the tower?" I asked.

"Yeah that's it. Nothing else. Why?" Damon asked with a peculiar gaze.

I suddenly got the picture of the room with huge metal beds. "I found this large room with these beds in it. I thought they were abnormally large tables at first," I recalled.

"Really? Well…what about them? Did they freak you out or something?" he asked in an awkward tone.

"Yeah, sort of. Who or what would need something that big? I posed the question

"How big were they?" he asked.

"I don't know. They were big enough to hold giants," I said with a shiver.

Now Damon looked at me dubiously. "Giants?" he questioned.

"Maybe…" I said. "I really don't know what possibly could…" Suddenly, I felt disturbed by the topic. I didn't want to think about it anymore. I just had to talk about something else.

"Can I see those guns sometime?" I changed the subject.

"Yeah sure, if you want to come to my house. They're hanging in my room," Damon answered.

"Don't your parents care that you have guns hanging in your room?" I intently questioned.

"I didn't tell them they were real," he spoke in an obvious tone. "I mean, they look fake, like replicas. They don't know they're real.

"Do you have siblings? One of them could get a hold of them," I said with concern.

"No. I'm an only child. My parents let me do whatever I want with my room," he said with a smirk.

I nodded.

"We've been standing here for a while, you want to start walking again?" he asked.

I really didn't think about it.

Crossing the street, we kept along the sidewalk passing more middle class homes. The conversation took a different path which made me feel a lot better. Damon told me that he played the guitar and wanted to put a band together. He was such a nice guy, if only he didn't smoke.

After our walk, Damon left, but we made plans for me to meet at his house tomorrow. Charsi was all over me about Damon. 'Where did you meet him?' 'What does he do?' And so forth. I told my dear nosy sister that we met on my college campus. What else would I tell her?

That evening, I had this strange feeling that wouldn't leave me. I felt as if someone was watching me. Paranoia is never a good thing. I ignored it continuing to brush my hair. I kept looking around the room cautiously. I turned back towards the mirror. I thought I saw someone behind me in the reflection. I thought it was my mom. When I turned around, no one was there.

But as I sat on the bed, something touched my foot. I looked down to see a woman lying on her side, reaching up to me. Her mouth formed the words; her voice came through sounding hoarse.

"Help me!" she forced out.

My initial reaction was to kick her away. I raced to my feet. The woman almost looked like my mother. Her eyes and mouth turned down in an expression of sadness.

"Find my daughter," she said and then disappeared.

Who was that? I looked around to find the room empty. Am I hallucinating? I left to go to the bathroom and get ready for the night. Maybe if I ignore these happening, it won't mean anything and they'll go away. I wanted to believe that, I really did.

When I returned, I was surprised by the new company. A woman with long red hair stood by my bedroom window.

"Aria?" I gasped.

The giant of a woman turned towards me.

"Hope. Are you okay?" The question felt like a dart thrown at me.

"What?" I could barely speak. I felt a drastic change of pressure in my stomach. "No! I'm not okay!" I let out. "What did you do to me? Why did you show up at my college and leave me there in some alternative world?" I tore at her.

"I sense some hostility," she said rather calmly. "You want to tell me something?" she asked.

"Yes!" I didn't hesitate to be sharp with her. "Why are you doing this? These strange visions, what are they? I don't know what they mean!"

Aria moved towards the window. "Come here," she coaxed. "You must see this," she said.

"Something outside my window?" I questioned. I walked over and stood by her.

"Look out there," she pointed. But I saw nothing but the backyard.

"What am I supposed to see?" I asked with curiosity.

Her face appeared emotionless. "Can you see them...dying?" she said hopelessly.

"What?" No one was out there, just the blackness of the night.

"Can you hear them?" she went on. "They are crying out for their injustice," she spoke with sadness.

I did begin to hear faint voices. I don't know if I actually heard them or if my mind made up the sounds. I started to see things, too. Fire fell from the sky and it was burning the people below! I saw monster tearing apart human beings! I remember this vision when I was on campus, but it quickly flashed in my mind last time.

"Aria, what is this? Why do I keep seeing these things?!" I cried out.

"You have to help them, Hope," she said simply.

41

"How?" I asked.

My question went unanswered. I found myself on a lone street. Fire continued to pour from the sky. The sky itself was full of smoke. People ran wildly through the streets. Suddenly, a woman ran towards me screaming. As she ran, flames exploded around her. I watched as her flesh fell from her bones. It made me so ill that I had turn away. I don't know what came over me ,but I just ran. This place was full of fear and anguish. I wanted to help those I saw, but nothing could make me get near any of them.

I stopped abruptly down the road. Huge creatures with sharp claws came at me. Their sharp talons dug into my skin, tearing it off. The pain wasn't as bad as I expected. I looked down at my arms. The skin was ripped off, but there wasn't any blood. I pushed the fiends away and ran, but they were persistent, chasing after me. As I ran, I looked around at the others there. They had no strength to push the monsters away, but I could push them away and not be as terribly hurt by them. Somehow I knew those people around me were in greater pain.

I kept running. I didn't notice at first that the swords appeared in my hands. Where were they earlier?! Spinning around, I swung at my opponents, hindering their path to me. Ahead, every tree burned, the grass burned, buildings, homes...the only building that wasn't on fire was a small church. I ran inside believing it was a safe haven. But safe didn't exist here. I saw the altar burning the crucifix that once hung had fallen and looked like an ordinary piece of wood. It didn't resemble a cross anymore. The altar stood untouched. As I examined it, something moved. Someone crawled around aimlessly. It horrified me to see a man moaning in pain. He wore a priest's robe and was severely burned to the point that his skin was falling off. He started muttering to himself. It sounded like a prayer. Then he cried out.

"Where is God? Why hasn't He come yet?" Then he burst into flames. I backed up, stumbling down the steps. I watched as he just burned, never stopping. He just kept crying out in pain. I closed my eyes, wanting it to all go away.

"No! I've had enough! I don't want to see it anymore!" I screamed.

Everything went deathly silent and the priest was gone. The altar now was afire. I stood alone. The fire ceased and a message was left behind in ash.

Where is your god now? These were the same words I saw before.

Suddenly, I was in my bedroom again, by the window. Aria stood there, silent. Then she spoke, "You've seen it now Hope," her voice came out in an eerie tone. "Your mind will never let go of it. Their pain...their cries..." she said.

"What was all that? What does that message mean, 'Where is your god now?'" I asked expecting a meaningful answer.

Aria just stood there, not saying a word.

"Come on! Just tell me!" I urged.

Her eyes pierced through me. "Those people were left to suffer God's wrath," she said.

"No wait! That's not God. I mean there is a judgment but..." I faltered in defending my beliefs again.

"Those people felt abandoned by God," Aria explained. "They believed in peace too, just not in the same way. They were punished because they were not good enough to be chosen. They will never have their salvation, they will never find it," she said sadly.

Guilt struck me.

"Tell me Hope, do you think they deserve this fate?" she asked.

I felt tears well up in my eyes. The pain from seeing those people lingered down into my soul.

"No." I answered. The truth came to me. What I saw...was Hell.

Chapter Six:
A New Friendship

I remained sleepless for the rest of the night. Sleep didn't catch up with me until early in the morning. I slept until around noon, which surprised the rest of my family. Sleeping till the afternoon was not like me, but they didn't know what happened to me last night.

After I got up, I rushed to get myself ready for the day. I had to tell Damon everything. We were going to meet at the university campus.

"I'm going to meet Damon," I told my mother as I head towards the door.

"Oh, your friend from school? Charsi told me she met him. Does he really have white hair?" Mom asked.

I stopped in route and turned toward her.

"White hair?" I thought about that. It did look that way. "It's really light blonde, I think. He might have dyed it. His eyes are this bluish-green color," I told her.

"He sounds attractive," my mother said. I rolled my eyes knowing what would come next. "What do you think?"

"He's nice," I gave a short answer.

"What is his major," she asked.

"I didn't ask him," I told her.

"Well you should ask him," she suggested.

"Yeah," I agreed.

Then she spoke softer, "the last thing you want to do is start dating someone with no focus in their life."

"Oh Mom, really!" I quickly became annoyed. I really needed to go and she kept asking pointless questions.

"I'm just saying, you should really know the person before making a commitment," she continued.

""Mom! It's not like that at all!" I said being irritated.

"You know, Charsi was dating that one boy from her school for a week, now she's dating someone else. I'm sure glad you're picky about dating people," she badgered.

My mom didn't get it. I didn't date guys every week like Charsi because I'm not asked out as much as she is! And thinking about it just made me depressed.

"I need to go," I said. I turned and left. I didn't want to rude, but I also didn't want to discuss my personal life.

I waited for Damon for fifteen minutes. I stood at the same tree where we met before. Soon, ten more minutes passed. I did have his number, maybe I should call him. As I walked to my car, I saw him in the distance. He was talking to some girl. Her blonde hair was cut short, her black blouse fit tight around her figure, and her knee high stocking almost touched her short black skirt. Damon seemed close to her, because he hugged her before he got into a blue Mustang. He was about to leave; I had to hurry! This time, I was following him.

Damon's house was enormous compared to mine. I followed him all the way there. All of the homes in this neighborhood looked alike. I looked up at the two story home; its gray brick exterior made the place look elegant. There was a large oak tree by the side of the house; the leaves were a collage of colors, orange and gold blended together. I parked behind the Mustang and walked towards the door. I had some sore feelings. Did he forget we were supposed to meet?

The double front doors were beautiful. Looking at the wood frames gave me chills. I didn't get why? I rang the doorbell and waited. The more I gazed at the door, the more I was reminded of that castle. They looked identical. The doors opened, and I pictured the dreary interior of that castle.

The door opened completely. A woman with red hair wearing a red V-cut sweater and jeans greeted me.

"Hello, can I help you?"

"Y-yes," my voice cracked. I turned away feeling embarrassed. I wasn't here for a few minutes and I already did something stupid. "Is Damon here?" I nervously asked.

"Oh, yeah, he's here. I'm Daphne McKay, Damon's mother. Come in," she invited. She took my coat and I took off my black tennis shoes by the door. The house from where I could see was spotless. I saw a number of pairs of shoes on the floor mat. Compared with most floor mats in a home, this one was relatively clean.

The woman led me into the living room. I sat on a white leather couch with matching leather chairs. In front of me was an entertainment center. The room also featured a floor lamp in the corner by a cabinet full of antiques. The carpeting was light beige extending from the living room to the next room. A glass table was in front of me, on the glass was a game system with two controllers carelessly lying on the floor by my feet.

"I am so sorry. This place is a mess," Daphne sighed heavily as she picked up the game console, putting it in a long drawer under the T.V. in the entertainment center. She wrapped the cords around controllers, "I told those boys to clean this stuff up!" she mumbled, then pushed the drawer in with a satisfied sense of accomplishment. She looked at me with a smile.

"Do you want anything to drink?" she asked. "We have sodas, juice, water, milk, tea…" I didn't feel like a drink. I just wanted to see the person who just stood me up!

"I'm fine," I responded.

"Okay. I'll tell Damon you're here," she finally said. Why didn't she do that first? I was getting impatient.

The next person I met was a little red haired girl who came hopping over to me from the staircase. She carried a plush doll with red hair like hers.

"Hi." She looked me with gleeful eyes. "I'm Anna, are you Damon's girlfriend?" she asked. She was so cute.

"No, we're just friends," I said. Then two boys came running down the stairs; they were red heads too; twins I think. They were yelling; playing with toy planes. They were 'hand flying' them around the area, making air noises.

Watch out!" one yelled. "Another enemy!" They continued making plane and bombing sounds.

"Oh will you two grow up!" I heard a familiar voice. Damon came down the stairs looking sorrowful at me. "I'm sorry, we were supposed to meet, right?" I almost exploded, but I didn't want to risk losing a new friend. It was also strange that he was on campus, anyway. He must have forgotten about me when he talked with that other girl!

"It's alright," I said. I looked at the two boys again. "So you have two brothers and a sister," I inquired.

"Yes," he said hanging his head.

"I met your mom too." As I said that, the lady walked into the room. "There you are, Damon. Don't just stand there, show this young lady around the house," Daphne told him.

46

"Alright, let's go," Damon spoke sounding less than enthusiastic.

"Hey Damon," I said as we walked upstairs, "You said you were an only child," I reminded him. He stopped and was silent for a moment. "Oh, it's all right. You don't have to be embarrassed. I didn't mind meeting them," I said trying to make the awkward feeling disappear.

"No, it's just..they aren't really my siblings," he said, then continued leading me upstairs. His last sentence threw me off. What did he mean by that?

He never said anything else about the matter. He opened a door at the top of the staircase. Inside his room posters covered the walls. Some were rock singers, and others were dragons and fairies (but the fairies weren't wearing much, I noticed). There were some magazines scattered on the floor by his bed. The dresser set across from his bed had a bunch of stuff on it, CDs, notebooks, and other miscellaneous items. A Chinese lantern hung in the corner by the wall to the left of the dresser, under the lantern was a guitar; the jagged shape in bright blue gave it the aggressive look. The bright blue was painted against a black background. The interior of the room was pretty cool--cooler than mine, I decided. In some ways, Damon was a very artistic person. Among these items I saw the guns hanging on the wall between two posters.

I looked at Damon who now was sitting on his bed. He looked forward; his eyes didn't focus on anything in particular.

"Damon, is everything all right?" I asked.

He looked at me, his eyes were emotionless.

"Can I see the guns?" I asked.

"I don't know if you should touch them," he said guardedly.

I've watched people shoot guns, but never done it myself. My father had many types of fire arms. I watched him shoot cans in a field with his buddies when I was younger. I wanted to try, but he never let me.

Without saying a word, Damon got up and took the guns off the thick nails that supported them.

"Don't shoot anyone," he said with dry humor. I gently took them out of his hands. The weight felt lighter than the swords. There were names engraved on the barrel of the guns. One read: Michael and the other read: Gabriel. These are the names of the archangels who fight by the side of God. The one that had the name of Michael was gold plated and the one that had the name Gabriel was bronze plated.

"I really like these," I said. I'd seen different types of gun magazines that my dad owned, and these guns looked like revolvers. If I remembered correctly from one of the articles, there should have been a lever or button or something that released the loading capsule, but I couldn't find it.

"Hey Damon, how do you load these?" I asked. He took the gold plated gun, Michael.

"Well, usually for a revolver, you can open the latch on the side of the gun so you can put the bullets into the chambers. But these guns don't have one," he said, then looked up at me. "They don't need to even be loaded."

"All guns need to be loaded," I said. I may not know everything about them, but I at least know they need bullets. He lifted the guns out of my hands.

"These guns are so powerful," he said looking them over.

"Then maybe they shouldn't be used," I warned.

He laughed, "Maybe they shouldn't be used by you," he said.

Was he making fun of me? I wondered feeling a little embarrassed and hurt.

"Don't worry," he answered my thoughts. "I'm just messing with you again. Ya know, I keep thinking about that Aria chick. She needs to answer our questions!"

Oh that's right. "Uh, I did see Aria, last night."

Damon's expression quickly changed, his mouth tightened and his gaze focused intently on me.

"Why didn't you say so sooner?" he burst out.

"I was going to mention it," I told him.

He sighed heavily, "This woman is the reason why this crap is happening to us!"

Oh great, he's mad.

"I'm sorry," I began. "I wanted to tell you when I got here, but your mom answered the door, then your sister showed up, and then your brothers...then you showed me the guns..."

He gave a wave of his hand, "Don't worry about it. So what happened?"

"Well, I'm not sure how to explain it," I said.

I told him my experiences and mentioned the woman who asked me to find her daughter. That happened before I met Aria in my room. I wasn't sure if the two incidents were connected.

"It was so weird how I met her," Damon began. "I was just hanging out with friends at a dance club. I guess I was getting sort of buzzed. She suddenly appeared on the steps that go up onto the second level over the bar and dance area. She came over to us and just started talking to me, like she's known me for years. Then she asked me to dance. Of course the guys pushed me to say yes. I hate them so much!" he said with annoyance.

I couldn't help but laugh when he said that. I covered my mouth, concerned that I offended him, but he laughed lightly too. "So anyways, I followed her to the dance floor. As I did, she started asking me weird questions, like she did to you. I thought she was crazy, so I tried to ditch her. As I walked away, that's when she said, 'your sins will finish you.' I felt pain run through my body and I rushed to the bathroom. And like I said, when I came out, the place was dead; my friends and everyone else were gone. I walked outside and I saw that castle. The club and everything else on the street disappeared," he told his story.

I nodded. I knew that the time we spent in that castle inflicted us with unforgettable memories. Aria told us nothing; she just threw us into this! There were too many secrets kept from us. I had this feeling that not knowing the truth would cost us more than our sanity.

Time passed, we just hung out, playing video games. I had to admit, I don't play these often. I wasn't that good, but Damon helped me best as he could. We were playing as a team for this first person shooter. I'm terrible at these! As we played, I saw the guitar out of the corner of my eye.

"How long have you played?" I asked him.

"What? This game?" he replied.

I let out a small laugh. "No, that guitar?"

"Oh, about three years," he gave a short answer. He seemed enthralled in the game.

"Oh, how's that going?" I tried to keep the conversation going so I didn't seem boring. Damon pushed pause on the game before turning to me.

49

"My friends and I are starting a band, some of my friends and I have talked about it. My one friend plays the drums and other is learning how to play the keyboard," he explained.

"I see," I said with a nod. "I remember you were reading that music book when I saw you on campus. Is Music your major?" I asked.

"Between you and me," he slightly whispered. "I want to learn more about music, but I'm waiting a little longer to go to school."

"What are you doing right now?" I asked, keeping my eyes focused on the TV screen.

He shrugged, "I'm just reading about music, writing songs. I like to go sit on campus and read; gets me out of the house," he told me.

"So, you're not a student," I clarified.

"Not right now," he admitted.

I turned towards him; our faces were only inches away. I suddenly felt nervous, and jumped to my feet.

"What are you doing?" he asked as I moved over to this desk adjacent from the bed.

"Oh, nothing," I told him. The clock on his desk read 8:30PM. I finally looked over at him. "I should go," I said quickly.

"Oh, all right, that's cool," he said. I caught some disappointment in his voice, but I just felt like I should leave.

As I left, I couldn't shake this dreadful feeling welling up inside of me. I really wanted this to be a real friendship; not something that would fade away like my former friendships.

When I walked through the door of my house, my infuriating sister Charsi pestered me about Damon.

"What does his house look like? Does he have brothers my age? Are they cute?" she quizzed.

"His house is nice," I responded. "He has brothers, but they're nine and his sister is six. He looks different from his mom and his siblings," I told her.

"How so?" she asked.

"Well you've seen Damon, he has bluish-green eyes and really light blonde hair," I told her.

"You mean white. The boy has WHITE hair," she corrected.

"Okay. White hair, but the rest of his family are redheads. Well, his mom and siblings are, I haven't seen his dad, however," I hastily responded.

"Yeah what's up with his hair anyways? How does someone get white hair?" Charsi continued. "I know some people who actually dye their hair white or some other outrageous color. Did he do that? I know this guy at school who actually dyed his hair white, like snow colored white," she said.

"Does it really matter what his hair color is? My hair is black and yours is blonde, but we're still sisters," I reminded her.

"Those are natural colors though. White is not natural," she explained.

"All right, so he obviously dyed it!" I ended up shouting. Why was she being so irritating?

"That's what I'm saying!" Her voice rose drastically. She left the room in a frantic matter.

Geez! Why does she always overstate everything? I got it the first time, he had to of dyed his hair! It doesn't matter anyways. I really didn't care about Damon's hair. But something he said earlier came to mind. 'They aren't really my siblings.' He said he was being sarcastic, but it was strange how he said that.

That night I tried to relax while reading. I took a break from reading text books and read one of my fantasy novels instead. It was 11:30 when I began to feel tired. But I didn't want to sleep. I tried to sit up to keep myself awake. As I read the words on the page, I felt drowsy. I abruptly closed the book and tossed it to the floor. Getting out of bed helped me not to think about sleep.

Suddenly, something hit my window. My thoughts were obstructed by the tapping sounds on the glass. My heart jumped and I prayed it wasn't her again.

Chapter Seven:
Out on the Town

Should I go over there? I heard the sound again. I turned to the window, someone was down there. They had something in their hand. Tossing the object, it hit directly in the middle of the glass. I took the chance of opening the window to see who it was.

"Hey! What's up?" A voice called to me.

"Damon? What are you doing throwing stuff at my window?" I whispered loudly.

"I was bored. What are you doing?" he returned in a loud whisper.

"Reading," I called down.

"You're reading in your room on a Friday night?" he asked.

Who made the rule that everyone has to be out on a Friday night? Not even Charsi was going out tonight.

"What do you want to do?" I asked wondering where he was going with all this.

"Can I come up?" he asked.

"Oh sure, let me throw down a ladder," I joked.

"You have a ladder in your room?" he asked thinking I was serious.

"No, I was kidding…never mind, just meet me at the front door," I called to him.

In the next few moments, Damon and I stood in my room. He looked around, studying the place.

"Wow, you have a lot of books," he said looking at my bookcase. As I remember, his room didn't have any books. There were magazines, but no books. Damon went over by the shelf looking closer at my collection.

"Have you read all of these?" he asked with curiosity

"Almost all of them, I just got three new books including the one I'm reading now," I responded.

He still stood there looking over my books. "So, do you just read fantasy books?" he asked.

"I have some mystery books too. Many of those books have been there for years," I explained.

"Oh, can I see those swords you have?" Damon's eyes brightened when he asked me.

I went under my bed and retrieved the box and opened the lid. He looked at them for a second before lifting them out of the box.

"Oh, they're short swords?" he asked.

I had no idea how to explain how the weapons changed.

"No...uh...in that other world, the blades are longer. Just like how your guns don't work for real here. The blades of the swords are actually shorter in the real world." I tried to explain. But as I gave my explanation, I felt kind of dumb for not having a reason for it happening.

Suddenly, I heard someone's footsteps coming down the hallway. Instinctively I closed my bedroom door.

"Why did you do that?" Damon asked me.

"No reason," I answered quickly.

"You're not allowed to have people in your room or something?" Damon imposed. "HEY, HOPE HAS A BOY IN HER ROOM!" he shouted.

"Will you keep it down?" I demanded.

Suddenly Damon gave me the weirdest smile. "Let's get out of here." He said with a laid back attitude.

"What? Where do you want to go?" I wondered.

Damon swung one of the swords around, "the place I was talking about earlier," he said.

He thought that answered my question? "What?" I had to ask.

"Fantasy Nights of course, hello?" he replied in an obvious tone.

"Oh, uh...I'm not twenty-one," I said with a disheartened feeling.

Damon looked oddly at me, "You've never been there before, have you?" he asked.

Before I answered he quickly added, "Its fine. You can actually get in when you're eighteen. However, we have to get there before nine because after nine, you have to be twenty-one to get in. But don't worry about being able to drink, I'll hook you up!" he said giving a sly smile.

My mind raced between excited and nervous. Maybe I really have been too much of a 'good girl' all my life. I lost friends in the past due to my morals and fears, but I'm an adult now. Even though I met Damon through really disturbing circumstances, he was the best friend I had right now. How could I say no?

It was going on eight-o-clock now. My mom was in her room and I think my dad was in the office downstairs. I saw light coming from Charsi's bedroom as Damon and I walked into the hallway. I wasn't going to tell anyone that I was leaving. I figured I could make the choice to go out without anyone's permission.

The parking lot behind the club was so crowded with cars and people. I got to ride in Damon's mustang. He seemed so proud of his car. After finding a parking spot way in the back, we made our way to the line to get into the place. The blaring music was muffled a little from the building. For some reason, I couldn't stop shaking.

"Are you cold?" Damon asked. I wasn't sure if I was cold. The temperature outside was surprisingly nice for early October. Maybe I'm really nervous. But why would I be shaking?

When it was our turn, Damon proudly showed his license showing he was of age to drink. The guy at the door had a tall forbidding stature. He stamped Damon's hand then looked at me.

"Um, I'm not twenty-one yet," I said quietly.

"You can come in if you're eighteen, you just can't drink unless you're twenty-one," he said in a gruff voice.

I showed my ID and he took a marker and put an X on both of my hands.

We were inside now and suddenly I felt overwhelmed by the number of people. Music blasted while people sat and talked at the bar. "This is the same place you came to before?" I asked with surprise.

"Yeah, and I've also gone to X Cape," he said.

"Escape?" I asked.

Damon glanced oddly at me. "The letter X and then CAPE," he spelled out the word.

"So, you drink a lot?" I asked.

"I'm drinking legally now. I came here on my birthday last month. It's also the same night I met that red headed wench," he mentioned.

"I see," I said looking anxiously around.

"I've drank since I was sixteen. I couldn't get into bars, but I got alcohol another way. An older friend usually hooked me and my friends up since we couldn't drink legally, ya know. Usually, I drank when I went to parties at someone's house," he said.

The place was so loud with the music and chattering of everyone, so no one heard him say those things. As he told me this stuff I couldn't help but feel empty. I really have been a 'good girl' and I've never experienced life. I wanted to experience what I never did before. I wanted to be spontaneous and crazy! I wanted to just have fun!

"So, you want something to drink?" he asked.

Wow, that didn't take long.

"I guess," I answered hesitantly. "What should I get?" I asked.

"I'll get some drinks, but be careful because they do have security checking to see if the right people are drinking," he whispered to me.

"Oh, uh, no problem," I said softly.

As the night went on, Damon and I played pool. He quickly made friends with these two guys who we ended up playing against. They looked like biker guys or something with their heavy leather coats and facial hair. I told Damon that I was not too good at the sport, but he assured me that it wasn't a problem. With his skill, he could take on both guys and win. And he did just that. He even bet money. He seemed so wild, just going to a place like this and betting money against guys who looked like that. But he actually won! I got a few balls in too, (including the cue ball a few times,) but it was still fun.

"Where are you from boy?" One of the guys asked.

"I'm from around here," Damon answered casually.

"Those were some pro shots you got in there," the other one told him.

Damon just held the cue stick and grinned. He won two hundred dollars! I couldn't believe he had that much to bet with!

Finally, Damon was ready to buy some drinks.

"So, what do you want?" he asked. I had no idea.

"Uh, what should I get?" I asked innocently.

"You want beer or liquor?" he asked.

Again, I didn't know.

"What do you usually drink?" I asked.

He laughed. "Okay, I'll get you something, just hold on." He went to the bar and got something that looked like fruit punch, but I doubt that was what it was.

"Here," he said giving me the class. "Go easy, I don't want you getting hammered," he said with some playfulness.

"No! Get her hammered!" The one biker guy cried out. "Isn't that the whole point?" he asked with a smirk.

"Yeah, she'll be a cheap date!" The other one chimed in.
I couldn't help but look at them with a dirty glare. Why did they have to be that way, saying stupid comments like that? And those two biker guys made me nervous to begin with.

Damon rolled his eyes, "Whatever," he said. I kept looking at the drink a little afraid of it.

"Just try it," he coaxed.

"What is it?" I asked.

"A Sex on the Beach," he replied.

"A what?!" I cried out.

One of the biker guys leaned forward from the stool he sat on, "I think she wants more than a drink," he whispered to Damon with a sly smile.

Damon glared at him, and then looked at me. "Uh, let's go to a table by the dance floor," he said as he grabbed my arm.

We sat at one of the round tables that circled the dance floor. I looked up to see the second level of this place. There were more pool tables and arcade games up there. I saw the stairs that led up there. Now I knew what Damon was describing earlier. A bar waitress came by with a tray full of tubes with different color liquids in them. Her white blouse and short black skirt rimmed tight around her body. Her black high heels clicked as she walked. She slinked over to Damon, and bent over so she was in his face.

"You want something, honey?" she asked sweetly.

Damon turned to me. "Well?" he asked me.

I didn't know what any of that stuff was. I did notice the waitress has long locks of blonde hair. Damon mentioned earlier that he thought blondes were cute.

"Um, what is in those?" I asked.

The waitress named every color of liquor she had. I still didn't know what I wanted.

"Just pick your favorite color," Damon suggested.

"Uh...red," I decided. The lady handed the vial to me and Damon got a yellow one. I think mine had a strawberry flavor and his was like a Piña Colada. I at least knew what those were.

"All right, down it!" Damon encouraged.

"Down it?" I questioned.

"Just take one big gulp. I'll do it with you. Come on, one two..."

"Wait, there's too much," I protested.

"No there isn't! It's a shot, you're supposed to drink it all at once," he said.

I nodded, but I wasn't sure I was ready for this.

"Okay, one, two... three!" he said and we both gulped the colored liquid down. It tasted really good--so good that I wanted another one.

"Uh, I kind of like it," I said shyly.

"Oh yeah? You want another one?" he asked.

Now did he ask me that because he really wanted to get another one or to see that waitress again? But when I thought about it, Damon really didn't seem interested in her. He was interested more in...me. My thoughts would be wrapped around this one for a while.

It was sort of funny. I hadn't finished the first drink Damon got me and yet I was having more shots. After about four of those, I started to feel dizzy. No, I felt drugged. I held the glass with the drink Damon got me in one hand. I was trying hard to finish it. Suddenly, I couldn't hold onto the glass and it slipped from my hand, landing and breaking on the floor. Everyone within five feet heard it. I couldn't believe this feeling that came over me. Someone could have punched me in the face and I wouldn't have cared.

"Okay, you're cut off!" Damon said jokingly. But I suddenly didn't feel well.

"Uh, Damon..." I looked over at him, but he looked blurry. Was I losing my sight?

"Ready to go?" he asked.

I nodded slowly.

On the drive home, I had the window down. The breeze cooled me off. After drinking so much, I felt so hot. I was so relaxed, I just felt like talking.

"So, your parents know about you drinking?" I asked with a drunken slur.

"What? Who cares?" he replied.

"I was wondering cause most parents don't want kids to drink under age," I kept slurring my words.

"Well, of course they didn't know. I usually spent the night at a friend's house during the weekends, they never knew, he told me.

"They never checked to see what you're doing?" I asked.

"No. They really didn't have a reason to," he said.

"Oh," I answered. I was sort of out of it, but I wondered how Damon could drive? He had about as much as I had to drink. He was sort of swerving, I noticed.

"Damon, did you dye your hair?" I asked suddenly. I don't know where that came from. I did have that question on my mind, but I didn't want to ask him before.

"What?" He kind of laughed at the question.

"My sister wants to know, cause she thinks the colurr of yourrr hair is diffant," I slurred out.

"Are you all right? I can't really understand what you're saying," he said.

"Yourrr siblingggs all have red hairrr and so does your motder," I continued.

Damon became silent.

"What about your fatder? What color hair does he have?" I kept asking questions.

"Why are you asking so many questions?" he asked, sounding somewhat irritated.

"I just wontdered. You said you didn't have siblings," I continued slurring.

"I didn't say that!" He'd suddenly gotten defensive.

"Yes, you did. When we first met," I reminded him.

"This all began with that woman. Who is she anyways?" Damon uttered, his voice deepened.

"Who?" I asked innocently.

His gaze stayed steadily on the road, but I still felt this intense emotion steaming from him.

"Damon," I tried.

He let out a groan. "Will you stop?! You're too drunk anyways! Just go to sleep, or just stop talking!"

I guess I was sort of drunk, but it was his fault! He kept giving me those shots to drink. I drank too much!

When Damon dropped me off, he barely said a word as I left the car. I went to the front door and turned the knob slowly. The door opened a crack and I looked back as Damon drove away.

What did I do? I wondered.

I made it to my room and fell onto my bed. I fell asleep instantly.

Chapter Eight:
Confession

Waking up the next morning, I still felt a little intoxicated. My dear sister decided to knock on the door.

"Hope, come downstairs for breakfast," she said outside the door.

Oh God, I didn't feel like eating. I dragged myself out of bed and to the door. I didn't bother with putting on day clothes or brushing my hair. I just slumped down the stairs in my nightgown.

When I got to the table, my family saw how disoriented I looked.

"Hey there," my dad said. "Had a wild night?" he asked, ending it with a smile. I was out drinking underage, didn't he care? He probably didn't know that part. I looked at him; his flaxen hair was so neat and he was wearing a tan polo shirt. Even on a Saturday his casual dress is nice. Actually, I looked like a wreck compared to everyone else in this room.

"Sit down, have something," my mom coaxed. I sat in my usual spot across from Charsi. She looked at me with this look of, "What sort of mischief did you get into last night?"

I never thought I would have this sort of conversation with my family on a Saturday morning during breakfast.

"So," Charsi chimed in at this point. "What's going on with Damon?" She emphasized his name playfully.

I really didn't want to talk about Damon right now. The one time I meet someone like Damon, I messed it up.

"Everything is fine," I lied.

Somehow, days passed, then weeks... and life was back to the way it was before. I became bored. As the time went on, I really wanted to see Damon. I began to feel depressed, not just subtle depression, real and painful depression, like I felt back in high school. Those memories came back, too. Just feeling alone... it hurt so much. No one understood why? Of course, no one ever asked, either.

Eventually, one Sunday, things changed. Usually I let my mind drift while the pastor gave his sermon. Today, the talk was on the book of Revelations. There are things mentioned in this book that are coming true, I guess. I wondered if there was anything about having nightmares and strange things happening that suggest they were real? As I sat there, the pastor asked a lingering question.

"Where is your God now?"

I popped out of my haze.

"Does anyone know who asked this question and why?" he asked the congregation.

My full attention was on him.

"As Jesus hung on the cross, the Pharisees mocked Him, asking him that very question. If someone were to ask you that question, what would be your answer? There are some who cannot answer this question," he said and took a long pause.

So, he jumped from Revelations to the four Gospels? Where is he going with this? I wondered.

"But we should know that God is the stronger one and He will always be. We are His children. He will look out for His children. We just need to confide in Him," the pastor finished.

I want to believe God is on my side, I really do. But why am I seeing such terrible things? Aria told me that God turned away from those people I saw in the other world, and that is why they hate God. But I didn't turn my back on my faith.

When service ended, my family stood around talking with other people from the church. Charsi had her little group of friends. And yes, even here, I am invisible. As I stood there in the back of the church, I couldn't help but over hear these two women talking about this Catholic Church on the other side of town, St. Mary's. I'm usually shy when talking to new people, but before I realized it, I walked right over to them. Actually, I have seen them in church many times.

"E-excuse me," I began. My voice came out soft and shaky. They turned towards me with a pleasant glance planed on their faces. "Um, you spoke of a church, where are you talking about?" I asked.

They looked surprised by my question. The ladies were older, one may have been my parents' age, and the other much older. I think they were mother and daughter. The older of the two wore this large rim hat covering her gray curls.

"Oh, you mean St. Mary's? It's on Waltz Street," her gentle voice chimed.

The other lady spoke next. "Yes, there is a priest there who we listened in on for some of his talks. His name is Father Daniel. He is a great person to talk to about anything in the Bible. He knows it all! And he is so kind and thoughtful, on fire for God. So much different than the other priests there," she informed me.

That last comment sort of shocked me. Different than the other priests? From the way she said it, that sounded like a good thing.

"I don't normally go to Catholic Masses, but when this man speaks..." The woman sighed, "he is just so inspiring.'

Something told me to see this guy. It was an internal voice screaming at me. At that moment, I felt like I needed to meet this priest. He may be able to help me.

"Can you tell me how to get there?" I asked

The older lady took a pen from her purse and grabbed a flier off the table outside the sanctuary. She quickly scribbled the directions onto the piece of paper.

"It's not too hard, it's right before the freeway," she said handing me the paper.

I nodded. "Uh, thank you," I said.

"Not a problem dear," the eldest one said. "You take care now."

After church I sat in my room on my bed once again. I'd spent a lot of time there lately. I just sat there, staring out my window. I wished to see something hit my window and see Damon down there, looking at me with that smile. Suddenly, I was startled by my mom's call for me from the other side of the bedroom door. I had it closed because I didn't want to talk to anyone right now.

"What?" I shouted so she could hear me.

"Come downstairs, you have a guest," her voice hinted that she knew I wanted to see this person. I dragged myself over to open the door. My mom stood there on the other side with a smile.

"It's your friend," she said before walking towards the stairs.

When I got down to the last step, I saw Damon in the foyer. His expression was full of disdain. Charsi stood in the doorway between the foyer and the kitchen, just looking at us.

You're not keeping anything from me. Her annoying look said.

"Charsi, can you come here please?" I heard my mom's voice. "I need your help," she yelled to her. Charsi slowly turned away like she didn't want to miss out on something.

"I..." Damon began with this shaky voice I never heard from him before. "I need to talk to you." I led him into the living room. Our living room was sort of a mess today. The coffee table cluttered with stuff and the cushions on the couch were uneven. We sat down anyways. He kept looking ahead, facing the TV. The news was on, but I doubted he cared about that right now.

"A-are you alright?" I asked after too much silence. He kept his head down as he shook it. "No," he breathed in. "It happened again." He looked up at me. His hair was messier than usual, like he didn't comb it at all.

"Do you want to go upstairs and talk?" I asked him, being concerned.

"Let's go for a walk, I need a smoke," he said. I nodded even though I didn't like the fact that he smoked. He really needed to tell me something, I could definitely see that.

Once outside, he went for his pack of cigarettes in his pocket. His hands were shaking as he took out the pack. He retrieved one, put it in his mouth and lit it. I noticed his lighter was a flip top and it was gold with this fancy blue design on it. He blew out the smoke with a heavy sigh.

"As you probably guessed, I saw her again. I began yelling at her to leave me alone. She just stood there with this irritating smile. Then she told me that I didn't have much time left...I don't get it! She also said that god was the enemy we have to stop." As he spoke, Damon's voice became more dramatic. "I have no idea what the hell we're supposed to do! Aria is crazy! We have to contact her somehow, both of us. Maybe she keeps seeing just one of us at a time for a reason. Maybe if we gang up on her, she won't mess with us," he said crossly.

That idea made sense, but there was no way to find her. She only shows up once in a while...hold on.

"Damon, do you realize that Aria only comes to us at night?" I asked him.

"Yeah, I still want to do that séance," he said.

"No, uh, I don't think we should," I said, not wanting to entertain that idea.

"Well what else can we do?" he asked, being bewildered.

I thought about it. I'm not sure why I had to think about it. I should just say 'no.'

"We have to try something," he said after a moment of awkward silence. "I can't take this anymore. I just want this to stop!" Damon inhaled on the cigarette again and blew out. "I know some friends who could help us too," he said quietly.

A few more moments of silence.

"Hope, I'm sorry for getting upset with you the other night. It's just that, with all this crap happening...I just didn't want to talk about the past," he apologized.

I asked him about his family. How was that discussing the past? Forget it. I won't ask him anymore questions. I'm not going to lose my only friend.

"We're doing it tonight. That's why I came to see you," he told me.

From my religious background, I knew that séances were not good, but right now, I was desperate.

And so, late that night I sat in Damon's basement with him and three of his friends. We all sat on the floor in a circle. One of his friends was someone I recognized, the girl across from me with blonde hair. I saw her on the school campus with Damon that one day. Part of me wanted to ask Damon about that, but I let it go for now. Seeing the girl more clearly, I saw her eyebrow piercing. Her outfit consisted of a black corset, frilly black skirt and net stockings. The guy next to me had black hair streaked in pink with a nose piercing. His heritage looked to be from an Asian descent. The other guy by Damon wore a cloak with full arm tattoos. Damon wore a black shirt with red and blue dragons twisting around each other and black jeans. Was I the only one that knew that black was not the only color that existed?

This is crazy! I thought to myself. I have class tomorrow morning and I'm spending my time doing this instead of studying. The girl, Terrace, took the role of leader.

"Alright," she began. "We are trying to contact Aria," she said.

"Is this really going to work?" Damon interrupted suddenly.

Justin, the guy wearing the cloak answered him, "yeah man, she's done this before. Don't worry about it," he said.

"Yes," Terrace said, "But I owe these successes to Justin," her voice was so light and airy. I thought I would fall asleep listening to her.

"Damon, you and Kei have not seen this before, I don't think you have either," she said looking at me. "But fear not, it is easier than one may think. This is a simple ritual; I do this by myself when I just pray. The spirit of the person I call comes to me," she explained. Damon nudged me and whispered, "She practices in the Wiccan faith."

Again I heard that term. What does that mean, Wicca? A Wiccan practices the Wicca faith, right? Isn't a Wiccan a witch?

Terrace placed a candle on a piece of cardboard in the center of our circle. Damon insisted on the cardboard because there would be candle drippings. Terrace lit it.

"Alright," she said. "We will join hands now. Close your eyes," she began speaking in this eerie monotone voice.

"We call now to the one named Aria. We want to know if you are here with us now," she chanted.

I began to feel lighter as if something was lifting me.

"Aria, if you can hear my voice, come to us. We await your arrival," Terrace continued.

The whole room went black. I saw Aria. She put a finger to her lips, and then jumped off a cliff. The cliff reminded me of my dream. I heard laughing. I saw Aria falling. I felt like I was falling with her. I saw the castle now. I felt as though I floated inside. I saw the ballroom where people danced, then saw the true forms of these people. They were demons, fangs, pasty skin, and black eyes. Then I went deeper into the castle. I went down a spiral staircase and into another room where I saw a portal open. There was intense sorrow coming from the portal and there I was surrounded by darkness and the cries of many tormented souls.

It became silent; I was aware only of the presence of the others in the circle. Everyone sat with their eyes closed.

"Where are you Aria? We want to understand who you are," Terrace spoke. I only heard her voice now. I knew I was wide awake when I saw all of that. The candle went out in a sudden puff of smoke. Everyone opened their eyes.

"The candle went out. What does it mean?" Kei asked.

"Not a damn thing," Damon spoke, frustrated.

"No!" I cried out. "More happened," I said. They looked at me with shock at my outburst. I told them everything I saw. They all seemed amazed and I was thankful they believed me.

"How fortunate are you to have Aria speak to you, Hope," Terrace said.

Not really, I thought to myself. I already had encounters with her before we did this. That was the problem!

"She didn't really say anything," I said. I wouldn't ever get that vision out of my head. I couldn't take it anymore! I stood up and walked out of the circle. I'm done with séances.

Everyone decided to just hang out after that. I watched part of this horror flick with the group. How can these people watch this crap after doing a séance? Well they didn't experience what I did. Forget it! It's almost one in the friggin' morning! I'm going home! Turning toward Damon, I whispered, "I need to go now." He barely responded and I just got up and left. No one even said goodbye. They were zoned in on the movie.

The next morning I felt so tired. I almost didn't make it to my ten-o-clock class on time. I had two classes that day. It was a good thing I recorded both lectures because I couldn't concentrate in class at all. I wanted to visit that church but I didn't want to go alone. When I called Damon asking him to come with me, he seemed really confused.

"You want to see a priest?" His voice came out of the receiver of my cell phone.

"I...I don't know what else to do. That séance thing just made it worse," I said.

I stood in my room with the door closed. I didn't want anyone in my family hearing this. Now I began pacing.

"Please Damon, please come with me," I asked pleadingly. "I sounded like I was begging. I hated that!

"Fine, but ...uh I haven't been to church in a while," he said hesitantly.

I wondered what that had to do with anything.

"That's all right. You don't even have to say anything just come with me," I told him.

"Okay, fine!" he said exasperated.

I got to ride in his car again. He sure didn't mind driving. I had lots of leg room. I liked this car so much. It was definitely the typical two-door sports car. The engine roared loudly as the car tore down the street.

"So, you really think a priest will help us?" Damon asked.

"I don't know," I answered trying to keep myself calm. I was already nervous enough as it was.

"Should I turn here?" he asked suddenly. I looked at the directions, then at the street sign. I had such a hard time focusing. My anxiety was making it hard to think normally.

"Y-no, keep going," I instructed him.

"Don't confuse me!" he complained.

"S-sorry, it's just that..." I stuttered.

He sort of glanced sideways at me, "If you don't want to do this, we don't have to," he said.

"I'm fine," I insisted.

"Okay, just tell me when you see the road I'm supposed to turn on," he told me. I gave a slight nod.

As we came to the next street, I couldn't tell what the name of the street was at first. A tree was blocking the way. I suddenly saw the letter spell out WALTZ.

"Oh here! Turn right here!" I spurted out. He quickly jerked the steering wheel, screeching the tires.

Son of a...couldn't you have given me more warning?!" he asked with irritation.

I wish I could have!

"Sorry..." I tried.

I saw the sign for the freeway like the lady said.

"It's before the freeway," I told him.

The church was not hard to miss. It stood tall with high archways. The structure was an old style Gothic architecture. The steeple stood tall on top of the church, reaching towards the sky. Damon parked in the lot across from the church. We crossed the street and made our way up the steps to two large doors. Roses and carnations were planted by the side, protected by a tiny wire fence. They probably looked good in the spring and summer, but they were wilting away now. I breathed in and pulled on the door handle. I held the door for Damon, but he didn't take it.

"Are you coming?" I asked.

His eyes went up the gigantic structure. "I'll wait out here," he said.

"I thought you wanted to talk to the priest," I reminded him.

He looked hard at me. "You wanted to talk to the priest. I came because you asked me to drive you here," he said.

"I didn't just want you to come for that. I had directions. I wanted you to come with me so we can both talk to this guy and he can hear both of our stories," I said.

"You said to come with you to this church. You said nothing about going inside," he made it clear.

Please, I obviously implied it.

"I just don't feel comfortable with this," he finished.

"Going into a church?" I asked.

"Yes!" he answered harshly. "Churches make me nervous, especially Catholic churches. Catholics make me nervous!"

"Damon, I..." Looking at him, I could tell he wouldn't change his mind. "All right. I'll be right back," I said giving up on convincing him to go in with me.

I knew there had to be more to why he wouldn't come in, but I wasn't going to press him on it.

I thought the church would be empty on a Monday, but I saw children waiting down the stairs. I saw a sign on the wall:

First and Second Grade-Room 2
Third and Fourth Grade-Room 3
Fifth and Sixth Grade-Room 4

I know kids go to Sunday School, but it wasn't Sunday. The sanctuary was up ahead. Stain glass windows surrounded the room. On the other side of the doors were bowls with water in them. Since I've never been in a Catholic church or know their ritual, I had no idea what these were used for. Now how was I supposed to find this guy? I walked up to the altar, the crucifix hung on the wall giving the feeling that God was there watching everyone. Interesting, my church doesn't have an altar like this or a hanging crucifix. We had pews just like this church, but instead of the altar we have a stage where the band plays worship music and the pastor gives his sermons.

"Hello? Can I help you?" I was startled by the voice coming from behind me. This man looked like a priest. His hair reminded me of how my dad kept his, very neat. But the priest's hair was light brown instead of sandy blonde. This guy definitely looked to be as old as my dad, however. His black robe covered down to his wrists and over his shoes. The white collar that showed his priesthood covered fully around his neck.

"Hi, I need to see Father Daniel," I told him.

"I am he," he said, "And you are?"

"I'm Hope," I replied quietly.

"Hope. Such a nice name. Your name means a lot, you know."

"Uh...You know anything about demons?" I asked. My boldness even shocked me.

"I know some things," he said with a smile.

"How about people who are demon possessed?" I asked.

"Yes. There are different verses in the Bible that pertain to demons and being demon possessed. My favorite verse is in the book of Mark, where a man was so over taken by demons that he was locked away from all other people. They bound him in chains and this is when Jesus came to this land and asked to see him. When he saw this man, he spoke to the demons. He asked them, 'who are you?' And the demons answered, 'I am Legion; we are many.' Jesus cast the demons out into a large group of swine, and the swine..." he said with a wave of his arm, "ran into the nearest body of water, Mark 5:1."

That was amazing. He didn't even have to open the Bible. I think I've heard that verse before.

"So, can people get possessed even today?" I asked.

"Yes, definitely," he affirmed.

I needed to be more direct. "I...see things. Um....I see people dying...and people burning in fire..." I told him.

The priest kept his eyes on me and for the first time, I could look directly at the person I was having a conversation with.

"Am I possessed because I see those things?" I risked asking the question even though I was scared to death of the answer.

"Do you want me to pray for you?" he asked.

I didn't care at this point. "Yeah, that's fine," I said.

"You must fight the fear the demons have instilled into you. Have a seat," he offered.

We sat on the first pew. The priest put his hand on my head and began murmuring in a foreign language. It sounded Latin, but I wasn't sure. He prayed for minutes at a time. How long was this prayer? Finally, he stopped and removed his hand. I felt the burden lifted away.

"What kind of prayer was that?" I asked.

"I was speaking with the holy spirit, in tongues," he said.

"I never heard anything like that," I said. He laughed a little. "It was done back in Biblical times. Jesus prayed over many," he explained.

I already knew that, but I didn't realize that is how he did it. I thought my mind would be clear from the clutter now, but of course, the thought of that woman crept into my head.

"Um, I have another problem," I said as I approached the other pressing topic.

"I keep meeting this woman and when I am around her, I see strange things. I don't know if they are really happening..or I'm just hallucinating. I see people in pain and I see these monsters, and... Uh, my friend sees it too. He didn't want to come in right now. But we've both experienced these things when this woman is around us," I tried to explain.

"This woman comes to see you and your friend often?" he asked.

"Well, that's another thing. She won't see us at the same time, and she makes sure we're alone," I told him.

"Does she give you anything? Any kind of drug or anything like that?" he asked.

That was a new concept I hadn't considered. Aria trying to drug us? But she never gave Damon or me anything.

"Who is this woman?" Father Daniel asked further.

Before I could answer, I became dizzy. My body felt heavy. I looked up at the crucifix. It changed in front of my eyes! I heard inhuman laughter. I saw blood fall from the eyes of Christ! The laughter grew louder. I saw the visions again, the people crying out in pain. If felt the energy within my body drain rapidly. I felt mental anguish and hopelessness. Then I heard a hollow voice speak, "I…don't want…to feel the pain anymore…" My mind shut down. I saw black. I fainted.

Chapter Nine:
The Test of Battle

I awoke in a bed, but it wasn't mine. I found myself in an unfamiliar room. As I looked around more, I saw it was a hospital room. There was a monitor next to me and a needle sticking out of my arm with a tube leading from it to the monitor. I turned my head to see Damon standing by the window looking out.

"See why I don't go into churches? Bad stuff happens," he said. He wasn't even looking at me, how did he know that I was awake?

"Damon? How did I get here?" I asked feeling dazed.

"The priest called an ambulance. They brought you here," he said somewhat irate.

"Where's here?'" I asked feeling groggy.

He still didn't look at me. He must be talking about Fallen Ridge Hospital. There was only one hospital in this town.

"Are you okay?" I asked him. He finally turned around to look at me; a look of disorientation crossed his face.

"Are *you* okay?" he asked the question more dramatically. "How did you black out?" he asked with concern.

I could only think of one name, "Aria…"

Damon closed his eyes, making a low groan, "Dammit! I'm gonna kill that woman!" he exclaimed.

"The visions. They were more vivid and just blending together. I heard this laughing, it wasn't human," I stopped speaking. I felt so tired. "I just want to sleep," I slurred.

"Sleep?" Are you sure?" he asked with some fear behind his voice.

"Yeah…" I answered as I drifted off.

The next time I awoke I found myself alone in the room. I don't remember falling asleep. I couldn't hear the normal bustling noises of nurses outside the room, nor did I hear the beeping of the machine. The IV was gone too. It was absolutely silent. Right now I was wearing this sheer operation gown. Was I operated on? I didn't want to think about that?

I got up, grabbing my clothes from a chair in the corner of the room. After I got my clothes on, I walked outside into the hallway. No one was around. My thoughts went crazy. *No! I'm tired of this happening! And here, of all places…a hospital!*

This was the type of place that was eerie enough while people were around and things were running normally. I looked through the window outside. Heavy clouds made the sky appear darker. The sun was completely covered. Where was Damon? I just wanted to leave.

I began walking down the hallway, through two swinging doors. I saw a vending machine right by the bathroom. I was not looking in any bathroom, not after what I saw at my school. The elevators were up ahead. I pushed the button, but it didn't light up. They weren't working, I guess. The exit stairs were at the end of the hallway.

This is so stupid! No one gave me an answer of why any of this was happening, not one that made sense anyway!

From the third floor where I was, I walked down to the first floor. I followed exit signs to the front doors of the building. The exit to this madness was right in front of me. I could just leave, but I thought about Damon. He might still be here. I had this feeling that he was trapped within the same insanity as me. I needed to look for him. There are three floors to this building so I'd start with this floor first. The main lobby looked normal, but I was disturbed by the musty smell. Where was that coming from? Magazines were in their usual spots, on the rack set on the tables around the room. The cushion seats looked inviting to sit on, but I didn't have time to rest. Through the next door into the operation area, the air became even thicker. Now the smell became more nauseating. One room was open, inside were the normal operating equipment one would expect to see. There was a sheet covering the table. Part of the sheet was soaked with something I pulled the sheet back to reveal the table covered in blood. This was definitely where the smell came from. Well, that's nice, moving on now!

I left that area and walked back through the lobby. There was a child's center in this direction. The office was open; children's toys were spread out in the far corner of the room. More magazines were put in their normal places.

Through the door into the back rooms, it was quiet except for a strange crunching sound. A few steps down the hall, I saw an animal chewing on something. It looked like a dog, but it also had wings extending from its back. It turned suddenly and I saw what it was chewing on. It looked like a human leg! That was a bit too

73

much! The dog creature just stared at me. Suddenly, it sprang at me, knocking me down. Quickly, I pushed it off. As it rolled over on its side, I saw that it was dead. I wondered how, then saw the blade in my hand, the swords returned to me. Both of the blades were long again. In the 'real world' the weapons appeared as twin short swords, but here they were twice as long as the hilt, which was pretty long. The creature I killed didn't show any blood, just as the demons I fought before. It evaporated into dust.

As I started down the hall again, another one showed up. This one jumped up at me too. The weapons took over, slashing the creature. I moved swiftly and spun around cutting into its side. It winced then tried to attack again. My body twisted around making the final stab into the dog's torso. The creature met the same fate as the other one I slew.

Moving to the right was an open door. I rushed inside and shut the door as I heard more of those creatures' howls behind me. More were coming. They traveled in packs like normal dogs. I locked the door; I prayed that they weren't strong enough to break down the door.

There was dim lighting in here that kept flickering on and off quickly. I was in another examination room. Cute, colorful pictures hung on the wall. The room appeared decorated for a child. A scale was in the corner and the sink sat opposite from the examination table. As I turned away from the sink to look at the table again, someone lay there. I stumbled back in shock. No one was there a minute ago. The woman lay there with her eyes closed. She was very thin. I held tightly onto the blades as I slowly approached her. She didn't even look alive. I stood over her, looking down at her face. Strange. She looked familiar. Suddenly she opened her eyes. I backed up. For a moment, nothing else happened. It was kind of disturbing, her eyes didn't really focus, just a blank stare. Then she turned her head towards me and sat up. I backed up more until I hit the sink. This hoarse voice emerged from within her.

"Where...is...my...daughter?" It sounded like she was pushing out her final breath as she spoke. I opened my mouth, but no sound came out.

"Do...you...know...where...she...is?" she asked.

I only shook my head.

"Here…" she said. A notebook was in her hand. I made the attempt to move. I couldn't stop my hand from shaking as I took it.

"Can…you…please…find…her?" she pleaded. Then she vanished.

What was that?! A ghost?! That was the same woman I saw before in my room. How am I supposed to find her daughter?

I looked over the notebook in my hand. The cover was light blue with stick figures of people and flowers drawn in crayon. I opened the cover to see words written on the first page.

This is the story of my child's birth. I wondered when I was a girl, if I would ever meet someone like in a fairy tale. Years ago I met a man who not only was that someone, but seemed to know all my dreams and my fears. His eyes made me feel warm. His hair was always kept so neat. I had a child with him who he decided to name Blood Child. The name was very strange for a newborn infant, but I agreed to it.

Soon we talked about marriage. He told me we were already committed to each other and did not have to be married in a church. He loved me. That was what I wanted to believe. He knew everything about me. At first, I felt so happy that someone knew me so well. But soon, it became scary. He knew too much. He knew things I never told anyone. Then he said he could make the dreams I never told come true. Suddenly, I felt uncomfortable around him. Even though I had his child, I did not feel I should be with him anymore. He made me do things that I hated and I felt dirty. He made me participate in these rituals some with my newborn child. It was like he planned that too. He had all these plans and I just followed along. Finally I could not take it anymore; I told him that I felt strange with him knowing everything about me. I told him that I did not want to see him anymore. He did not really respond to this. He did not laugh or cry, smile or frown...he said nothing and left.

After he was gone, I decided to change the child's name to Kiara instead. As my child grew, I noticed that she had some unique features. Her eyes were a brilliant blue, just like her father's. Her hair was strange too. Her bangs were stark white and the rest of her hair was black, like mine. As a child, she was scary to look at and it seemed that most people were afraid to go near her. It was her eyes that looked so cold; so unemotional. What could I do? She was my child. I pretended she was normal. Sometimes she scared me when she looked at me. How could I be afraid of my own child?

There were some blank pages. After that there was a page with huge lettering that read: *HE'S HERE! HE'S BACK! HE'S BACK!*

The rest of the pages either had childish pictures or were blank. I placed the journal on the bed.

Who is Kiara? I wondered.

I came out of the room to see four of the dogs crowding around me. Couldn't they find any mutant cats to chase? Swinging the blades, I struck at their jaws as they tried to chomp down on me. The dogs winced back in pain with each strike. I dodged the snapping jaws and swung for their throats. The dogs yelped as I hacked down at their necks multiple times. I kept striking the one closest to me until it fell and burned to ash. The others came at me and before I knew it, I had cut them down to the bone and they burned away. I had so much adrenaline that I kept moving at a fast pace down the rest of the hallway. But now another mystery presented itself to me. Once again the swords vanished.

"Why does this keep happening?!" I cried out.

I could barely restrain myself from losing control. Those weapons made me feel safer than having nothing.

Looking around anxiously, I decided that it was best to keep moving. Returning to the stairwell, my feet moved as fast as they could up to the second floor. Maybe Damon was up here. Down the long hallway, I came to a receptionist desk. This place was so quiet. Not a soul was around. The search for Damon seemed futile. I'd been finding everyone and everything except for Damon.

"Damon!" I called. "Damon are you here? There was no answer. Sighing, I continued searching the area. There were more bathrooms up here too. I really didn't want to go in them. I tried knocking on the men's room.

"Damon, are you in there?" I asked as I knocked. No response.

I went into the woman's bathroom. Everything appeared normal in here. I left and started down the hallway until I found the cafeteria. I wasn't interested in food, especially after seeing the buffet table. I think the potatoes went bad by looking at some brown mush stuff in a bowl... and I'm not going to comment on the salad (at least I think it was salad).

"Ugh, I'm...going to move on now," I said to myself.

Nothing out of the ordinary, just a few tables lined the wall. The bulletin board was cluttered with pamphlets, paper, and postage notes on information about the hospital's services. I've got something to say about your service. It sucks!

There were public restrooms over in this area too. I knocked on the men's bathroom door. Again no one answered. I should just go in there; there aren't any people around anyways. I pushed the door open, feeling sort of embarrassed as I looked around. I was about to leave when I looked over at the stalls to see blood dripping from one of the doors.

Not again! Forget it, I'm not going to look! My thoughts protested. Still I felt myself walk forward and push on the door. Behind the door, I saw the worst graffiti anyone could scroll on the bathroom wall. Public schools never had to see this! In blood was written,

> *God is dead!*
> *Satan is power!*
> *Blessed are the strong, for they shall possess the Earth-Cursed are the weak, for they shall inherit the yoke!*
> *Blessed are the powerful, for they shall be reverenced among men-Cursed are the feeble, for they shall be blotted out!*
> *Blessed are the bold, for they shall be masters of the world-Cursed are the righteously humble, for they shall be trodden under cloven hooves!*

Blessed are the death-defiant, for their days shall be long in the land-Cursed are the gazers toward a richer life beyond the grave, for they shall perish amidst plenty!

Amidst all of this was a cross, drawn upside down. I heard of that symbol before it's a mockery of Christianity. Why did I feel the need to come in here to see this? And this writing…It was written in the same type of language as the Bible, but the meanings behind the verses were the exact opposite from the Good Book.

These verses intrigued me. I had to write them down. There were notepads and pens on the survey table in the hall outside the café. I rushed back to the area to retrieve some pen and paper.

When I walked back into the men's room, I was stopped suddenly when I saw a living person in there. It was Damon, even better! He turned toward me,

"Hope? What are you doing in here?" he asked as if he were disturbed by my presence.

"I was looking for you!" I burst out.

"Why are you in the guy's bathroom? You're in the wrong bathroom!" he shouted at me.

At this point it didn't matter. "Well, I wasn't going to check the bathrooms after what happened to me on the school's campus, but if you must know, I was concerned enough about you to check anyways," I said in my defense.

"So? This is the men's bathroom, so get out!" he said in a tone that I couldn't take seriously. He was just joking, I realized, but now was not the time!

"Why does it matter right now?" I barked at him.

"I'm just messing with you," he said. "It's all right; I've been in all the girl's bathrooms in this place. There was no one around to scream at me. It's sort of cool being able to go wherever you want," he said.

What was he talking about? This type of stuff is not supposed to happen!

"Uh, did you see the writing in the stall?" I asked.

"Writing?" he asked.

When I showed Damon the offensive graffiti, his eyes widen with shock.

"Wow! This person is talented to be able to write in blood like this," he said staring at the wall.

"Aren't you grossed out by it?" I dubiously asked. *Seriously!*

"Well, it does smell bad, but this person must have felt a need to do this," he said.

"But why would someone do this? It's just wrong!" I exclaimed.

"Hey, there were artists who did all sorts of weird stuff to show their artistic views," he said still focusing on the wall.

I wrote down the verses onto the piece of paper I found as quickly as possible. The words sounded like they could come from the Bible, but I knew they didn't.

"Have you actually read the Bible?" Damon asked suddenly.

"Yes, I read it all the time. Well, actually, I've participated in Bible studies at church," I told him.

"Do you know what the upside-down cross means?" he asked.

"I was told it's the opposite of Christianity; Satanism," I explained.

Damon studied the cross. "Yeah, I've seen this symbol before. I know someone who has a Celtic cross tattooed upside down on his arm," he told me.

"Is he a Satanist?" I asked.

"I don't really believe anyone is a Satanist," Damon concluded. "I think it's something churches just made up to scare people."
I didn't agree with that, but I stayed quiet.

"He's a friend of Terrace's, the girl you met at my house. He was supposed to come too, because he knows about that stuff. He would have done the ceremony himself, but he couldn't make it. But he's not a Satanist!" Damon added the last part in rather quickly and with some harshness.

"We should get out of here," I strongly suggested.

"Yeah, anytime would be great!" he agreed.

I couldn't get what he said about Satanism and the church out of my head. What was his issue with the church anyways?

Now moving toward the stairs, we were intent on getting out of this place.

"You know the elevator isn't working, right?" Damon asked.

"I know," I passed back to him. We went from a fast pace walk to breaking out in a sprint down the stairs. Now on the first floor, we ran towards the entrance. As we were approaching the lobby, the floor boards weakened. We fell right through the floor! I lay on my back looking up at the hole.

"Damon!" I called. "Are you okay?"

"I think I broke my back!" he cried out.

It was completely dark down here. As I looked around, my eyes adjusted so I could see. There were rooms with steel doors and small square windows framing the top of the doors. Who would they put down here? This was too creepy. Damon got to his feet. He looked around frantically.

"Hope! Where are you?" he called out to me. I was right in front of him. "I'm right here," I said.

"Where?!" He stumbled about.

"Damon, what's wrong with you?" I got up and grabbed his hand.

"Oh there you are," he said.

"You couldn't see me?" I asked.

"I can't see anything!" he shouted.

I looked at him for a moment. I don't know what came over me, I just hugged him. That wasn't like me to just do something so impulsive. I felt him hug me back.

"We should get out of here," he said. He started to move away. "I wish we had a flashlight," he said.

The more I looked around, the more my eyes adjusted. How come I could see fine, but he couldn't see at all?

"Let's just get out of this place," I said taking his hand and walking.

"Do you know where you're going?" he asked.

I had no clue.

We got down the hallway when we saw a grotesque display. More monsters, plus one larger demon crowded around fires lit in trash cans. The flames were the only light down here. One demon was very large, similar to the one I saw at the museum. It appeared the same way, like an angel, but with singed wings. The skin appeared brownish and rubbery. His eyes were black and sunken into its deformed head. There were about five or six other demons. These creatures stood on two legs, their heads were round, eyes black and their arms and legs were abnormally long with overtly large hands and feet. Their skin appeared red and burnt. It reminded me of those victims I saw on campus.

80

"Wonder what they're doing?" Damon pondered.

"How do we get past them?" I asked.

Damon lifted his hands. He held the guns with the engraved names of the archangels. They appeared to him the same way the swords came to me.

"You know these things just appear when there's something to fight?" he noted.

But the swords didn't come to me like before.

"I don't have my weapons. I don't know how I can help you fight those things," I told him.

Damon looked at the group of monsters, then at me.

"I'll take care of them," he assured me.

"Are you sure?" I asked somewhat horrified by the situation.

"Yeah." He smiled. I couldn't believe he was so calm about everything. Either Damon was that brave or he lacked common sense.

I ducked behind some tall boxes. Damon suddenly jumped out and unleashed bullets at the monsters. The lesser demons were taken down easily, but each one taken down was replaced by more. They surrounded him. I wanted to help him, but the blades wouldn't come to me. As I watched Damon, he didn't even look scared. It seemed like he'd done this before. I thought I was safe until something grabbed me from behind. One of the demons held my arms; another one came and took my legs. At first, I thought they were going to pull me apart! But they ended up throwing me into the wall. The pain struck me, but it was not as bad as I thought it would be. I got up and regained my composure. Now the four demons were advancing on me. Damon was just dealing with the larger demon. I guess I'm being a good diversion. As the demons cornered me, I took this gigantic leap over one of the trashcans. I didn't know how I accomplished that. But I took the advantage, knocking the can over. The fire caught onto the boxes, trapping the monsters.

Damon shot endlessly at the winged demon. He was at least smart enough to keep a good distance from it. But the demon jumped forward, then slashed out with claws and sliced Damon's clothing.

"What the hell?!!" he cried out. The giant monster seemed to be laughing at him. It angered me suddenly. The demon continued slashing at Damon. He was hurt badly. He was bleeding!

As long as the fire burned, I didn't have to worry about the other demons attacking. The more Damon shot at his adversary, the more it got aggressive. It flapped its gigantic wings again, then pounded on Damon. Damon landed on his back. That thing started to tear him apart. It tore at his clothes and ripped his skin off!

Damon's cries pierced through me. He tried to shoot the monster, but it knocked the guns out of his hands. "Shoot it!" Damon cried.

Taking the guns, I aimed at the giant beast and pulled both triggers at once. The most vivid white light came from the barrels; the ear piercing blast echoed the hall; bullets penetrated the demon's thick armored skin. Cracks of white light spread through its body, then exploded. Both Damon and I were speechless for a second.

"Let's get the hell out of here!" Damon exclaimed.

I breathed in and nodded.

We started to run. Behind us, we heard high-pitched screeching. Looking behind me, I saw the demons coming after us. The fire must have died down enough for them to get through! Ahead were some stairs. We made it to the steps and upstairs to the first floor. The emergency exit was in front of us. As we approached the door, we noticed chains wrapped around the door handles. Behind us were the heavy footsteps of those creatures.

"It's locked, we can't get out!" he shouted. At that point, I didn't care if I had to break the glass of the door. I was getting out of there!

"Just shoot the lock!" I shouted.

Instead, he used the back of the gun to break the glass. We ran out into the parking lot.

"Where did you park?" I asked.

"Down this way," he said, leading us down a row of cars. We were almost to the car. Damon had the keys ready. As we approached the car three dogs jumped out from behind a van and blocked our path. Suddenly, I was far beyond irritated; I was right out angry. I felt the swords in my hands.

"Get out of our way!" my voice commanded. I sliced them up before Damon had a chance to move.

"Whoa, where did the aggression come from?" Damon asked almost laughing. I went to the driver's side and pulled on the door handle discovering it was locked.. I looked at Damon feeling exhausted.

"Can you unlock the door?" I asked in a weakened voice.

He did, and we both jumped in. It was then that I realized Damon's wounds on his the side of his face and neck were healed completely.

"Damon, didn't that thing cut you up badly?" I asked in astonishment.

He shrugged. "I feel fine." He looked into the rear view mirror. "Yeah, nothing's wrong," he said.

"But you were really hurt and you were bleeding," I told him.

"I guess I heal quickly," he said with a smirk. It was then that I realized how Damon could make light of any situation.

Chapter Ten:
Damon's Past

The sound of knocking woke me up. I found myself on the living room couch. I had no recollection of walking into the house last night. I heard the knocking again. It was incessant. I wondered why no one had answered the door yet. I got up slowly and stumbled towards the door. I felt that drugged feeling as I moved towards the foyer and to the front door. Opening the door, I saw a tall African-American man dressed in black pants and a heavy tan sweater. I was sort of surprised to see him, not because of his race, but because I've never seen him before. This man had to be the tallest person I've ever met. Not only was he extremely tall, but extremely well built.

"Hi, how are ya?" he greeted. "I'm handing out invitations to come have fun at our little get together at Fantasy Nights. Have you been there?" he asked.

"Yeah," I answered.

"Great! The party's on Friday, October 30th and it starts at six-o-clock," he said. I took the invitation, turning away for a moment to look at it. The invitation said, *costume party.*

"This is some type of Halloween party?" I asked.

"Yes, but you don't have to dress up," he said with a friendly grin.

"Why are you handing these out instead of mailing them?" I asked. I thought it was a good question.

He seemed taken aback from my question. "Well, I'm sure you will find out when you come," he said. He seemed so professional, like a door to door salesperson. "There's an old friend who wants to meet you," he finished and walked off down the walkway to a black truck. I closed the door and heard the truck drive away. I opened the pamphlet to find a map inside. Fantasy Nights was the same club that I went to with Damon. Maybe he would go with me. I looked at the symbol on the cover of the booklet; a curved moon with stars.

"Who was that?" The voice pulled me away from my thoughts. It was my sister once again getting into my business.

"Charsi...hi." I stuffed the pamphlet into my pocket, which probably crinkled it.

She kept looking at me as if waiting for me to speak. "Oh, the guy at the door, yeah, he was offering Bibles. I told him that we have a number of the King James Version."

"Oh, alright," she said, but she didn't looked like she believed me. I rushed upstairs before my nosy sister asked me anything else. It was none of her business anyways! If she knew anything about what was going on with me...I mean, everyone would know. She doesn't keep secrets well. I wasn't even sure what this event was about, and with all these strange things happening...I didn't need my family to know about it. But part of me wanted to tell them. I especially wanted to tell my mom. I usually told her everything. It didn't seem to matter though. I tried to talk to a priest and nothing was resolved. In fact, it seemed to get worse!

This party continually crept into my thoughts as the week went on. And with my mind so cluttered, I couldn't even keep the days straight anymore. The one thing I couldn't stop thinking about was how that guy just showed up. And even stranger, I found out that I was never verified as a patient at Fallen Ridge Hospital. No one called me or my parents about a bill or even about me staying there. I didn't get it. I didn't even want to try anymore.

The date of the party came closer and I still waited to hear from Damon. I kept calling him and just got his voice mail. It came to the day before the party. I thought of just going to his house. I had to get ahold of him somehow. I wasn't going to this thing alone.

I sat on my bed looking at the pamphlet/invitation to the party. On the bottom of the map there were some words in cursive writing.

Blessed be the night.

Weird I thought to myself.

"What's that?" I heard a familiar voice ask. I looked up to see my sister in my doorway.

"Charsi...it's nothing," I said. She walked over to the side of the bed. She looked curiously at me for a moment, then tried to take the pamphlet. I pulled it away as she grabbed for it.

"What is it?" she asked more directly.

"It's directions to Damon's house," I offhandedly spurted out.

"Is he your boyfriend now?" she asked with a pushy tone.

"No. We're just friends," I answered with shortness. Then softer, I said, "I could never date a smoker."

85

"Damon smokes?" she asked with an annoying high pitched voice.

"Uh, sometimes," I tried to play it off. "He only does it outside," I tried to defend him.

"Well, I couldn't date a smoker either," she agreed. She started to turn away.

"Hope, you would never keep a secret from me, would you?" she asked innocently.

"What kind of a secret?" I asked her.

"Any secrets. I mean, you can tell me anything," she said trying to come off as sweet.

Maybe when we were kids that was true. But she's not six and I'm not ten anymore. We used to be close, but now we're so different.

"Don't worry about it Charsi. I'm just distracted by all of the work I have to do for school," I pacified her.

She turned to me with a sharp glare. "Don't patronize me! I deal with school too. You think because you're in college, you're more mature than me!" she accused.

"Well, I *am* older," I reminded her.

"Yes, but not more mature," she said in a sophisticated voice. "I know what's going on," she kept on like a brat.

I'm sure you don't! I contemplated.

"You stay out at night and spend time with that boy all the time. You're sleeping with him aren't you?" she insinuated.

"What?!" I couldn't believe my little sister's words.

"No! Of course not! We're just friends!" I exclaimed.

"Then where are you going at night?" she interrogated me.

"Out. To clubs, hanging out with friends; I do have friends, Charsi!" I threw out harshly.

"What kind of friends? You're participating in séances, are you hanging out with Satanists now?" she continued with accusations.

"How dare you judge people like that?!" I screamed. "How would you know if I participated in a séance anyway?" I demanded.

"I found these!" Charsi said holding up a box of tarot cards.

"Where did you get those?" I asked being puzzled.

"They fell out of your bag!" she said strongly.

"First of all, those aren't mine. Second, don't come in my room and just take stuff!" I warned.

"Your bag was downstairs," she said.

"You must have moved my bag, because I didn't leave it there," I replied sharply.

"That's where I found it!" she insisted.

"No. I had it in my room. You must have taken it from here," I said as if it were truth.

"Are you saying those card are yours?" she asked, daunting me.

Now I was beyond frustrated with her. All of this because I participated once in a séance? The girl doing the séance didn't use cards! My mind was ready to explode!

"No! Why do you care what I do?" I demanded from her.

"Were you involved in a séance?" Charsi persisted.

She really wanted to know.

"I did it with Damon and his friends…uh they were trying to see if Damon's house is haunted." *Oh God! That's the best I can come up with?* "Look, I know I shouldn't do that stuff and something freaky happened and I'm never doing it again, alright?" I asked with some lingering annoyance.

"What about these?" Charsi asked referring the cards she still held.

"I'm serious. I've never seen them before," I said.

"Tell me where you found them or I'm telling mom and dad," she threatened. She did that tattle-tale voice. How is that being mature?

"Tell them what? That I'm doing séances? How exactly would they stop me?" I questioned.

Charsi gave a sound of exasperation. "Fine. We'll see what they say. I hear dad's car now," she said and walked towards the stairs.

"So you're going to tell on me for something so stupid and you think you're more mature than me?!" I screamed at her. I chased her downstairs, but she was at the front door and dad was coming inside.

I knew those cards weren't mine! Were they Damon's cards? If so, why would they end up in my bag? He wouldn't put them there, would he? I tried to even contemplate how he would get ahold of my bag, let alone put those cards in there. Plus he really had no reason to do it. I put my bag upstairs, zipped closed. It was upstairs this morning. Someone had to bring it down here. It had

87

to be Charsi. I couldn't stand it, I just wanted to scream! I didn't do anything wrong and now Charsi is ready to bad-mouth me to our parents for something so stupid! She doesn't even know what's happening to me! She doesn't even care how I've been suffering!

Speaking of the matter, the little witch just came in with my father who looked puzzled.

"Now," he began as he set down his briefcase. He looked over at me, "what is going on?" he asked calmly.

I was about to speak when he pointed towards the kitchen.

"Come on, let's sit down and talk," Dad said.

The three of us sat at the kitchen table. Right away, Charsi began babbling about finding the cards in my bag.

"Dad, those are not mine!" I protested. "They might belong to Damon, and I'm going to ask him about them," I explained sincerely.

"All right, what about this séance thing?" he asked.

"I did participate in it once, but I won't do it again. It was scary." I wasn't lying about that either. "I am not a Satanist, alright?" I said strongly.

My father sighed and looked at Charsi. "Now, I know you are concerned about this matter, but don't jump to conclusions," he told her.

"But she is out almost every night, all night. Aren't you wondering what she's doing?" Charsi asked him.

"Well, she is a grown up," he stated. "She can be out late as long as she is keeping up with her studies, it doesn't bother me," Dad said flatly.

Charsi stood up, pushing her chair back with a screech. "You always make a big deal about where I'm going and who I'm with all the time! You never even met this Damon and you don't care that she's always out with him?" she fussed.

"Well, your mother met him and said he was a nice kid," Dad said. He looked at me now. "Maybe you should invite this boy to dinner so we can all meet him and find out more about him," he suggested.

"Sure, whatever," I said. I took the cards from the table. "I'll ask him about these too." I turned back towards my dad, "You know, just because someone does things differently, doesn't make them a bad person," I said.

I saw the expression on Charsi's face; she looked like she hated me now. Why does she care so much about what I do with my life? Is she jealous?

The next day, I drove to Damon's house after class. I stood at the door waiting for someone to answer. No one came and I wondered if anyone was home. The garage was closed and I didn't see anyone's vehicles in the driveway. As I started to leave, the door opened and Damon ran out past me. A tall man with dark hair came to the door.

"Damon! Get back here!" he yelled.

"Leave me the hell alone! You have no idea what's happening to me!" Damon shouted back angrily.

The man at the door just noticed me. "Are you here to see him?" he asked in an exasperated tone. I nodded. "Well you better go catch him," he said before closing the door. That was kind of rude!

I started running after Damon.

"Damon, hold on," I called. He stopped just short of the woods behind his house.

"He doesn't care," Damon said softly with his back towards me.

"Who? Your dad?" I asked assuming the man at the door was his father.

"Yeah. He doesn't care that I've been having a hard time," he said. I moved around Damon so I could see his face. He kept his head down; he wouldn't look at me.

"He wants me to go to school," Damon continued. "I told him that if I did, I wanted to major in music, but he told me he forbid it! He told me to choose a real major. Music is all I'm good at though," he explained.

"It's hard to make your family understand you, I know. Right now, my sister believes I'm a Satanist," I said feeling sort of shameful.

Damon looked up at me. "Where did she get that idea?" he asked. I took the tarot cards out of my coat pocket. "Are these yours?" I asked.

Damon looked oddly at the cards wrapped with a rubber band.

"No. I don't own tarot cards. Terrace does, but I don't know how you would end up with them," he responded.

"Where did these come from then?" I wondered. My thoughts drifted to the incident that happened with Charsi. She acted like a child trying to get me in trouble with our dad. And she called herself more mature than me!

"What are you thinking about?" Damon interrupted my thoughts.

I let out an exasperated sigh. "My sister just frustrates me, ya know? She tries so hard to make me look foolish. She thinks she's so mature," I told him.

"Yeah, well I thought I was mature at twenty-one, but I guess I still can't make my own choices," he said with disappointment and apathy. Damon started walking into the woods and I followed. He led the way farther through the trees. We treaded up a hill a ways before Damon stopped, sitting down on a nearby tree stump. "I wish I could just move out," he said.

There weren't any other stumps for me to sit on and I wasn't sitting on the fallen wet leaves, so I just stood.

"Why don't you?" I asked.

He looked at me with tired eyes, "I would, but I really don't have the money and I'm trying to get a band together with my friends so we can start playing and get paid. My dad wants me to go to school and he is willing to pay for it, but I don't want to major in something like business or engineering like he wants me to. He thinks playing music is a waste of time," he finished explaining. Suddenly, Damon stood up in an aggressive pose, "You know, I shouldn't have to listen to him! He's not my real father anyways!" He let loose the confession as if a long guarded secret was finally released.

"What?" I didn't expect to hear that.

"Huh?" He looked confused.

"You said he's not your real father."

Damon became silent.

"Damon, what is going on with you and your family? First, you tell me that you are an only child, then I meet your brothers and sister. Then you say they're not your siblings, and now your father is not really your father?" I inquired.

Damon still wouldn't speak. He wouldn't answer me. I guess I should respect his privacy, but at the same time, after what the two of us have been through, I felt I had a right to know. He wanted to keep his secrets. Well, too bad! It was bad enough we both shared the same nightmarish visions, we had to at least trust each other.

Finally he spoke. "No, that guy is not my real father and those kids are not my real siblings. And the woman you met is not my real mother. The McKays adopted me," he confessed. He suddenly took off, walking down the other side of the hill; I quickly followed him.

"It makes sense," I said. "You don't look like them. Can I ask you about your hair?" I tried to gain another secret.

He let out a lingering sigh. "Yes, it's white, my real hair color." He answered in a tone that was upset about releasing that information.

He kept walking, quickening his pace. I raced after him, almost tripping over broken tree limbs and piles of leaves trying to keep up. "Ever since the visions, I keep thinking about where I came from. I don't know my real parents. But I never really cared before because I had a good family," he told me.

"So what age were you when you were adopted?" I asked.

Damon stopped abruptly; I almost walked into him.

"Seven, he answered. "I don't remember anything before that age.

I was twelve when my mom had my brothers," he explained.

We didn't say anything for a few moments, then Damon asked, "Did you get something delivered to you about a party at Fantasy Nights?" I almost forgot about that.

"Oh...yeah, I got something. I thought it was weird though. I asked the guy why he was delivering the invitation but he really didn't answer me about it," I told him.

"I think there is more to this. The guy who gave me the invite to me said something about meeting an 'old friend.' I have no idea what he was talking about," Damon explained.

"I was told the same thing," I responded.

"Do you want to go?" he asked as if it were all up to me.

"I don't know if I do. Something is telling me to go, but…" I paused trying to come up with a reasonable explanation for this event.

"Okay. Let's go to this thing," he said suddenly.

"Well, alright. I was told it was a costume party," I recalled what was said.

"Screw that! I'm not dressing up!" he burst out.

"Well, you don't have to. I don't know if I will either," I said.

"No, you should. I can picture you as a gunner chick or something," he teased.

"Can I borrow your guns?" I asked.

"After what I saw at the hospital? Now way! You'll blow up people!"

We burst out laughing. At that moment, I felt like I could tell Damon anything.

"You know, I've been thinking about things and I need to talk to you about this dream I've had a couple of times," I began to explain.

"Another vision?" he asked.

"No. This is a recurring dream I've had. In this dream, I am pushed off a cliff. I kept dreaming this when I was a child, then it stopped when I got older. I didn't have this dream again until the night I met Aria. And during the séance; I told you I saw her. The cliff was in the vision I saw of her. She fell or actually jumped off the cliff, and somehow I fell with her. I saw the castle and I saw these people dancing, but they were actually vampires or something," I tried to explain this phenomenon as best as I could. I wondered what Damon thought of this. He just stared at me. "I was pulled deeper into the castle and I heard this wailing and these desperate cries, like thousands of people in pain," I continued telling him.

Damon suddenly let out a snicker, "Geez! You poor thing. I think you're getting the worst of all these visions,' he said with slight pity. He had no idea.

"What would you say if the dream actually happened?" I asked.

"If you were actually pushed off a cliff, you would be dead," he said bluntly.

"I know. That is why it doesn't seem real..but it was," I told him. His eyes narrowed as he looked curiously at me. "How do you know? I mean, how could you survive something like that?" he asked.

"You've seen what's happened to us. We aren't normal, Damon," I said.

He was silent for a moment. "What exactly happened?" he asked further.

I would never forget. Memories of the incident flooded inside my head.

"When I was ten, I went with some friends to this park and there was a wooded area that went uphill to a drop off point. It was a good, I don't know, fifteen to twenty feet up," I explained.

"This happened in Fallen Ridge?" Damon asked.

"Yeah, well we were just outside the town a little ways. We rode bikes out there. These kids…" I couldn't believe this. I started feeling the tears swell up inside me. I tried to resist the emotion, "these kids were my friends…at least I thought they were," I said as my eyes filled with tears. Breathing in, I tried to hold them back. "These kids hated me so much, that they…pushed me…they pushed me off the cliff," I finished choking out the words.

Damon's eyes questioned me. He didn't believe me! Suddenly, I felt so angry.

"I'm not lying!" I screamed.

Damon drew back from my reaction.

"I'm not saying you are!" he retorted.

I just felt like he mocked me. Maybe I was overreacting, but the feeling wouldn't leave.

"Those people…they had no right…" I began mumbling, more emotion building. The memories just exploded in my mind. "THEY HAD NO RIGHT!" I screamed as loud as I could. I let go of everything. I just pounded my fists into the nearest tree. It didn't hurt me at all. I did it five or six times. Then, I stood still.

Suddenly, the wood of the tree trunk cracked; the whole tree fell over! Damon jumped back as it fell and hit the ground with a loud thud.

"Y-you just…!" he cried out.

I looked at the fallen tree. Normal people can't accomplish that feat. Now the tears came. I collapsed onto the ground, just crying my eyes out. I put my hand to my face. Then, I felt something touching me. I looked up to see Damon with his hand on my shoulder staring at me with caring eyes.

"Have you told anyone else this?" he asked sympathetically.

I shook my head.

"So, you weren't hurt...at all?" he asked again.

"No, I was fine. I never mentioned it to anyone. No one knew... how unhappy I was," I explained through my tears. Damon suddenly wrapped his arms around me. I didn't know how to react. I just cried more.

"I know. Sometimes, I wish God would just kill me already," he said. I looked oddly at him. That was a strange request.

"Why are you saying that?" I asked him. He looked away.

"Because I'm so screwed up, maybe?" he replied.

"No. You know what? Forget this!" I exploded. "It's stupid! Maybe we're the normal ones and everyone else is messed up!" I lashed out. Damon suddenly broke into hysterical laugher and I had to join him. I think we both just snapped from the insanity.

Days before the party at the night club, I thought about what I would wear. It was supposed to be a costume party. I guess I could find something to wear. I stood in the basement looking at costumes I wore in previous years for Halloween.

"Hope? What are you doing?" I turned around to see Charsi.

"Nothing," I answered harshly.

"What's your problem?" she asked crudely.

I can't believe she would even ask that.

"What are you looking for?" she kept prying.

"I'm going to a party and I need a costume," I replied.

"Hey, I have a costume for you," she said.

"Aren't you worried that I'm going to a Halloween party?" I asked.

"No, why would I be? I'm going to a party too. It's just that the costume Mom got is too skimpy and Dad doesn't like it. But she can't take it back so I'm stuck with it," she explained.

"What is it? A barmaid?" I asked jokingly.

"Yeah, like I'd dress up as a barmaid! It's an angel costume. The title of the costume is called Avenging Angel and it doesn't cover much, but Mom said I could wear it because I'm sixteen," she bragged.

"But Dad disagreed?" I asked. She nodded. "Well, I guess I could look at it," I agreed.

I followed Charsi to her room where she showed the outfit to me.

"Can you fit into this?" she asked. She took a small piece of clothing from the bed and held it up to me.

"Is that a sash or something?" I asked.

"This is the top," she said.

"Wow, how much does it cover?" I asked looking at the thin piece of cloth.

"It covers what it needs to I guess," she replied.

"Let me try it on first," I said.

A moment later I had the costume on and looking at myself in the long mirror on the closet door. I liked the colors, purple and black. A lot of skin showed like Charsi said. I wondered what Damon would think? The sleeveless top covered the chest area and made a triangle shape at my abdomen. The top was black with a purple border. The skirt was the same, only there were purple stripes going down the sides and the skirt reached just above my knees. There were leather pieces that were supposed to cover my arms and legs. I also saw a black halo and black wings. This was an angel? Angels wear white, not black. I decided that I wasn't going to wear the dumb looking halo.

"I guess I could wear this," I said.

"It looks good," Charsi commented. "So who are you going to this party with?" she asked being nosy.

"I'm going with Damon," I told her.

"Oh," her voice rose musically, hinting she knew further intentions.

"So what costume are you going to wear?" I asked.

"I don't know," she suddenly sounded annoyed. "Now I have to think of something else because Dad thinks I'm too young to show any part of my body," she whined.

"It's strange," I agreed. "You know, sometimes I'm surprised you and I are allowed to dress up for Halloween," I went on.

Charsi narrowed her eyes. "Why?"

"Because some churches say it's an evil holiday," I told her.

Charsi shrugged, "It's just for fun. But I know what you mean. I have a friend who isn't allowed to dress up. She never gets to go out and get candy or do anything. I feel bad for people who let their religion keep them from enjoying life. They don't understand. They think if you do anything fun, it's bad," she explained intelligently.

It made me feel better that my sister said that. I was beginning to think that she was one of those people who judged others that way. There are people who take things too far.

Chapter Eleven:
An Old Friend

The night of the party came finally. It seemed to take forever getting here. Damon picked me up at the time he said. He also kept his word on not dressing up. Instead, he wore a black t-shirt along with black jeans. When he saw my costume, he thought it was the coolest he'd ever seen.

"Wow! I never thought you would be the type to wear something like that," he commented.

What did he mean by that? I wondered a little worried.

My family had dinner before he and I left. It went well and Damon put up with my parents' stupid questions. We left for the club right after. The place was crowded when we got there. It was about seven-thirty. There were a bunch of people just standing around outside. We pushed past everyone. Everyone acted like it was such an inconvenience to let us through. We weren't sure where to go.

"We're here," Damon said. "Now what?"

From the crowd, a tall dark skinned man walked towards us.

"That's him" I said to Damon as I pointed to the man.

Damon nodded. "That guy is so tall, look at him!" The man's head could clearly be seen above everyone else's. He smiled at us.

"Hey, you made it! Wonderful! Come with me," he invited us.

"So, are we the only two you handed out those invitations to?" Damon asked.

The smile on the man's face faded.

"Now, let's not waste time with talk. You're friend is waiting for you," he said sternly.

I became a little nervous. What's going on?

The man took us to the back behind the bar. We went through a door that said *Employees Only*, then up the stairs and through a thick oak door. On the other side was a lounge room. There were a few couches and chairs with a red interior. The music was muffled a little by the walls. One of the walls was completely glass. We were able to look down through the windows at the people in the club.

We sat down on the couch right before the door opened. A girl walked in. I noticed her heavy mascara and blue eye shadow right away. Her outfit consisted of a black tank top with a leather jacket and leather pants. She also wore a spiked collar with matching bracelets. Her expression was calm as she sat across from Damon and me.

"Damon…Hope, it's been a while," she said to us. I didn't know who she was and I wasn't sure if Damon knew either.

"You remember me?" she asked. Neither of us spoke. Her eyes dropped down in a sudden disappointment. "It's me, Kiara," she said.

Kiara! I almost jumped off the couch in excitement. Finally something made sense! That woman I saw in my room and at the hospital; she was looking for her daughter… Kiara.

"Oh, right," I said trying to make her think we knew her. "Nice outfit. I like the whole Goth look for a costume as you can see with mine," I rambled on. Now I was babbling. I gave a slightly nervous laugh.

"Actually, this is how she usually dresses," the man said as he laughed. Kiara gave him a harsh jab into his shoulder. From looking at how muscular this guy was, I doubt he felt that.

"Yeah, I usually wear this much eye liner!" she sternly spoke as she jabbed him again. "I usually don't even wear this much eye make-up," she said to us. She turned her gaze towards Damon. "I see you didn't dress up. Still the same, I see," she joked with him. Damon barely uttered a sound in response. "And always so articulate," she kept teasing.

"I'm sorry, who are you?" Damon finally asked. "And who is he?" He pointed at the tall man.

"This is the manager of this fine establishment, Lyell. I have been helping him out for a little over three years now," Kiara explained. She looked for Damon to catch on, but even I could see how lost he was. "I guess it has been a while, I changed my hair too," she said. Part of her hair was cut short around her ears and the rest were in small braids falling down her back.

"I'll help you out," she went on. "Hope and I met in seventh grade. We had gym together," she said jogging my memory. "I remember meeting you Damon in ninth grade. We always sat in the back during history," she reminded him.

"Were you the girl who always asked for paper?" Damon asked her.

"No. I never took notes. I didn't have to. It was a stupid class anyways." She said that last part as if she were too good for it. That must have been your other girlfriend," Kiara said hotly.

"What?" Damon didn't get it yet.

"Did you two date?" I asked.

"Not when we first met. He didn't talk to me for some reason," she answered. Damon turned to me with a bewildered look. "It was a year after that we officially became a couple, remember Damon?"

"Can you tell us something that makes sense?!" Damon's confusion turned to irritation. "Not that I wouldn't love to spend time going down memory lane, but I noticed that we are the only two up here and I'm wondering why?" Damon spoke directly. "This guy came to my house and gave me the invitation," he said while pointing at Lyell. Then he turned his finger to Kiara. "Then you came in here and started talking to us like we're old time friends, giving us a bunch of memories? What's the point?" he questioned with absolute frustration.

"Damon..," Kiara sighed. "You always were a guy who wanted it straight to the point. But I think you know why I wanted to see you two. You have the visions, right?" she asked.

"How did you know about that?" I asked with shock and some fear.

"Because, I have them too," she explained further. "It happened one night this past summer, August 23rd," she told us.

That date sounded familiar. Wait, wasn't that the day I fell asleep in class and had that dream? Not just that, it was the day I had my first supernatural experience myself.

"Hey, I had my first vision on that day too," Damon informed everyone.

Him too? I thought to myself.

Kiara nodded. "I expected that," she said and turned towards me. "You too?" she asked.

I nodded.

"How do we know we can believe you?" Damon asked.

Kiara's face contorted in shock and dismay. "Hello? Didn't you just hear me? I just told you I have visions! And you have them too. You think it's coincidental?" she spoke with attitude.

"So, what do you want to do about all of this?" Damon asked with exasperation.

Kiara's eyes focused on us, showing determination.

"We find out why these visions are happening and stop them,' she stated flatly.

"That's it?" Damon asked, sounding aggravated. "We've already been trying to do that! That's what that witch said!" he exclaimed.

"Who?" Kiara asked.

"You know someone named Aria?" he asked.

Kiara responded by biting her lip. "I know her very well," she answered.

I couldn't believe this. Would all the mysteries be solved tonight?

"Yeah," Damon said, "I've met her several times, so has Hope."

"See, I knew her before she changed," Kiara said.

"What do you mean?" I asked.

"Aria was the sweetest woman you could meet, then she changed. I'm not sure how yet, but we are going to talk to her and find out what is really going on," Kiara said with certainty.

"Sounds like a plan,' Damon commented. "At this point I don't care. She better have an answer for us!" he demanded.

"Don't start acting so tough now," Kiara said rolling her eyes.

"What are you talking about?" Damon asked.

"Forget it. We'll talk more about this later. You came here for a party," she said as she stood. "So, let's have some fun!"

As the night went on, things loosened up and we started having fun. Kiara introduced us to the bartenders and the D.J., the security guards, and other workers. We had some drinks; I just drank pop. I wasn't going to drink alcohol after the incident last time I came here. Kiara played pool with Damon and me, then she and I danced... but Damon wouldn't come onto the dance floor. Finally, Kiara had enough and just pulled him off the chair.

"You're going to dance whether you like it or not!" she told him jokingly.

Kiara seemed to have her way of doing things. I'm usually not one to get on the dance floor either. Tonight, I actually felt confident enough to make a fool of myself and not care! I haven't seen this Kiara in a while, but she brought out this feeling inside of me. I was happy.

Chapter Twelve:
My Secret

Friday was my party night. The next day, I had to study. I had papers due and so much to read. Finals were coming soon, so I studied every waking hour for them. Some people, like Charsi have a photographic memory, but not me. But, I realized that since these nightmares began, I have been not only more alert and faster, but smarter too. I wondered how that happened. I noticed this as I studied for my history exam. I didn't have to read everything over again like usual, and I read faster too. Maybe something good could come out of the chaos.

"Hope?" I heard the voice at my door. Why did I leave it open?

"Yeah," I answered. I turned to my sister who seemed to like to pester me while I was doing something important.

"Can I have my costume back? I need it for tonight," she asked me.

"But Dad doesn't want you to wear it. Did he change his mind?" I asked.

"He said it was all right if I wear another shirt under the top of the outfit. I'm wearing a plain black shirt and putting that top on over the shirt. I guess he doesn't mind the skirt, it was the top that bothered him," she explained.

"Oh, it's in the closet," I told her. Charsi helped herself to the bag where I had the costume. "Where are the wings?" she asked.

"The wings? Oh, they're in the car. I took them off while I was dancing because I kept hitting people with them. It was funny at first, but I sort of poked this girl in the eye with the tip of one of the wings," I told her while trying not to laugh.

"Really?" Charsi asked and laughed a little herself. "Can I have your keys so I can get them?" she asked.

"Yeah, here." I pulled the out the intertwined pile of keys and key chains from my purse and tossed them to her. Charsi did an almost miss catch.

She left and it was finally silent again. Charsi is one for talking for an excessive period of time. I was starting to get somewhere after the minutes of silence, but then Charsi came pouncing back into the room. She looked upset. What was bothering her now?

"Hope, why are there cigarettes in your car?" she asked with her nosy attitude.

Oh my God, I can't believe this girl!

"Those are Damon's. I told you that he smokes," I reminded her.

"Well, why do you have them?" She continued to pry. I wasn't going to explain it. I didn't have to.

"Don't worry about it," I said ignoring the question.

"I just wondered," she protested.

"No, you thought I was smoking them. Why do you care so much about what I'm doing?" I asked, starting to show my own attitude.

"You're changing, Hope, and it's scaring me!" she exclaimed.

My eyes stared daggers at her. "You are afraid that I'm changing? Why? Because I'm not sitting at home every night like before? I found friends now and actually have a life and you can't take it because you're usually the popular one and it's scaring you because you feeling like you're losing your place!" I blasted at her.

Charsi looked surprised by my allegation. "I don't care if you are going out with friends. But you have been acting strange lately and you might not think I'm smart enough to figure it out, but I have!" she cried out. "Being out at night, doing séances..."

"That was only once!" I stated. "And there was a reason for doing it!"

"Really? You betrayed God because you wanted to play silly games!" she accused me.

I lost it. Standing up now I stared my sister down. She back away suddenly. She's never done that before.

"I haven't betrayed God!" My voice thrived above hers. "He betrayed me! I'm the one losing my mind; seeing terrible visions!" Charsi was a girl who flipped out if her nail polish chips off. Telling her about my nightmares and hallucinations made her beyond fearful.

"Visions? So it's true, you're doing dark arts," she interjected.

"No. I didn't do anything for these visions to happen, they just started over the summer and I keep seeing..." I stopped speaking in mid-sentence.

"Seeing what?" she asked, sounding concern now.

I gave up. I told her everything.

"I see places where people have died and these monsters are roaming everywhere. I've seen people on fire, running around in agony and blood is everywhere…I see Hell," I confessed to her. Charsi just stared at me for a moment. Then she started calling out. "Mom! Mom!" I ran after her. Grabbing her by the arm, I held onto her. She tried to struggle away from me, but I wouldn't let go of my grip. "Let me go! You're crazy!" she cried out.

"No, Charsi! I trusted you with this information so you can't betray me!" I shouted at her.

"I never said I'd keep it a secret!" she shouted back at me. She kept twisting, trying to get away, but I held her tightly. "Let go!" You're hurting me!" she protested.

I thought she was being dramatic, but her arm where I held her looked bruised. I didn't think I held on that tightly. How did I do that? She looked at the blackened bruise.

"Look what you did! I'm showing Dad!" she whined in her usual bratty voice.

"Charsi," I warned, "Stop this! I don't need more enemies. It seems I'm already hated enough," I told her.

"What do you mean?" her voice quavered as she spoke.

I stood right next to her. Charsi was so much shorter than me. I was bigger than her and if I wanted, I could really hurt her. I shuddered at that thought. I shouldn't even think things like that.

"I will talk to Mom and Dad when I'm ready," I told her.

"Tell them tonight," she demanded, "or I will!"

"I said when I'm ready!" I warned her again.

"Tonight," she spoke more directly.

I guess I had to tell them now. "Fine," I said.

I went back to my room, but now I had a hard time concentrating. How does my sister manage to act like that?

That night, I wondered how I could approach my parents with this topic. Well, I guess I could start by telling them about the night this started, when I met Aria. And I'll have to tell them the truth about meeting Damon. I guess it's appropriate. I've needed to talk to my mom about all of this for some time now. Charsi felt the need to remind me before she left for her little party.

"Remember what I said," she whispered harshly.

Yeah, like I forgot?

Mom was in her room. It was just her, and I'd rather tell her first anyways.

Somehow, my mother sensed I was there even though she had her back towards me.

"Hello?" Who's at my door?" Her voice sounded musical, so pleasant and inviting. That helped me relax a little.

"It's me, Mom," I said.

"Hi Honey," she greeted. She saw my expression and already figured something was wrong.

"Are you all right?" she asked me. *Don't cry Hope! Don't cry!* I still felt like I would though I couldn't stand it!

"Mom," my voice cracked, "I needed..to tell you…" I couldn't do it. I couldn't talk to her about it. What would she say? Would she freak out like Charsi and go running to Dad, telling him I needed therapy or something like that?

"Come in," she beckoned. I walked into the room, but I felt so uncomfortable. When I walked in, worry crossed her face. "Hope, you don't look well at all," she connected.

I breathed in. "Mom, Charsi thinks I'm getting into things that I shouldn't. She's actually upset because I have a social life right now," I explained.

"Charsi has been worried about you. She asked me what I thought of Damon and if I thought you should be seeing him," she told me.

"What did you tell her?" I asked.

"Well, I told her that you are old enough to choose your own friends just as she is. He is a nice boy. I don't see anything wrong with him," she said smiling at me.

"Mom, you know that I haven't turned my back on God, right?" I asked nervously.

She scrunched her eyebrows. "Why would you ask that?" she said with seriousness.

"Well, Charsi does. She found those tarot cards; they aren't mine. I don't know where they came from. Damon never saw them before either," I told her.

I just kept skipping around the topic. I needed to just say it really fast.

"Mom, I keep having bad dreams," I blurted out. I told her about the first dream I had when I was at school.

"Really? That sounds like a nightmare," she replied.

She got it in one.

"I've had other dreams too. But they don't feel like dreams. Is it possible to have visions?" I asked, then bit my lip, wondering how she took that.

"Hope, we all have dreams we can't explain. But they're just dreams," she explained trying to make everything sound okay.

"Mom, can I show you something?" I asked. She nodded.

I ran to my room and grabbed the shoe box under my bed. Inside were those blades. They looked like antiques that would fall apart if I used them. I knew they were different in the other world, but whatever! This would be enough proof.

I brought the swords back to my mom. She looked curiously at them, but she took them and held them in her hands.

"These do seem familiar," she said. She stared at them as if she were in a trance. "Yes, I've seen these before," she said assuredly.

"Mom, where have you seen these before?" I asked being puzzled by her response. Her gaze became dreamy.

"The Eternal Battle..." she said sounding spacey. It was too weird. "The Watchers...Sons of God lusted after daughters off men...Giants roamed the Earth..." she spoke, quoting scripture.

"What are you saying?" I demanded. "You're not making any sense!" She didn't respond.

"Mom!" I yelled at her. She suddenly snapped out of it.

"Hope, I'm sorry. My mind went blank for a moment. Tell me if you have any more dreams, alright?" she asked being a bit startled.

"Do you know what's happening to me?" I asked in desperation.

"No," she said. "Your father will be home soon. Don't mention anything to him," she let the words roll off her tongue. She spoke in this eerie tone that really freaked me out! She acted as though she was in this dreamy state.

"But if I don't say anything, Charsi will tell him," I explained sensing my secret was safe with Mom.

"I'll talk to her. Go back to your studying," she simply said. She gave me the swords and went back to folding clothes.

"I can't go on like nothing is happening. I know this isn't it, I know more is coming and I can't ignore it," I explained.

"It will be all right," my mother said as she lamely assured me with a kiss on my forehead.

I went back to my room, but now I couldn't study. I felt tired, but I didn't want to sleep. I just felt the torment over and over. I couldn't take it. I let out frustration, screaming as loud as I could.

Chapter Thirteen:
The Ritual

When I realized that I had just screamed like some girl getting slaughtered in a horror movie, I knew everyone had to have heard it and would come running. But apparently, no one did. Maybe no one cared. I sat on my bed. I wanted to see Damon. He was the only one that understood. We went through this madness together. I layed down, thinking of him.

I think I fell asleep. Images flashed through my mind; they were so fast. I felt like I was moving. I found myself in a cave of some sort. The air felt cold and damp, smelling with mold and mildew. It was dark, but I could make out the jagged rock walls of the cavern.

Where am I? Is this a dream?

No. I felt wide awake. *I don't want this anymore.* This place felt so cold. I realized that I wore the same clothes I had on earlier that day. As I walked, the air became thicker. I breathed in deeply, but began coughing. The air now became filled with toxins. I gasped for air. I thought I would pass out, but I didn't. My heart pounded hard and I could barely breathe now. There were cement stairs leading downward. I didn't want to go down there, but I felt myself walking.

The steps went down into this room, it felt like a tomb. There wasn't any light, but somehow I could still see. There were stone walls all around this place. In front of me looked like a stone altar. Three lit candles sat on a huge stone forming an upside down triangle from where I stood. Above the altar was a crucifix, hanging upside down. What did all of this stuff mean?

As if my question would be answered, I heard this chanting coming from all around me. There wasn't anyone there that I could see, but I still heard multiple voices. Before my eyes, there were figures of people appearing around me. These people were covered in cloaks, some black; some red. The ones in red were fewer and stood in front of the ones in black. They seemed to be praying. They were not aware of my presence, which may be a good thing. I stood there watching these men mutter among themselves. Someone stood at the altar now, he wore a gold mask. In his hands were two daggers, one had that S-curve like mine and the other had a long, flat blade. He raised the weapons above his head and then plunged them into the altar. I heard the crying of a baby.

No! They wouldn't...a baby?

But I didn't see the child. I just heard it crying. Then the floor under the altar began to crack and a rumbling sound could be heard from below. Something sprang up from beneath the floor. It was gigantic. The creature was covered in reddish-brown scales around its deformed body. The thing stood on two legs and its arms were massive in size. The hooded men bowed down to this thing. They stood again and removed their hoods revealing scales for skin, pointed ears and reptile like eyes. Their attention turned to me. Now they could see me! Staves randomly appeared in the hands of the black-hooded men. The red-hooded men held flails. Those things hurt! Let's see, what do I have? Um...nothing?

Quickly, I turned and ran back towards the narrow passage. As I ran, two of the men in the red robes rushed past me to block my path. The other two men in red cloaks came up behind me. Four of the men held their flails up in the air ready to strike. I had nowhere to go! Suddenly, the two in front of me used the double ball and chain maces to swipe at me. Instinctively, I put my hands up to fend off the blow, but instead of getting my hands mangled, I held something that blocked the attack.

Guns.

Looking at the pistols, I recognized them right away. These were Damon's. I noticed the names of the archangels curved into the side of these unique firearms. The cloaked men still tried to charge at me. I guess they were that stupid. I began firing, sending out streams of white light, forcing them backwards. The thunderous sounds of these weapons should have been enough to make me lose my hearing for good. But the sound didn't affect me. This was the first time I ever fired pistols like these or of any kind. Somehow, I was an expert at it.

The larger demon kept its distance, so I just took care of the weird reptile men attacking me. I was able to easily take each of them down. This was so much better than using those swords. As each one of these enemies fell, I felt a power emanate within me. I felt stronger and more confident. Even when several surrounded me, I shot them before they came five steps in front of me. Above me was a ledge that looked safe. It was kind of high jump, but I still attempted it. I sprung up into the air and actually landed on the ledge. I looked down to see the enemies beneath me.

Now I was eye level with the giant scaled demon. He looked straight at me! I was at least ten feet up from the ground, so this creature had to be at least ten feet tall. What was this thing? I shot more rounds, but it just retaliated with anger. It let out this terrible roar which shook particles of rocks from the cavern walls and ceiling. It shook me so much that I lost my balance and fell backwards. I landed on the ground hard on my back. I was still okay to move. I got up quickly and shot desperately at this monster. The bullets pierced its eyes, making it stagger backwards. If I took out the eyes, it wouldn't be able to see me. That was a demented thought, but it would work. I aimed and shot, trying to accomplish hitting its eyes. Suddenly, it grabbed me by one thick claw and threw me across the room into the other wall. The impact of my body actually broke through the solid rock. I thought I was dead. But I still got back up. I felt some pain, but not enough t to stop me from moving. I sprang back to my feet. I couldn't believe that none of my bones were broken!

The beast was not done. He came at me, moving at inhuman speed. I jumped back on the ledge, shooting down at it. Some of the hooded guys were still moving around down there. Bullets pierced through their robes, and they fell and burned away. I got them easily, but I still had the giant to worry about. I wasn't paying attention, and it grabbed me again. Holding me tight in one enormous hand, it spoke to me in a foreign tongue, yet somehow I still understood him.

"WHERE IS YOUR GOD NOW?" The words from this creature pierced my mind. It hurt just to hear them.

I woke up suddenly. But even safe in my own bed, my heart still raced. That question burned within my mind. I had to find the answer.

Chapter Fourteen:
Mother's Journal

Where is your god now?

The question repeated itself over and over in my mind. The question was asked by those left by God. I was awake now, I think. These things were really happening, which meant if I died during them, I die in my world too. The blasts from those guns still echoed in my mind.

After class, I drove to that club Fantasy Nights. When I got there, no one was at the door, it was wide open. The place was dead. I guess that was expected at four-o-clock on a Monday. I sat down on one of the bar stools. Finally a woman wearing a bright pink jacket zipped up to her black sports bra approached me. Is that acceptable to wear to work? This woman looked over thirty, busty, with short bleached blonde hair.

"What can I get ya honey?" she asked. Her voice sounded very rough. It was so weird. She called me 'honey.' Was she hitting on me? I'm a girl, too, for crying out loud!

"Uh, I actually need to talk to Kiara. Is she here?" I asked. They lady showed a smile, her hair was whiter than her teeth. She probably smoked.

"No problem honey, I'll go get her," she said and left. *Okay, stop calling me that. My mom calls me honey,* I kept thinking to myself.

After waiting uncomfortably for five minutes, Kiara finally came out. I guess Kiara did go for the Goth look. She had on a black shirt with red lettering that read: 'I'd rather choose death over you!' Her black jeans with the hanging chains made an intense fashion statement. And the black army boots were a nice touch too. I sometimes wonder how I would look in something like that. I never would be one to do it though. I always cared too much about how others saw me, but I was getting to the point where I didn't care so much anymore.

"Hope, I'm glad to see ya," Kiara greeted me.

"Uh... hi Kiara. I don't want to impose on you or anything, but..."

"Don't be silly! It's cool. I think we should talk more, you me and Damon. Is he here too?" she asked.

"No, just me," I said.

Kiara looked somewhat disappointed. "Damn, I wanted to talk to him too. Never mind, you can just pass the info along," she told me.

"About what?" I asked now feeling my anxiety rise a little bit.

She spoke in a low whisper, "Lyell is still looking into the issue with our visions…we shouldn't talk here though. Janet can be nosey sometimes," she informed me.

"Janet?" I asked.

"The lady you met. She's the head bartender. She has to know everything," Kiara whispered.

"Oh, the one that called me honey." I said recalling her.

Kiara rolled her eyes. "Oh God, she has a name for everyone, cutie, baby, honey, darling…she's just being friendly, but it gets on my nerves sometimes," she said.

That makes two of us. I thought to myself.

"We can go up to the lounge any time you want," she invited me.

"Sure," I said and followed her lead.

We sat upstairs in the chairs looking out of the window into the club.

"Hope, I know Aria. I met here when I was younger actually. She helped me through some hard times, but she is acting strange now and I'm afraid for her. She's been having a hard time. I think it has to do with her being involved with this cult," Kiara explained.

"What kind of cult?" I asked, wondering. If they worshiped an upside-down crucifix, she'd need to change religions quickly!

"It's your basic cult. They do these rituals, claim they have the blood of Christ inside of them…it's really messed up," she clarified.

"Blood of Christ? People in cults don't believe in Jesus," I stated.

Kiara gave me the strangest glare. "You don't believe in all that 'Jesus died for your sins' crap, do you?" she asked with an irritated tone.

That kind of offended me. What did she mean by that?

"I don't understand what you mean," I told her. As I spoke, someone interrupted as they opened the door.

"Lyell!" Kiara screeched. "Don't just open the door without knocking! I have no idea if it's you or someone else!" she chastised. She seemed a bit paranoid.

"Who else you think is gonna come up here this time of day? Besides, Janet is the only other person here and the old lady is breaking glasses in the kitchen!" he said with a chuckle.

"Again?" Kiara questioned. "She's gotta get rid of those fake nails," she said with a laugh.

Lyell suddenly looked over at me, then turned back to Kiara again.

"Is the other one here too?" he asked.

"His name is Damon," Kiara replied with a half smile.

"Oh yeah, your other boyfriend," Lyell joked.

"She came here by herself. We've been talking," Kiara explained.

Lyell took a seat on the couch, and gave a heavy sigh. I know that feeling.

"So I told Hope about Aria and her strange affiliation with her religion," Kiara said.

"Yeah, the church has always been messed up," Lyell agreed.

"The church? How did we go from cults to church?" I asked feeling a little lost.

"Is there a difference?" Lyell asked. He and Kiara laughed. I didn't get what was so funny.

"I think Hope is offended by our religious discussion," Kiara spoke in a mocking manner. "Come on, you know how the church tells people how to live. They say one thing and do another," she finished.

"Okay, so this particular church tells people to do bad things?" I asked, trying to figure out what they meant.

"They teach people to be narrow minded and prejudiced," Kiara told me.

"That's not right," I agreed. "But not all churches are like that. Mine isn't," I defended.

Kiara looked over at Lyell they just gave this knowing smile to each other. It bothered me. I got the feeling they were just making fun of me.

"Anyways Lyell," Kiara began. "Is she willing to come here and talk with us?" she asked.

"Sorry," he responded. "She's doing a good job avoiding us. She wasn't home and I checked that church, but the priest there told me to leave," he said.

"That's so stupid!" Kiara shouted as she pounded the cushion. I felt a harsh wind from her motion even from where I sat. "I don't know why Aria is doing this! Yes, I left home but..."

"You left home?" I asked. I didn't mean to pry, but I felt like this big secret was being kept from me.

"Also, Aria is upset that Kiara is working at a bar," Lyell explained. "And she's drinking underage," he added in a whisper.

"Lyell! Be quiet!" Kiara shouted.

"It's all right," I said. "I won't say anything. I'm not twenty-one yet either."

"I'm going to be twenty-one on the Spring Equinox," Kiara mentioned.

"What's that?" I asked wondering what that meant. She gave me this look like, 'I can't believe you don't know that.'

"It's the twenty-first of March; the first day of spring," she explained.

The mention of that date swam in my head. It was more than a shock to me. "That's my birthday too," I told her. I was born on the first day of spring, and I was going to be twenty-one years old, just like her.

"Excuse us." Kiara told me suddenly. She got up, gesturing for Lyell to come with her. They left the room with me sitting there by myself. What were they saying that I wasn't allowed to hear? I was really annoyed now. I couldn't stand it when people left me out. It reminded me of my childhood. Before, I wouldn't have eavesdropped, but I wasn't going to be left out this time. I walked over and put an ear to the door, and found out I could hear quite well through it.

I heard Kiara's voice first, "See, there is a connection between me and her," she confirmed.

"No. It could just be coincidence." Lyell objected.

"We look alike though and our birthdays are the same." Kiara noted. "She doesn't have the white in her hair, but it's black like most of mine and our faces look alike. I mean, we could be sisters," she said. I felt my heart pound.

"You are jumping to conclusions again." He warned. "I know you have this fantasy of finding your family, but you really believe your father had more kids?"

"He could have. Look at the two of us. Our eyes are the same except for the color, mine are violet and hers look silver. But people in the same family can have different color eyes. Our faces have similar features and we both are having these visions," Kiara explained.

"Okay, say that she is your sister or whoever, what is it going to matter? She doesn't know you. You have no history together," he retorted.

"It does matter! If she is my sister then…that is all I need," she said.

"I don't know…I think you are just wasting your time," he told her.

"Well, I don't care what you think!" she exclaimed.

I heard pounding as footsteps came up the stairs.

I hurried back to the chair where I originally sat. Kiara was first to come in, followed by her partner in crime.

"Well, I bet you wondered what we talked about," she said.

Oh sure, that's why I listened in. I hated not knowing what someone says about me. It feels too much like high school.

"Kiara," I started, "you know where Aria lives, right?"

"Yeah, I do," she said.

"Can you tell me so I can talk with her?" I asked. Kiara suddenly tensed up when I mentioned that idea.

"Hope, I really need you to trust me. I know we haven't known each other long…well, we knew each other in school, but we didn't really hang out that much. I was just in a few of your classes," she said, changing her demeanor. I noticed how sad she looked all of the sudden.

"I just need you to come back here with Damon, then we can decide what to do," she told me.

"Why does Aria care so much about what you do?" I asked Kiara.

"Like I said, she is part of this cult and I hate to say it, but I almost joined it and I chose not to, but she will not leave me alone about going to church. I don't need to go there, I have my own religion. Please, just don't try to find her," she requested.

"I guess I understand," I said, feeling so confused about everything. I couldn't stand it. What didn't I know about Aria?

"Can you two meet me here on Friday?" Kiara asked. I had no idea what else I'd do, "I'll talk to him about it," I told her.

I spent the week involved in my studies. Until Friday came, I wondered what exactly would happen. My room used to be a comforting place, especially when studying. Now I didn't feel right there. As I turned towards the door, my mother surprised me. She stood there at my doorway. Her demeanor looked unsettled, like she was really unsure of what she was doing.

"Oh, mom, I didn't see you!" I cried out apologetically.

"I'm sorry if I startled you." She said that with the corners of her mouth curved down.

"Are you all right?" I asked her.

"Yeah, I'm fine," she said casually. I wasn't sure if I could believe her. I wondered if this was a good time to ask her about what happened the other day. The day she was acting so weird when I showed her the cursed blades.

"Mom..." I tried hard to force out the words. "Did I scare you the other day? You know, when I was talking about the dreams I've been having?" I asked timidly.

She was quiet for a moment. "No. I mean, that is all I think they were, dreams, but..." she stopped.

"What about when I showed you the weapons?" I asked her.

"What?" She asked. Now I was really upset. How could she forget?

"I told you about the dreams, showed you those daggers and you started mumbling or something," I reminded her. My voice sounded a bit drastic, I think it surprised her.

"Mumbling? Hope, I don't understand," she said, acting dumbfounded.

With extreme frustration, I suddenly pounded the wall with my fist. "Of course not! Nothing is supposed to make sense, right?" I screeched.

"W-what? Hope, I don't know...." she said. I don't know if I was going to cry again, but there was just this intense feeling of anger and pain I couldn't get past. I turned away from my mom. I didn't want to even see her right now.

"Hope, I don't want to scare you, but you need to know that I have not always chosen to be a Christian," she began that so eloquently.

I turned to her. Right now, she didn't even look like my mother anymore. She became a stranger to me.

"I met someone before your father and at that time, I did not follow God," she explained further. "This man showed himself well and I believed he loved me. We joined this religion together, and I did things I am not proud of. I never told you much about my childhood, but I became very rebellious and your grandmother worried so much about me. Grandfather died when I was a teenager; about Charsi's age actually. Grandma had four kids to raise. Being one of the middle children, I did not feel anyone really paid attention to me. I know it sounds cliché, but I did what most teenagers do when no one sees them, I got into trouble a lot," she said.

"Mom, it's all right, if you stopped believing in God for a while, you can still be saved," I said. My mother looked at me with question.

"Mom, you are saved, right?" I asked, feeling fearful.

"The term, 'saved' always bothered me," she admitted. "That term Christians use to say that a person has accepted Christ and know that they are forgiven for their sins. I know the exact night I asked for forgiveness. It's just that I think you need to understand more about how you came into this world," she said. It seemed that she finally would tell me the truth. She didn't explain why the term upset her. But I was more interested in what she just said. How I came into this world? Was this it? Was this going to explain every strange thing that happened to me?

"Hope, your father…" she started.

"Amira," Dad's voice was heard from their room. "Have you seen my plaid tie?" he called out.

"Which one?" Mom asked.

"Any of them!" he yelled.

"I'll be right back," she said. My mom left me, which bothered me because I knew she was going to tell me something I needed to hear. Can't Dad find his own stuff? I couldn't explain why, but I began to become very irritated with my dad. First the lecture about séances and Satanism, and now this? It just seemed like he kept getting in the way. Then I thought about something, or the thought was just placed inside my head. It sort of scared me.

If he is such a bother…just get rid of him.

What was that? That voice inside my head again.

While I waited for mom, Charsi graced me with her presence.

"Aha! I got you now!" she said.

"Charsi, I have all these books and paper on the floor where I am trying to study. Can this wait?" I asked, becoming irritated.

"You should study at a desk, not on the floor," she said, sounding so smug.

"Well, why don't you give me yours since you're so concerned," I said sharp and somewhat threatening. "I just need to get this stuff done!" I finished.

"Do you know what I have?" She asked in this taunting voice. She held a notebook. It was red with a brown trim.

"What's that?" I asked.

She rolled her eyes, "A journal."

"I know that! I mean, what's in it?" I asked with curiosity.

"Do you want to read it?" she taunted.

"No. Should I?" I asked with suspicion.

She gave me this playful smile. "You can read it, I won't tell."

"Charsi, I don't have time to play these games!" I said.

"This is stupid!" I heard my dad's voice. "I can't stand going to these company meetings! And they make it at such an inconvenient time, and I hear we're not even getting paid for it!" he fussed.

"Here, I found a tie for you, dear," Mom said.

"Not that tie, honey," he said a little calmer. "I need to look professional."

Which tie did she give to him? Anyways, it seems that they would be busy for a while.

"Alright, let me see the notebook," I said.

Charsi suddenly had this outraged look on her face. "Oh my God! I can't believe you would read Mom's diary!" She objected.

"You just offered it to me and…" she was trying to trick me.

"I only read the first entry," she admitted. "But I found it in your bag, so you must have stolen it," she chided.

"What the hell?! Charsi! Stop messing with my stuff!" I yelled at her.

The expression my sister's face changed to shock, "Did you just swear?"

"Hell is not a swear word," I argued. "Forget it! Just don't touch anything that belongs to me," I warned her.

"I'm not touching your stuff!" she yelled back.

"Forget it! Just hand it to me!" I demanded. As I reached for it, Charsi pulled it away.

"And what do I get for letting you see it?" she asked.

Something inside me awoke, in this dark voice I responded, "I'll let you keep your organs intact!" I flared.

Charsi gazed at me with these wide terrified eyes, "W-what are you…?" she stuttered.

I snatched the journal from her during her stunned state. Opening the cover, I saw there was some cursive writing.

To my daughter Amira,

Let this be an outlet for all of your fears, doubts, and pain.

Love, Mom

This was given to my mom by her mom--my grandma. Why did she write that? Fears, doubts, and pain? Was mom sad a lot?

The next page had a date followed by some more of the same writing.

Oct. 6
What is your religion? That is what my friend asked me today. I told her Christian to make her happy. Actually, I joined a group where I can find spiritual enlightenment. In church I feel like I have to

put on this act for everyone. This place is different. I can be myself. I don't think I can tell anyone. My family, they probably would not understand. They will say I am in a cult. But I'm not! These people understand the truth. They understand me!

This confirmed what Mom said earlier. She wasn't always a Christian. I guess it doesn't matter. That was left in the past, right?

"Which entry talks about me?" I asked.

Charsi didn't respond, she just gazed at the floor, it wasn't like her at all. I turned the pages until I found an entry that read,

March 21,

My daughter, Angel Cry. That is what he named her. What a strange name, but that is what he wanted to name her. She is so beautiful. She has eyes like mine, a unique color, too. I think they are silver. Her hair is black like mine, too. I am twenty-one with a baby. Many would frown upon that, but I feel it is right. Xander has arranged for her to be baptized in our religion. He told me it was done for many children who will find strength, pride, and fulfillment in their lives. I am so glad to have found a wise man to guide me. I would be lost without him.

My birthday is March 21, just like Kiara's.

"Charsi, what did you think about this?" I asked with questioning eyes.

She wasn't paying any attention to me, she stared at the floor.

"I'm sorry I snapped at you, but why do you try to play those games with me?" I asked.

She looked up at me. "You're not really my sister," she said in this hollow voice.

"Of course I am. Just because I have a different dad…" I thought about that. The man my mom is married to was not my father? Then who….?

"No," I shook my head. "I can't believe this! It has to be a trick…." I looked intently at Charsi, "This is a lie! You made this up, didn't you?" I accused her.

Charsi looked surprised by the allegation. "No! Why would I? How would I....?" She questioned.

"Admit it! You're mad because I have a life now and it's more interesting than yours!" I blasted.

Even though I was mad, I couldn't help noticing how hurt Charsi looked. But I still continued. "I know what you did...back when I was in middle school! You and your air head friends made up this letter and told me they were switching me to a different school for mentally disabled kids..." I suddenly remembered that so vividly.

"Come on, you remember something that long ago," she said.

"I remember a lot of things you did to me Charsi, and I'm not taking it anymore! I didn't believe you about that anyways," I told her.

Charsi gave her 'yeah right' look.

"Just get out!" She didn't move. "I SAID GET OUT!" I pushed hard enough that she flew backward into the wall. She staggered, trying to hold her balance. We both looked at the wall, an indentation was left there. I didn't think I pushed her that hard.

"Get away from me! You're crazy!" She screamed and ran out of the room. I was sure she would tell our parents...I didn't care anymore.

I had little time to find out more about this journal. Was it really my mother's? Well, maybe it was, Charsi would not take the time to write all of these entries. Still, she may have written that one about me. I heard those three coming towards my door, I had just a moment to throw the book under my bed before they walked in.

"You know, this is honestly an invasion of privacy," I said. "What do you guys think I'm doing in here?" I asked them.

"I'm curious about this myself," my supposed father said.

"She threw me into the wall!" Charsi cried. She showed our parents the dent in the wall.

"Oh my God!" Dad exclaimed. He looked at me, a bit angry and a bit afraid.

"What is going on between both of you? Why are my girls fighting a lot all of the sudden?" He asked both of us.

"Actually, James," I began with hostility. "I'm not sure that I am your girl!" I said, flaming mad.

"Hope!" My mother cried. "What are you saying?" She asked with a shocked look.

"I read part of this journal…" I began.

"Which journal?" Mom asked, "Mine?" That was a very accurate guess.

"It might be," I taunted.

"Hope, I need that back!" she said urgently.

"Mom…you hid stuff from me all this time and you still are! You know why I'm having those visions…" I started.

"Hope, give the book back to your mother," James demanded.

"Sorry, I can't do that," I said. "I want to know where I came from. I want to know who I am and what the things I see mean!" I demanded.

"What are you talking about? What do you see?" James asked.

My mother stayed silent.

"Tell him!" I urged her, but mom didn't look like she was about to talk.

James looked at her, then me, "Enough of this!" James walked towards me.

"Please…" I felt this darkness inside me return. "Do you think that I am afraid of you?!" I challenged. My voice sounded dark and disturbing.

This strength grew inside me. Like in the dreams, I felt a need to defend myself. I felt a strong wind whirl around me; it blew the papers around the room. I was surrounded in darkness all of a sudden, I couldn't see anything.

"What's going on?" I heard Charsi's voice.

"Hope!" I heard my mother. "I'm sorry! I'll explain everything! Just stop!" She pleaded. I was not sure if I could. Hearing my mother say that did calm me down, I could see again, their faces came into view. The wind died down. The paper picked up by the wind floated back down to the floor. My mother ran over to hug me. I looked over her shoulder at Charsi and James. I don't think they ever expected me to do something like that. They looked terrified of me. Maybe they should be.

Chapter Fifteen:
Fighting Through Lies

"You know I love you, right, honey?" Mom asked. My mother's attempts to apologize always seem to begin with this type of question. I couldn't look at her. My eyes stared past her. "Is this why I've always felt like I don't belong?" I asked.

We sat alone in my room; my door was closed. After what happened, my mom told James to take my sister somewhere and that she would talk with me. At first, James was too scared to leave his wife alone with me. He almost called the police, but what would they do anyway? They probably wouldn't believe his story. I realized that I was stronger than any normal human, knowing that made me feel invincible. I suddenly felt no fear.

"Hope, having a special gift is not a reason to feel ostracized," she said.

"Gift?" I spoke with no emotion.

"You always could see things others could not. You've also been stronger than others; I mean physically stronger," she continued.

"James is not my real father then?" I asked. My voice remained monotone.

My mother was quiet, then after a moment of awkward silence,

"No. I don't want you to ever meet your real father," she said firmly.

"Why?" I asked.

"Because, he is an evil man. He... tried to kill you when you were an infant," I finally looked at my mother. She was crying.

"I turned away from my faith," she said in between sobs. "I had become a witch a Satanic witch," she cried out.

"You were of the Wicca faith?" I asked.

She shook her head. "No, there's no way a person of the Wicca faith would do what I've done.

"I thought they were the same thing," I said. I recalled that they were known as the same; that is what most Christians say.

"They are not the same. A Pagan or Wiccan believe in their gods or goddesses and perform their rituals. They are different than satanic rituals. It is a common false belief as such. Did you read the entry about the ceremony?" she asked.

"I'm not sure. I read something about a ceremony, but it didn't go into detail about it. And there was this child named Angel Cry," I told her.

"I know it sounds silly. I liked the name Hope, but he did not. He wanted to name you Angel Cry," she tried to laughed again through her tears.

"I could not leave him. It hurt so much when I was away from him. He always made sure he knew exactly where I was. He told me that we were bonded. So I always had to be with him. I was so drawn to him, like being under a spell," she explained.

"Where did you find this guy?" I asked.

"He just appeared one day. I met him in college. I went to this party with some friends, that's where I met him. I always caught myself in his eyes. Those cold blue eyes. There was never any emotion in them, but they drew things out of me that I didn't know existed," she told me with a faint smile.

"So, that child is me? Angel Cry was my real name?" I asked her for the truth.

My mom put a hand on my arm, "You should read that entry." She opened to a page where the writing looked very shaky. It was not dated.

Taking the journal, I began to read the messy scribble. Normally, I would have to keep asking what a certain word was when I read handwriting like this. But, not only could I read the writing, I could see the images of the past clearly in my mind.

> *March 21*
> *"Our child is to lead the path of a new faith," he said.*
>
> *"Our daughter is to be raised higher than any other being," he said.*
>
> *I had no idea what that meant. I guess I was too afraid to question him.*
>
> *The night of the ceremony, I held Angel Cry in my arms wrapped in a blanket. There were a select few people who witnessed this event. Everyone sat in a circle around this stone altar. A triangle of candles were lit, two sitting on the edges and one in the middle at the opposite end. We were underground*

and it was very warm down there. I had to wear this black cloak which made the heat worse. In fact, everyone wore a black cloak except for Xander and a few others who wore a red cloak. I guess they were at a higher rank than the rest of us or something.

The High Priest wore a red robe with a black sash and collar. He also wore this ceremonial mask; it was gold. I don't remember much more than that; I really wasn't supposed to look at the priest.

There was another woman there with a baby in a blanket. She was so tiny and frail. She stood beside me; she wore the same garbs I did. Xander took the infants from us, one in each hand. Then he placed them on the Altar. There they lay, inside the triangle of candles. During all of this, I noticed a young girl sitting in the circle, directly in front of the altar. She couldn't have been more than eighteen. I clearly remember her long red hair.

When I looked back at the altar, the priest uncovered the children, now they wore nothing. The priest started chanting. Everyone began chanting around me. The only ones who weren't were Xander, the two other women, the one standing next to me, and the girl with red hair, and myself. Soon the many voices began to sound like one voice. It was strange. I felt a little hypnotized by the chanting and my eyes focused on the burning candles. Suddenly, I heard crying. The priest held two daggers, one in each hand. He raised them above his head. My heart skipped; he was about to stab the children! My child… I sprang to my feet and ran for my baby. I grabbed Angel Cry just before the knife cut her. The other child was not saved by her mother. I heard the most awful cry from the other baby as the dagger pierced its chest.

At that moment, the priest shot a glare at me. He started yelling in this foreign language. Xander spun around towards me, "What have you done?!" he cried out.

The others in the room broke their chant.

I felt numb as I answered, "I saved my child."
Now even the priest was silent.

Xander stared coldly at me, then raised his hand, and struck me across the face.

"This is my child," I said to him. I remember being very frightened of him, but the thought of losing Angel Cry scared me more. "Why would I give her up to be killed?"

"She will not die. She will live on as a god! You have no idea what you are doing!"

"Yes I do! I am saving my baby!" With Angel Cry in my arms I tried to run out of that place. The others in this ritual stood up to block my path. When I looked at them, they no longer looked human. Their slanted eyes, their pointed ears…they looked like demons!

Xander pushed past all of them. "Give me the child!" he yelled at me.

"No! You will not hurt her!" I screamed.

Xander tried to take her. I don't know what happened, but he didn't succeed. As he moved towards us, this light emerged from Angel Cry. It pushed Xander back, throwing him into the altar. The others were blinded by the light too. I just ran and I never looked back.

I wasn't sure what to say. I only looked up at my mom. "So, my father tried to sacrifice me?" I asked her.

"Hope, I gave you your name after I escaped that night. It seemed to fit because I had hope after that night…hope that things would get better," she told me.

"Are things better?" I asked.

"Of course. You have grown up and are such a beautiful young woman. You have a future now," she said with a smile. My mom looked a lot calmer now. "You know, I was able to get in contact with your grandma, (my mother.) After how I acted towards her and my family before, I did not think she wanted to see me again. But, she embraced me and she was so thankful I came home with you. She told me she was so scared for me being with that man."

"How old were you when you met him?" I asked.

She sighed, "Twenty."

"I'm twenty, about to turn twenty-one," I noted. "I met someone else who is turning twenty-one too. And on the same day…" I thought about Kiara. "Mom, what about the other baby? Did she die?" I asked, fearing the answer.

"I would think so. I don't know how her mother could just stand there and watch. It sort of made me angry," mom remembered.

My theory seemed outlandish, but I wondered if the other infant was Kiara. But, just because this girl had the same birthday as me didn't mean I had any relation to her.

"Don't think too much about it," Mom said to me. "I just thought you should know. Maybe now you won't have those nightmares anymore," she said.

No, she didn't understand. They weren't just nightmares, they were really happening! I thought about the reoccurring dream I've had since I was a child, the one where I got pushed off a cliff. That really happened too. There had to be a connection between that and the ritual…

"Mom, something happened to me when I was younger. I went to the park with some friends; it was outside town a little bit," I began.

My mom shook her head. I don't think she remembered at all. That really bothered me.

"I know they were from school and there were some older kids there too. We went through some thick woods; I don't think we were allowed to go through there. Um, something happened while I was with them….We walked up this hill to a cliff that looked over the water. No one else was around. I looked down from the cliff, I heard a boy shout, 'don't fall,' and then it felt like someone pushed me. I fell down all the way…." I told her.

127

"Hope, if you fell off a cliff, you wouldn't be here," my mom said. She was doing it again! She knew I was telling the truth!

"Listen to me!" I pronounced each word with precision. "I was pushed off this cliff. People were laughing, calling out 'die witch!' I didn't dream this! It happened! Just like all of the other things I've experienced!" I explained in desperation for truth.

She didn't say anything. I couldn't believe it. How could she be so blind?

"Why would these kids push you off the cliff-side?" she asked.

Like I know? "People have always felt strange around me. Like they knew something was different about me," I explained.

"They believed you were a demon," my mom concluded. "It had to be Xander's curse. A few days after the ritual, I got a letter from him saying that I could keep you, but soon I would not want you anymore," she said and smiled, "But that never happened. You were never a burden to me," she assured me.

"I need to be alone for a while," I said as I walked to my door.

"Wait, Hope," my mom hugged me. "Please promise you'll be all right," she said.

"I promise," I said it without thinking it through. I didn't know what would happen.

When Friday came, I was excited to finally catch Aria in the act and find out what was going on. Since Kiara was with me too, there was no way I could sound crazy anymore. I sat up in the lounge waiting for Kiara. It was eight-o-clock and the early drinkers were showing up. Kiara came in and slammed the door shut.

"Are you all right?" I asked.

"Aria won't come!" She complained loudly.

I stood up, "Well, fine. Let's go to her house then. I am going to speak with her about everything myself!" I declared.

Kiara shook her head. "No. That won't work. She can refuse to see us," she said.

"I don't care! This has to end!" I said, being fed up. She got quiet suddenly. "Kiara, we have to talk to her. I don't care if we have to camp on her doorstep. I can't go on like this. My mother told me about my real father. His name is Xander..." I told her.

Kiara spun around, "Oh, sure, you're mom is willing to be honest with you!" She blasted at me suddenly.

"What are you talking about?" I asked puzzled at her outburst.

"Look! You're mom is around and she cares about you! Mine isn't around for me!" She cried out. I knew that her mother was dead. I wanted to tell Kiara that I saw her mother, but I just couldn't bring myself to say it.

"I...I'm sorry Kiara," I began. "We will find out what is going on, all right?" I tried being empathetic.

"Don't start telling me it's going to be all right! Nothing is ever all right!" Kiara screamed. She looked so angry. I didn't know what to say to her.

"Kiara..." I walked toward her. "I know how you feel. It is frustrating and painful..." I began.

"No! You don't know how I feel! I'm alone! I have no one!" She cried out in frustration.

"That is not true! I'm here. I'm having the visions too! And so is Damon, we are all going through this," I tried to comfort her.

"You know what, I don't get it!" her voice softened. "This has just been going through my head, just bugging me. Why does it seem like Aria has two personalities. I mean, she acts one way towards me and another way towards someone else. And you act like she is a different person than who I know. I just don't get it," Kiara revealed.

"She's just trying to confuse all of us," I concluded. That was all I could come up with.

"I need a cigarette," Kiara spoke curtly as she tore out a pack from her pocket. Now putting the rolled up nicotine paper in her mouth, she flicked the switch of the lighter, igniting it. She breathed in and released the smoke. Both she and Damon like their cigarettes.

"Does that really work?" I wondered, asking her.

"What?" She asked abrasively.

"Smoking those things," I managed to say even with her intimidation.

Kiara did not say anything. She had her back to me and took another puff.

Lyell came into the room at that moment. "Hey! Hey! There's no smoking in the lounge!" he protested.

Kiara glared at him, "You're not my damn mother!" She blasted him.

"What's your problem?!" He asked, outraged by her attitude.

129

Kiara responded by pushing Lyell aside then stomped down the stairs. Lyell looked at me now.

"What's with her?" He tried asking me.

I felt that rage build up again "I don't know! I guess things didn't go well when you tried to get Aria to come here?" I asked, trying to get some answers.

"She asked Kiara to come to her house. Kiara refused to go there. She wanted Aria to come here," Lyell said.

"Well, it can't go both ways, someone has to make an effort here. I just need to see Aria; I don't care if I have to go to her house to speak with her," I said and realized that was what I needed to do. "Can you give me her address?" I asked Lyell.

He looked earnestly at me. "Shoot! I'll show ya where her house is," he said.

"Really?" I was surprised, I barely knew Lyell. I didn't expect him to do anything for me.

"Yeah, we can go right now," he said.

In the next moment, I was getting into his truck and he drove out of the parking lot and down the road. He turned the truck onto Burken Street and pulled to the curve. I've never been over in this area before. Shows how much I get around. Such a small town, and I haven't seen it all yet? It was dark out of course; during this time of year it was dark by six. The porch light wasn't on and the house was crowded by trees. We walked up to the porch and I could see the color of the house was white and it looked like a ranch home.

Lyell knocked on the door and we waited a moment. He knocked again.

"Hey, Aria!" he yelled.

No one came.

"Man, why isn't she comin'?" He mumbled to himself.

"Maybe she's not home," I said.

"She was here when I came by earlier. She's just not comin' to the door," he fussed.

She's probably afraid to come to the door when someone is yelling her name outside her home.

"Aria! It's Lyell! Answer the door!" He suddenly yelled.

"I don't think she's here," I said again to him. He let the screen door slam closed.

"Man, I'm sorry. She should be here," he told me.

"It's okay; I know where she lives now. I'll come by some other time," I said.

When we got back to the club, Lyell asked, "Are you going to stay for a while?"

"I came here to talk to Kiara and Aria. Since Aria cannot be found and Kiara is upset with me, there is no reason for me to stay," I told him.

"You don't know why she's mad?" Lyell asked.

"I think she is mad because Aria didn't come, but she also seems to be mad at me for some reason too," I said shrugging my shoulders.

"Yeah, I don't know what her issue is," he protested.

Lyell drove us back to the club. When we got out of the truck, I realized that no one waited outside. Normally; there was a long line to get in. Also, it was quiet, no music played. Lyell went inside and I heard him calling for Kiara. I was only a step inside the entrance when I heard him scream. When I walked into the club, I saw all of these people impaled with spikes into the floor, walls and even the ceiling. I guess by now, I was used to seeing the gore because I barely uttered a word about it.

"Oh! Hell no!" Lyell cried. "What happened in here?! Kiara! Where are you?!" He was answered, but not by Kiara. This gigantic monster jumped through the glass from the lounge and landed in front of us. This creature looked about the same as the one that attacked me in the underground cavern. His eyes were dark holes, scales all over its body.

"What is that thing?!" Lyell yelled. "Hold on! I got my shot gun in the truck!"

Lyell spun around and began to run back towards the front door. Right before he placed a foot at the door, the monster grabbed him. Lyell gave murderous cries as the demon held him tight. It all happened too fast. The demon looked at the man in its hand and swallowed him! And I realized I would be next. Somehow I was able to jump up high enough to where the pool tables were on the second floor. I held onto the railing and pulled myself up and over it. The monster was too big to come up the stairs so it decided to throw tables, chairs and bar stools at me. I hid under a pool table to avoid the flying objects. I rolled to the next pool table and got under it before I was hit by a flying stool. I rolled to the next table and the next until I sat there on the other side of the room. Ahead of me was a row of arcade games. I got up and ran toward them. As I ran forward, I barely missed the strikes of this demon. I made it to a pinball machine and crouched beside it. There was an exit door at the other side of the games. I would try to make it over there.

As I prepared for the next stride, I heard the sound of metal clanging together. I also realized that objects were not being thrown at me anymore. I crawled over to the railing and looked down. While crouched down, I heard the shriek of metal hit something. I looked down onto the first level to see Kiara was in combat with this creature. She held these long rectangular blades; I've never seen these types of swords before. She wielded them as if they weighed the same as paper. She could jump high too. She kept jumping up and cutting at his midsection, then swiftly moved so she was behind it.

This creature was just as dumb as the other one. It had no idea what she was doing; he just stumbled around trying to squash her. She slashed at the back of his legs. She kept going at this quick pace and the monster tried to grab her and failed. It began to look confused and irritated. Now it pounded its fists into the floor trying to crush Kiara. She managed to jump on its back and slice into the giant. It yelled in pain as expected. Hysterically, it tried to grab her with its stubby arms, but could not reach her. It fell backward. Kiara jumped off it before she was crushed under its weight. The last thing she did was stab into its stomach, cutting it open. I had no idea what to think. Lyell fell out of the stomach cavity. I expected again to see blood coming out of this thing, but that didn't happen.

"Lyell..." Kiara said with relief as she hugged him. That was the first time I saw her give affection to anyone. They were talking softly to each other. I ran to the stairs to where they stood. When she saw me, her expression hardened.

"Did you guys talk with Aria?" she asked me.

"She wasn't home," I answered.

"That is such crap! She has to be there!" Kiara fussed.

"Sorry," Lyell said. Kiara looked angry again, and then her expression changed; her face began to fill with sorrow, she looked like she was going to cry.

"Whatever," she spoke faintly. "I guess we're going to have to try to get a hold of her another way."

"I'm thinking of going to her house again," I said.

"It won't do any good!" she exploded. "Just give it up!"

She let out a long sigh.

"We gotta clean everything up here," Kiara said solemnly.

"We'll take care of it," Lyell told me. "You should get home." He said to me.

"Are you sure? How are you going to explain this to the police?" I asked him.

He looked at Kiara. They must have had a telepathic experience because he didn't say anything, but she nodded to him.

"Just go home, Hope," Kiara said. She and Lyell just walked away towards the lounge. I didn't understand why she said that, and why they were so casual towards the situation. I drove home, but I didn't know how they would take care of it. How do you cover an incident like that?

Three months seemed to fly by since September. It got closer to finals week and I tried really hard to concentrate on my studies. My mom told me not to stress too much; she knew I had gone through a hard time. But I didn't want to use that as an excuse. I wanted to do as well as Charsi always has, or even better. I thought of my dear sister with a heavy sigh. She was avoiding me. I understood why. I must have really scared her. But she asked for it. Why wouldn't she just leave everything be? She kept trying to prove that I was part of some cult or something. When I tried to tell her about the dreams, she just freaked out about it. I can't think about her right now.

I tried to focus on the words in my textbook. The words looked normal, and it should be easy to comprehend them. But I kept reading the same sentence over several times and it did not make any sense! My head hurt.

"Hope? How are you doing?" My mother asked at my door. She held a plate with a sandwich on it. "I thought you might be hungry..."

My head hurt so much, but I ignored the pain. Pain didn't affect me anymore.

"Hope..." she hugged me; I could barely feel her. "Honey...it's all right."

I didn't respond.

"How can I help you?" She asked me.

"I don't think you can," I plainly spoke. "Kiara...this girl I met... she has the same dreams as Damon and I," I told her.

"Damon? He has these dreams or whatever they are too?"

I nodded. "I met him in the dream."

"Wait a minute! Who is Damon?" She asked. "Where did you meet him?"

I just looked at her. If she didn't get it by now...She had abnormal experiences, but she just wanted to deny everything. That was fine. I didn't need her sympathy.

"So you met Damon in this dream and then again at school?" she asked.

She finally got it.

"I didn't believe he actually existed until I saw him on campus a few weeks later," I told her.

"He was going to his class when you met him again?" She asked.

"He doesn't even attend that college. He just hangs out on the campus green sometimes," I told her.

"He doesn't go to school? He told us..." she rambled on.

"Just forget it. Forget everything I've told you," I said.

"I want to help you," Mom insisted.

I stood up, looking at her with this dead stare. She backed away.

"Where were you before?" I asked. My voice never wavered; it stayed at an even tone.

"Where were you when I was pushed off that cliff?" I took a step towards her. "Where were you when I was alone and scared?" I asked her again.

"I didn't know that happened! You didn't say anything about it!" Mom shouted then burst out crying. I don't know what came over me. I was just sick of her crying. Why did I have to pay for her mistakes?

"I didn't know anything!" She kept crying. "You didn't tell me anything! I thought it was all over! I went to a priest, Father Daniel and asked if he would baptize you. I wasn't raised Catholic, but I needed to find someone who could help me!" she cried out.

She met Father Daniel? I found another connection. For some reason though, I didn't want to tell her about it. I was on my own. I knew that now.

In the middle of our discussion, Charsi's voice intervened. "Hey mom, I needed to know…" She saw Mom was talking to me. "Oh, sorry, I'll catch you some other time," she said. Right Charsi, my mom was in my room, who did you think she was talking to? Did she want to avoid me that much? Not that I care, she should avoid me!

"It's fine, what do you need?" She asked her. Charsi kept her gaze away from me.

"It's no big deal. I'll ask you later," she said and left our presence and that was the end of it. I had no intention of apologizing to her.

"Things are getting a bit out of hand," Mom admitted.

I said nothing.

"Hope! Will you talk to me?!" she asked frantically.

"I need to rest now," I said. I felt so numb.

Chapter Sixteen:
Finding Truth

Everything felt so awkward for the next month. Finals were a blur. I really didn't care how I did in my classes. The holiday season came and went. Mom and James kept things under wraps about what was happening to us. The rest of our family had no idea what occurred in our home. I didn't talk much to our company; they weren't my family that is how I felt. I had no family. My father was a murderous demon and my mom was a lying witch. As time went on, I started to get very depressed. I have not seen Damon or Kiara for some time. The New Year is supposed to bring new beginnings. But in truth, the New Year scared me. I didn't know what to expect.

I guess I shouldn't complain. I did make the Dean's List. It made me feel a little better. Charsi got mad because I did better than her. Ha! That will show her! Now she can't say any of her usual snide comments, telling me to study more! It was quite funny. She tried to blame it on the fact that I pushed her into the wall and damaged her brain. She could sit and whine all she wanted, it didn't matter to me.

"How can I forgive her?" Charsi complained during dinner. "Look at me, I'm falling apart, my grades are lower this term, my family is too weird, and I can't tell anyone about it, and above all, my sister is trying to kill me!"

"You know what, Charsi?" I exploded. "We are not really sisters, so you don't have to worry about it anymore. You don't have to make excuses for having a strange sister or come up with any stories about me suffering some accident when I was younger and that is why I'm not as smart as you. Besides, I did sort of have an accident when I was younger...I was pushed off that cliff," I finally let out. My mouth formed a sly smile.

"But I didn't die..."

Everyone in the room was silent. They looked so freaked all out. They had these expressions of fear and confusion on their faces

"Will both of you stop this?!" James reprimanded.

"It's all right," I said. "I'm not really her sister and you're not my real father. I can live with that. But I can't live without knowing what my purpose is!"

"What do you keep going on about? Of course you are my daughter and Charsi is your sister," James told me.

I looked over at Mom; she remained quiet. Now I knew how Kiara felt.

I thought I could trust you mom. You of all people…. You betrayed me. I thought to myself.

I left the table at that moment. There was this horrible, uncomfortable silence as I left. Things will change now….forever. I couldn't stand this house any longer. I grabbed my coat. As I walked down the snowy driveway, I gazed up at the sky. The sunset was sort of pretty. The sky blended with blue and red and some pink in between. I thought about Damon. I missed him so much. He understood. He knew what I've felt. Kiara went through these visions too, but I didn't feel like dealing with her. She seemed very unstable, but then again, how stable was I lately? I walked down to the end of the road and back. I felt so cold, I didn't really want to go back, but I needed to be in the warmth of the house.

I walked up the stairs to my room, but something stopped me.

"So, can you tell me how this happened?" I heard James' voice. Mom and James' room was to the right of the stairwell. The door was closed. I didn't have to press against it, I heard them fine from where I stood.

"I don't know…" I heard my mom answer in this hoarse whisper. "You knew I had Hope when we met, so why does this shock you so much?" She asked.

"You're saying I shouldn't be shocked? She pushed Charsi into the wall and then that weird blackness thing? What *is* she?" he asked.

"It's not her fault!" Mom's voice became hysterical. "She's just upset! She almost died when she was just barely born!" she defended.

"Do you think she should see someone?" He asked softer.

"I don't think that would help," she replied.

"What are you doing?" I heard a voice behind me. Charsi once again picked the perfect time.

137

"Nothing that involves you," I said sounding smug.

"What are Mom and Dad talking about?" she tried.

"I don't know. I don't really care," I said and went towards the bathroom. I turned to see her put an ear the door.

"I think they're talking about you," she said.

"So what if they are?" I asked. It was unbelievable how much she was testing my patience. Maybe she was the dumb one. She was quiet for a moment.

"Hey, I just heard Mom tell Dad about where you are from," she told me.

"I already know where I'm from," I said.

"So what? You think you have special powers or something?" She asked hastily.

"Something is happening to me, I can't deny that," I said softly.

"You think you are from some divine origin? Do you think you're some superior being? You are just a lost soul Hope! You got into things you shouldn't have and now you are possessed by demons!" she chided.

"Possessed? If only it were that simple. I see demons Charsi. I see Hell," I said.

Charsi shook her head in disbelief. "No! I swear if you hurt my parents, I'll..."

Was she threatening me?

"You have no idea what you just said. You have no right to judge me!" I charged her. I felt the darkness surround me. It felt like I was on fire inside. My sight blurred and the darkness filled around me as it did before. I felt heavy, like I would just fall to the ground, then I heard Charsi scream. My vision returned as James came out of their room.

"What happened?!" He cried out. My vision returned and I saw that the wall caught on fire. He gasped as he stumbled back from the fire. Then, he pulled Charsi down the stairs, and yelled, "Amira, don't come out of the room!" I stood and watched as he returned with the fire extinguish we kept by the basement stairs. With a few quick movements of pulling the pin and the handle, the fire was quenched with some hissing sounds.

Charsi stood at the bottom of the stairs looking up at me. She started shaking so hard she fell to the floor. Now my mom came out, she looked directly at me. I didn't know if she feared me or hated me, maybe both. James looked at me with extreme hate.

"Get out!" He fired at me.

"Don't blame her!" Mom yelled at him. "I tried to tell you..."

I turned away, walking to my room. I wasn't bothered by his words at all. I didn't know why I didn't care. I just didn't. From my window, I gazed out at the night. It was black, no stars in the sky. Snow began to fall. I wanted to forget everything...

"Hope?" That sounded like my mom. I really did not want to speak to anyone, especially her. *I've had it with all of them!* I remember thinking *They don't care about me. They just laugh at my pain.*

"Hope..."

I realized the voice did not come from the door. It was from behind me. As I turned around, this white light blinded me. I had to gasp at the sight; I stood in this green field by a stream. The sky was so blue and I felt the warm sun. Flowers of all colors and shapes surrounded me. It was beautiful for a change. No horrible monsters, no blood or gore.

I saw someone standing by the stream. The familiar face turned to me. "Hello again," she said.

"Aria?" I asked. She smiled. I felt so tranquil while standing here. Even though I was mad at this woman before, I didn't feel any anger right now.

"Why?" I asked, breathing deeply. "Why is all of this happening?"

"Haven't you figured it out?" she replied.

"Was I supposed to? How am I supposed to know what is going on?" I questioned her.

"You've learned about your abilities. You're not like other people," she told me.

"So, am I a demon? A monster?" I asked.

"No, there are no demons, just lost souls. Lost souls who need you, Hope."

"Lost souls who need me? What can I do? I feel like I'm out control," I said.

"Hope, you have more strength than you believe. Look at everything you overcame. You fought against your enemies. And you're still alive."

"You knew about all of the things I would face. Why didn't you warn me?" I asked.

"I told you not to make this hard. You didn't ask for my help, so I didn't give it to you," Aria explained.

"What are you talking about? You show up unexpected, gave me some strange exchange of words, something weird happens and you're gone. I wanted to talk to you a while back and I couldn't find you. I met Kiara, a friend of yours I guess?" I asked hoping her answer would not confuse me more.

"Kiara?" Aria interrupted.

"Yeah, I guess she thinks of you as somewhat of a pest. She's not even sure who you are," I told her.

Aria made the weirdest smile. "You've met Kiara?" she asked.

"Yeah," I tried to ignore the awkward feelings I got from looking at Aria. "We're trying to find out why we are having these nightmares. So what happens now? Are you going to tell me what is going on? Do I have to keep guessing?" I wondered.

Aria moved over to me and put a hand on my arm. "Hope, you know you are not the demon here. The demons are the ones who persecuted the people on Earth. You have seen those poor souls, they look wretched now, but they were once vibrant and well," she explained.

"So, how can I help them?" I beseeched.

"You want my help now?" She implored.

"Well, I don't have much of a choice. Look, I hate the idea of Hell. We are taught about it in church and how everyone has to get saved. But honestly, if God is so loving, why would he send anyone there? It doesn't make sense. But of course, we're not supposed to question either," I said.

"Hope, you've lived in this life with no purpose. You've been mocked and betrayed by those you trusted. Your heritage is the reason why. They are jealous of you as they should be," she explained.

"So, what is this heritage?" I inquired.

"We are descendants of the righteous angels that fell from Heaven," she said.

What was she talking about?

"Righteous angels?" I asked being puzzled.

"More specifically, we descend from the Watchers, angels who watched over humanity. They were told by God to punish humanity, but they refused. They took pity on the mortals," she continued.

"Wait, what are these monsters I've seen?" I asked being perplexed.

"The angels that stand on God's side," she said.

None of that made any sense. It was completely backwards from what I knew. But the one thing I did know was that I saw these monsters hurting people. I saw their souls in complete agony.

"Hold on! I was told my father was this monster who tried to kill me!" I blurted out.

"No!" Aria said with such harshness. "You're mother lied to you! He cared about you Hope. He didn't want you to suffer, but she ruined your chance for greatness!" She exposed to me.

I didn't know what to believe. "My mom wrote a diary about what my father did," I told her.

"This is the last chance you are getting!" I suddenly felt frozen by her cold stare. "Either come with me or suffer in this wretched world with the other lost souls!" she bellowed.

Now I was confused.

"Wait, you just said…" I began.

"Where is Kiara?" she asked, switching the topic.

I didn't know if I should tell her. She was acting even stranger than before.

"Um, don't you know already?" I asked.

Aria's stare became really intense. I felt compelled to speak even if I didn't want to.

"She's working at the club, Fantasy Nights," I let the information loose.

"Oh yes, that little hole in the wall," she replied. Aria turned away, I had no idea what she was thinking.

"Aria…?"

"We're done now," she said dryly. Her words cut through me.

I was back in my room now. What just happened? Well, I guess I could just tell Kiara about all of this.

The club was packed, which surprised me since the last time I was here disaster struck this place. What about those people? How did Lyell and Kiara get this place running so quickly again? Sure it had been over a month, but weren't people scared to come here? How did they make the repairs so quickly too? I saw Kiara at the bar.

"Kiara!" I called. She first looked at me like I was a stranger. "Hope, what's going on?" she asked.

I stood next to her shouting so she could hear me over the techno music.

"I talked with Aria again... I said. She rushed me up to the lounge and shut the door. I looked around the vacant room. Did anyone else ever come up here?

"What is going on with that woman?" Kiara asked suddenly. "What did she say?"

"She told me that...we are descendants of righteous angels who fell from Heaven. The demons we've seen are actually angels and God is this evil being who wants our destruction," I repeated Aria's words.

Kiara blinked a few times. "That does not sound like Aria. Aria is very religious," she said adamantly.

"Religious? That is the last word I would use to describe her," I blurted. "It was really strange, but I guess she does have a split personality. She wanted to know where you were...I thought she knew you worked at this club," I explained.

"She does!" Kiara cried out in frustration. "What the hell?! I don't get her at all! Where did you see her?" She asked angrily.

"I saw her in another vision. But this one was different. I was in this field by a stream. It was peaceful; I just felt this overwhelming tranquility," I revealed to her.
Kiara sat down in one of the chairs just staring straight ahead.

"That church has brainwashed her," Kiara said.
Kiara told me how much she hated the church. I wonder, what are her beliefs?

"Do you believe in God?" I asked the question before I really thought about it.

"Which god?" she asked, focusing her eyes on me.

"I mean God. What is your religion?" I asked her.

"I have my own ideas and beliefs. I don't go to church or anything. I believe we are here to find our own destiny and understand ourselves. Aria took me to church when I was younger, but I spent most of the time being told I was sinful and going to Hell," she reluctantly revealed.

She smiled suddenly; she looked just how Aria did earlier. "You know what? I'd rather go to Hell!" She stated, ending her speech in an eerie smile. I was not sure if I really liked her. Everything she says and does goes against my morals. I was not sure if I should trust her at all. On top of that, she really scared the crap out of me. Ever since I met her, all I had to do was see her to remind me of my past. I did not want to go back there.

"Why wouldn't you want to be in Paradise?" I finally asked.

"What makes you think there is a Paradise? What if Heaven is actually Hell? What if everyone is being tricked?" She did sound like Aria. How in the world could they be in such disagreement when they sounded so alike?

She looked serious again. "Let me guess, you're a Christian, right?" She asked as if being certain.

I felt hesitant to answer, but I did anyways.

"Yes. Why do you...?" I began to ask.

She stood up suddenly. "I knew it! You are just like all of the others, sitting there judging people! How can you believe in a place as terrible as Hell? Even worse, you believe people who are not like you should go there!" She accused me.

She greatly misunderstood.

"No. God doesn't want people to go there. That is what they choose. Because of sin, we have fallen and we need to be saved..." I tried to explain.

"Now I get it. You're just messing with me! Aria and you have been working together all this time!" She made more accusations.

"What are you talking about?" I asked, shocked by her outburst. Was she insane? I tried to continue, keeping her on the right track. "So what about the Bible? It says that..." I tried again.

"The Bible is made up of a bunch of stories," she said sharply. "Everything that has happened to us, everything that shouldn't be real, is. Did it ever occur to anyone that maybe God is the Devil, just like it said in that poem?" She asked defensively.

"Poem? Which poem?" I asked.

"I saw it too. At the fountain, just before the castle. It's true," she said.

After all of what she said, I had to admit I was a little frightened of her. She really lost her mind. I was afraid I would soon be there too.

"Forget about what you knew before," she spoke quickly. "You have to go by what you know now. I'm not going to believe in a book or religion that says a bunch of stuff we are not allowed to question. I want to live my own life. And I want Aria out of it!" She said with anger. Her voice grew with every word she said. She became more dramatic the longer we stayed in this conversation. Maybe I should let it go for now.

"I'm sorry Kiara. I didn't want to upset you. You have no idea how much I hurt right now," I told her in all honesty.

I turned away, tears were falling from my eyes. No. I decided. I won't show weakness to her! Opening the door, I sprinted down the stairs.

Walking back to the bar, I saw Lyell sitting in a chair across from a couple of girls, one was African American and the other was a blonde.

"Hope," he called to me. "Come join my crew," he invited me. The girls giggled. *Yeah, right,* I thought.

"Lyell, I need to know something," I said.

"Yeah?" He looked past the girls at me. The girls threw this glare at me.

"It probably would be best if we could talk alone," I hinted.

"I see," he said and got up. "I'll be right back, ladies." Lyell took me back behind the bar. People were scattering around back in the kitchen.

I didn't know if we should talk here either.

"What did she do?" he asked suddenly.

"Who?" I asked.

"Kiara, I saw her drag you upstairs," he said.

"Yeah, I told her I spoke with Aria recently. I think that started her anger," I told him.

"She's always angry. If she shows any happiness at all, she is usually drunk," he remarked.

"So why do you let her work here?" I asked.

"There is more history between us than anyone can understand," he explained gravely.

"I see. So, you and Kiara still get business even after what happened?"

Lyell narrowed his eyes. "What do you mean?" he asked.

"The day the monster attacked and we found those people dead?" I asked him.

"Why would they care? They don't know what happened," Lyell lowered his voice.

"I don't understand," I said, becoming confused.

"They don't have the visions we have, Hope. They will never know the power we have. Besides, we said we'd take care of things," he reminded me.

"I didn't know what you meant by it. How did you take care of things anyways?" I asked.

"Wow, you really are clueless. No wonder Kiara needed to find you," he replied.

"What?" Now I was really confused.

"I'm sorry," he spoke softly. "I'm not trying to be rude or anything."

I felt like I was the only one that didn't know the big secret.

"You're going to have to explain everything to me. What exactly am I missing here?" I sincerely asked.

"You have the gift, but you barely know how to use it. You are lost in the events that happened and you cannot tell what is real and what isn't. Maybe telling you this will clear up some things for you. When you see people who are dead and demons roaming the area, you are not exactly dreaming, of course you are not exactly awake either. You are having visions, but they are visions you can interact with and change. They are things only those with our gifts can see. We have the power to fight the demons or we can choose to join them in their mayhem," he explained the details for me.

"So, you and Kiara are fighting these demons too. How do we make it so we can all have the same vision at once and fight these demons together? I mean, Damon and I had the same vision while we were met in this castle and at the hospital. Other than that, I've been alone when I see those things," I revealed to him.

I wanted to ask Lyell about his beliefs, but I really did not want to get into another religious discussion tonight.

"Did she tell you about what she planned to say to me?" I asked.

"No. But, she told me she wanted to talk to you about your false beliefs," he said in a sorry tone.

"But they aren't false beliefs! Not to me!" I protested.

"That's fine. Just understand she has different ones than you," he said.

"I can accept that, just not her putting down my religion," I told him. I still had questions about that night the monster attacked the club. It seemed like Lyell was trying to distract me from what I really needed to know.

"So when these visions happen, we're the only ones who see them? So, the incident the other night with the place getting attacked, that didn't really happen?" I asked, starting to get confused again.

"It did and it didn't....think about another time when you saw things that were messed up and then the next day they were normal again," he replied.

I knew exactly what he meant. The first night this began, last summer on campus. I found everyone dead, even my instructor. But after that night, everything was fine, my instructor was alive and well and so was everyone else. If that many people died with unexplained deaths, there would have been news cameras and all these people checking out the scene, police officers, ambulances, and everything. None of that happened. No one else in the normal world knew any of it happened.

"That's it? We defeat the evil and things change back to the way they were?" I asked, trying to be sure I understood.

"Don't make it too complicated. Just accept all of those things that happened," he said.

Accept what happened?! That's it? Does he realize what he just said? My family is afraid of me for what just happened! I almost killed my sister twice!

"I know there is a lot I don't understand," I admitted. "But we defeated the monster and nothing changed. You had to have done something else," I pressed him.

He was quiet for a moment. "I need to get back to those girls, before they suspect something," he said then started to walk away. I didn't want to stop talking to him. I had to find out what else I didn't know.

"Lyell, I think something is really wrong with Kiara. I didn't say anything earlier, but I...think I met her mom," I confessed to him. He stopped in mid-step, turning to me with this sharp glare. "Her mother is dead. And I wouldn't ever mention the subject again, to her or to me!" he warned.

He left by the door into the bar area. So now what do I do? No one wanted to give me a straight answer.

In my car, I turned the dial on the panel, blowing heat onto me. I got home to a quiet house. It was almost midnight. The T.V. and couch looked inviting. I sat down and picked up the remote to turn it on. The light from the screen engulfed the whole room. I sat there just staring at the screen. I really am not in the mood to watch T.V right now. I was so tired.

I wanted to go to sleep; as if that were possible. As I came to the stairs I heard a knock at the front door. I really did not want to answer, but the knocking was so insistent. When I opened the door, I saw Damon standing there in his usual casual way.

"Hey!"

"Where have you been?!" I cried out with more emotion than I intended.

"Uh, doing stuff," he said giving me an awkward glance. "Can I come in?" he asked.

"Yeah." Damon walked inside and saw the T.V. was on. "What's on?"

"Nothing. I'm just bored," I said. I should tell him about talking to Kiara.

I shut off the T.V.

"What's wrong?" he asked. I guess he could sense I was upset.

I just shook my head and walked toward the stairs. I felt like I was in a daze again. Damon followed me as I moved through the living room to the stairs. We reached the top of the stairs where Damon immediately saw the burnt piece of wallpaper hanging in shreds.

"What the hell happened? Something caught on fire?" He asked, surprised.

"That's one of the things I need to talk to you about," I said. We went into my room; I hit the switch on the wall turning my nightstand lamp on. I went over to sit on my bed. Damon noticed the dent in the plaster by my door.

"What is going on in this house? You guys have anger management issues?" he joked.

"I do," I said quietly. "I pushed my sister into the wall and tried to fry her," I told him.

"Hold on! What?"

"Strange things keep happening…I'm not myself anymore," I said.

"Is everyone asleep?" he asked.

I nodded, "yeah, probably."

"What else has been happening?" he pried.

I told Damon about meeting Kiara again. The incident of talking with her about Aria, going with Lyell to Aria's home, and coming back to find people dead, impaled on pikes and the monster attacking us.

"So Kiara killed this monster, it was like the one we saw in the basement of that hospital?" He asked with curiosity.

"No. It was worse. I saw the same type of creature in one of my other visions too," I told him.

"What was it?" he asked. His voice held tension when he spoke.

"A Nephilim," I responded.

"What's that?" Damon asked, never hearing the word before.

"An offspring of a fallen angel," I said, like it was something I've always known.

Damon looked serious for a moment than cracked a laugh. "W-what? How do you know?"

"I just do," I answered.

"So, this monster was at the club. Then you went back finding the place normal with people again. You had this religious discussion with Kiara and learned more about the visions from Lyell," he repeated what I told him.

"Doesn't it freak you out?" I asked.

"It sort of freaks me out that you've gone postal on your sister, but I'm getting used to seeing the demons. I mean, it's no different for me. I see things get screwed up and then everything is normal again," he responded.

How could he be used to seeing such horrible creatures? And everything else too?

"I can't believe you tried to talk about the Bible to Kiara," Damon said switching topics.

"Why?" I asked.

"She doesn't want to hear about God or the church. She has her own beliefs. See, I did remember her right when we saw her that night at the party. I just didn't want to say anything," Damon told me.

"Why? You don't like her or something?" I asked.

Damon turned away from me. "Hope, do you remember much from high school?" he asked me.

"Nothing I want to remember," I admitted.

"Yeah, me too," Damon agreed. "It actually made me cringe when she mentioned meeting me freshmen year. I found that yearbook too. I found her picture in it and sadly, mine too. I can now show you what I looked like with black hair and blue streaks!" He said laughing a little.

"Really?" I asked, thinking about how that would look.

"Yeah, and I found your picture too Hope," he mentioned.

"I don't remember you," I confessed.

"Well, for one, I look different now. I went back to my natural hair color and I don't look like such a wimp anymore," he said rolling his eyes.

"You shouldn't be so hard on yourself," I said, and realized I was guilty of exactly that. I hated thinking of the past, as much as he did.

"Well, it is interesting," Damon went on. "We all have pictures in the school yearbook. You know, Kiara was really smart, but she never showed it. She never did her homework, but did well enough on her tests to pass. She barely got out of high school, but she never seemed to care. I didn't see her after that. We hung out after I graduated and she was still a senior, but then, one day…she just disappeared. I saw her again at the party," he said with a tinge of regret.

149

"Really? I wonder what her connection is to Aria. I still don't know that yet," I replied.

"I do," Damon spoke softer. "Somehow, every time I've seen her during these visions, I don't recognize her at all. But after the fact, I know that I once knew her very well. I can't believe I forgot Aria. I've seen her many times--Kiara lived with her," he recalled.

"Wait a minute!" My head was spinning. "Kiara lived with Aria? So she was her...guardian?" I asked trying to understand.

"Yeah. Amazing, huh? The woman who has been giving us problems took care of Kiara when she was a teenager. But I don't understand something. The woman I met back then cannot be the same woman we met recently. Something is messed up," he said trying to figure things out.

"James is not my real father," I told Damon. I'm not sure why I just mentioned it at this moment.

"What are you talking about?" He asked being surprised at what I said.

"I found out from a journal my mom has and she told me too. This whole thing started when Charsi would not leave me alone about how much time I spent outside the house," I confided in him.

"Why should she care?" he asked.

"Exactly," I spoke sharply. "She is just used to me being at home, while she always had friends and I've always been alone! She has no idea who I am! I hate her!" I cried out with explosive anger.

"Um, Hope?!" Damon spoke. My hands felt warm. I looked down to see them burning! It scared both of us. Damon jumped back just staring at them. After a few moments of shock, the fire died down.

"What the hell is wrong with you?!" he cried.

"I don't know!" My voice shrieked. Then I turned to the closed door, praying no one heard me. I looked at my hands. There was no indication that they were just on fire. I didn't even feel any pain.

"Has it always been this way?" Damon asked. "You don't get along with your sister?"

"She's not my sister," I replied.

"Just like my brothers and sister aren't really related to me?" Damon inquired.

"Yeah…." I agreed.

"Well, she is your half-sister if your mom is her mom. You just have a different dad," he explained.

"Yeah," I agreed again.

"Hey, I don't mean to change the subject, but I had one of those vision things and instead of having the guns, I had those swords," he told me.

"Really?" I responded knowing the connection. "That's probably because I had the guns in my last vision," I said.

"Hey, you stole them from me!" he teased.

I shook my head. Only Damon would make a joke at a time like this. I think that's why I really like him.

Chapter Seventeen:
The Nephilim

Damon and I didn't try to figure out why we switched weapons. We found out during the battle in our joint vision that the guns were more powerful in my hands. We didn't try to figure that one out, either.

Since my mother mentioned Father Daniel, I thought about seeing him again. I wished my mom would come with me to the church, but she right out refused. When I asked why, she only said, "There is no purpose in going there." *Father Daniel.* I had that strange experience the last time I was there. But when he prayed over me, I felt this heavy burden leave. While I talked to her, I noticed something I never did before. I always thought her eyes were brown, but today they looked gray, almost as light as mine. I guess one might say that I have silver colored eyes. They were always seen as very unique, I guess it fit with everything else.

When I arrived at the church, it was deathly quiet. From the entrance way, there were some stairs leading up to the second floor. There were many rooms up here, but I heard voices coming from the room at the end of the hall. It sounded like a couple of men were having a heated conversation. I crept down towards the voices. I was right outside the room now. I've been doing a lot of sneaking around lately, but this is how I found out everyone's little secrets.

"What are you telling me?" I heard one of the men's voices. "You are not satisfied with the church, feeling it does not meet your needs, but you do not want to leave?" he asked.

"I don't want to leave because it won't change anything. The church will keep going on like it has been. People need to hear the whole gospel, not just parts of it," the second man answered.

"And what do you think we are leaving out?" The first man asked further.

"No one ever speaks of the passages that talk about fallen angels having offspring. You may not think the topic of fallen angels is important to discuss in today's society, but truthfully, it references to the 'End Times,' the time of 'The Rapture," the second man replied.

"The verse you speak of does not say that giants roam our world now, but that they once did. It is why God flooded the world for forty days. None of them are around today," the first man informed.

"What about the story of David and Goliath? Goliath was this giant of a man taken down by David, a much smaller man. It is said that Goliath had sons as well," the other man said.

"Wait, where does it say that Goliath was an offspring of these fallen angels?" The first man asked.

There was a pause, "It doesn't say specifically, but it does tie in with him being a giant. And there is a whole book devoted to speaking about fallen angels and offspring in the book of Enoch," the second man retorted.

"That book was never part of the Bible!" The first man raised his voice drastically. "Don't be fooled by those who claim there are lost books, those stories would still be in the Good Book if they were real."

"What about references to being baptized in the Holy Spirit in the four gospels and Acts? Speaking in tongues, perfect prayer to God?" The second man asked.

"You are speaking of the time when Jesus walked the earth. Many miracles happened back then," the first man responded.

"Are you suggesting that miracles do not happen in today's time?" The other man asked.

"Yes, they happen, but in a different way. We don't have the power of God. It is blasphemous to believe so!" the first man exploded.

"But we do have the power of God. We have the power of Christ! With the Holy Spirit, we have the power to heal the hurt and sick as Christ did. We have the power to pray perfectly to God, finally praying in His language of our needs instead of using our meager language," the second man exclaimed.

"I'm sorry." The first man's voice subsided, "I sense that you are confused about what the Bible says. And I sense that you are lost in its translation and are misinterpreting the metaphoric language for literal meanings. Please, come to the conference next weekend. The teachings can help clear up some of your misunderstandings," he said.

I heard footsteps coming to the door. I moved away before it opened. The man saw me standing there, "Hello. Can I help you with something?" The man who asked me appeared to be quite older than Father Daniel. He wore the same garments, the black robe and white collar.

"Um…" I wavered. Looking around the corner, I saw the priest I needed to see. He looked very bothered, vigorously organizing his desk. "I just need to see him," I pointed to the busy priest.

"Oh. Well, go right in, I'm sure he won't mind," he responded rather hastily. I stood there looking into the room as the other priest moved on down the hall.

As I walked in, I felt so out of place. The priest looked up,

"Hello," the priest greeted me.

"I thought it was you in here, but I was not sure." I began. "Um…"

"Come in." There was an uncomfortable looking wood chair across from him. I thought that churches could afford nicer chairs from the money that is collected from people. Behind him was a small short shelf with a variety of books. There was not much else in this room. It was so tiny and plain.

"Um, I don't know if you remember the last time we talked," I said. I choose to remain standing. I didn't plan on staying long.

"Oh yes, yes," he responded confidently, a little too confidently.

"You remember I asked about demons, if it was possible to be possessed by them?" I asked.

"Yes. Um…now remind me of your name," he said.

I didn't think he really knew who I was. "My name is Hope. It was a while since I came here. You prayed for me," I reminded him.

"What is going on? What exactly has brought you to me today?" he asked.

"My mother told me that you baptized me as a baby," I said.

"Oh really? What is her name?" he asked.

"Amira Eden."

He looked curiously at me, "I knew an Amira once; that was a long time ago.

"Did she bring a child for you to baptize?" I asked.

154

"Oh, it's been so long. I remember this woman came to the church about twenty years ago with a child. She ran into the church and started screaming for a priest. She cried out 'I need a priest! My baby is cursed!' I was the only one there and I was new to the priesthood. I did the blessing on the child. I remember this child had dark hair like her mother, and her eyes were light silver, almost white," he recalled.

"What was this child's name?"

The priest sat back in his chair.

"Angel Cry," he uttered and looked up at me. "That was so long ago...," he stated.

I felt emotion build up inside of me. Emotion that has been trying to get out since all of this began.

"I'm Angel Cry," I forced myself to say.

His eyes grew wide. He sprang out of his chair and raced towards the door.

"Wait!" I called after him. I chased him down the hall. He ducked into the room left of the stairs. I heard a lock click.

"Please..." I called through the door. "I'm not going to hurt you." My voice was cracking. I felt tears run down my face. "I just need help. I came here because I was scared. I don't know what's happening to me!" I cried.

It was silent for way too long in my mind. Then I heard his voice, "I knew your mother quite well actually. After that night, we became good friends. But I told her..." his voice faded.

"What?" I urged.

"I tried to baptize you, but the holy water almost killed you. I...I asked your mother what she knew about this. She just kept talking about a curse put on you by your father. I...told her to kill you!" He finally revealed.

I couldn't believe his words. I didn't want to believe them.

"You weren't a normal child," Father Daniel continued. "You see, I can sense demons. You weren't really a demon, but you weren't really human either." He kept talking about me in the past tense. It was disturbing.

"Do you know what demons are Hope?" He asked through the door.

"I know they are evil spirits, the Bible refers to them as such. But I'm being constantly attacked by them now. I didn't think they could have children."

"They are actually the fallen angels that went against God while they were still in Heaven. Satan was once known as Lucifer and had a team of angels who rebelled against God and were tossed out of heaven for eternity," Father Daniel continued.

"Wait, fallen angels and demons are the same things? I never knew that. I thought fallen angels were thrown out of heaven and the demons were made by them."

"There were also the Watchers, another group of angels who desired human women and had children with them. Those are the Nephilim," he further explained.

Nephilim? That creature I saw. I knew what he was called even though I've never heard that word before.

"Actually, there are passages in the Bible that confirm such beings. One is the book of Genesis; Genesis 6:1-4.

"And it came to pass, when men began to multiply on the face of the earth and daughters were born unto them.

The sons of God saw the daughters of men that they were fair; and they took them wives of all which they chose….

There were giants on the Earth in those days; and also after that, when the sons of God came unto the daughters of men and they bore children to them the same became mighty men who were of old, men of renown," he quoted scripture.

"Sons of God are angels and daughters of men are born of human beings," he explained.

Alright, that was understood, but what about demons?

"The offspring of the angels and women were monstrous beings. God sees this happen and this is actually how the flood of the world comes to pass," he finished.

"That's interesting," I had to admit that. "But those offspring were killed right?"

"There's a book that was cut from the Bible, it never made it into an English Bible. It didn't even get into the King James Version in 1611, but there is a book that explains the coming of fallen angels."

"Why was this book taken out?" I felt so weird, yelling through this door. "Can I please come in?" He didn't answer my question. Instead, he kept talking about the original topic.

"I wonder if it has to do with the book being so strange and sort of frightening. But I also wonder if someone in high power of the church did not want this book to be known."

"Why? I don't understand," I said.

"The problem is that not everyone of the church is saved by Christ. Some are mis-preaching the Word," he answered.

"I had a conversation with someone about religion." I breathed out a sigh. "She thinks the church tries to fool everyone," I revealed.

"Some churches do. Maybe she had a bad experience from going to church. What exactly doesn't she like about the church?" He asked.

"She thinks God is the Devil...or something like that," I said, still not believing she said that.

"She is not the first person to think that. In fact, people in the church believe that. That's why more people aren't getting saved. Not everyone in the church believes in Hell either," he said gravely.

"I know Hell exists," I said. "I've seen it!" I cried.

There was some more silence, and then the priest actually opened the door. He seemed very afraid, but I could see some sympathy in his facial expression.

"I've seen it too." He spoke gravely. "Those giant monsters down there...are the first Nephilim God destroyed in the flood. There are other demons that roam from Earth to Hell. I've tried to tell others about it. I want to talk to the whole congregation, but I seem to keep rubbing the elder priest the wrong way," he said with sadness in his voice.

I didn't know what to say right now.

"I know you have kindness in you," he continued. "It's not you who I ran away from. Sometimes, this gift of seeing demons and Hell can get to me sometimes."

Tell me about it! I thought to myself.

He walked out into the hallway. "Please, come back if you need anything," he offered.

I didn't get it. One minute, he was scared to death of me and then he's willing to see me again the next. I'm not sure if this visit helped me or not. I'm even more confused now.

Chapter Eighteen:
My Father's Legacy

When I came out of the church, it was completely dark out. The sun sets around six during the winter season, but it was two in the afternoon. The sun was covered as if there was an eclipse. I did not have time to worry about it. I had to get home. I needed to tell my mom about what I learned. While driving home, I kept thinking I was being followed. Maybe it was all the strange things happening to me or my mom's story about the demon was now beginning to get to me. I ignored the feeling, trying to convince myself I was being paranoid.

I was home again. I had not been out so much since, I'm not sure when. Ever since I met Aria, my life has changed. It became interesting. Once again, I found no one home. Were they avoiding me now? They must be afraid of me?

They should be afraid of you! You are greater than them!

How did I keep hearing that demonic voice in my head? Voices inside my head meant that I really was crazy.

Upstairs in my room, I settled down on my bed. Laying there in the dark, I tried hard to clear my mind.

"Well, you're not going to learn anything by just laying there," the male voice shocked me. I quickly sat up. There was a man standing there, but the darkness shrouded his appearance. I did notice that he was a very large guy.

"Oh great, someone else who wants to be my friend?" I wondered.

"I'm the best friend you have right now." His voice sounded so hollow and eerie.

"Who are you?"

"You don't recognize your own father?" He shrewdly asked.

At that moment, I raised myself off the bed with feet on the floor.

"My what?"

He stared at me; his eyes looked so cold. The lights were off, but I could see him clearly. His eyes stuck out even in the dark. They were two brilliant blue irises staring down at me. It sort of freaked me out. I think I prefer Aria. It gave me an eerie feeling as he talked to me like he's always known me. But what struck me the hardest was what he called himself.

"My...father?"

He gave me a peculiar look, "Let me guess, you're at the top of your class?" He didn't hide the sarcasm.

"Why are you here?" My voice came out a bit sharp.

"Well, I would have been here sooner if I knew where you were! I have looked for you since that day your mother took you away from me," he said.

"She took me away from you because you tried to kill me!" I shouted at him.

"Please, Amira never really understood your true ability. You were to become a god," he said.

"You know, lately I have been called crazy, but you are the one who is crazy! I know who you are, my mom told me everything!" I said.

"Really?" Xander asked. "And what did your dear mother tell you about me?" I looked up at the tall man. I felt the sudden rage swelling up inside of me. "Get out of here! I know what you are demon!" I lashed out. He gave a thunderous laugh.

"A demon? That is the best you can come up with? There are no such things as demons! Humans want to call us monsters. They are the monsters! They create war on themselves, greed, gluttony, lust, every sin is what they make it," he continued.

"Strange, you are not the only one who confirms that demons do not exist. What about fallen angels? I have proof they exist," I told him.

Xander laughed again with a stronger mocking laugh. "You have no idea what exists outside the human world. Humankind wants to make up their god and their angels and miracles. There is no such thing, it is only those who choose a better destiny," he replied.

He walked closer and put his hands on the sides of my face, a feeling I did not really need. He spoke softly now. "Angel Cry, my daughter...I know you have suffered much in this mediocre society. They can never understand our ways. The ones who fear you have right to, now you can show them all your true power!" He said hypnotically.

"What did you call me?" I asked feeling fearful.

"I called you by your rightful name."

"That is not my name! And I'm not going to hurt anyone!" I shouted. But my words betrayed me. He was speaking the truth. I had wanted to hurt others lately. I'd been thinking so much of the past lately, and I want everyone who hurt me to suffer.

"They hurt you." Xander knew my thoughts. "Will you just let others make you feel less than what you are? You have the choice of being a god and creating a new world. Those ignorant beings will never understand us!" He said with conceit.

I had nothing to say. He was right, many people have hurt me. They made me feel like an outsider, no one understood me. I tried to remind myself that my mom did tell me the truth...after the fact of having lost myself in an alternate reality. She could have told me sooner...

"By your quiet poise, I'm guessing you are considering my offer?" Xander casually inquired.

What was there to think about? This guy standing here in front of me was a demon or fallen angel by what the priest said.

"I'm sorry. I'm already looked at as crazy. Joining you would just confirm it," I told him.

"See, you are quick witted and bright. You are brave enough to give me such an insult. Obviously, the people you know don't give you enough credit," he said in attempt to flatter me.

I wondered if I deserved much credit. It hurt to think of myself as so useless.

"Just think about the offer then," he said, then opened the window and jumped out. His massive leap didn't surprise me too much. I guess that is how he got in. Did I leave the window open? I suppose I cannot worry about that. Now I had another problem that I was sure would show up again.

I felt the chill of the night before closing the window.

It struck me as odd that the whole time that monster was in my presence, neither the guns nor the blades appeared. No one else was here right now. I didn't feel right. As I moved to the window, the sun came out again. It was so dark a moment ago, but the day returned to normal. The environment changed whenever an evil presence was around. That concluded that I couldn't trust Xander. I just felt like I needed to be around someone. I went out into the hallway, turning toward the main bedroom. The wallpaper still was not fixed yet, neither was the hole in my room. I wished it would get

161

repaired. It was just a reminder of what I did. That was back in December. It was March. It seemed so long ago that I pushed my sister into the wall. I can't help but admit that I felt some joy thinking about it. Do I really want to hurt others?

The door of my parents' room was closed. I knocked, but there wasn't any answer. I opened the door slowly to find the room empty. The king size bed was made up and everything was so neat and tidy. My mom cleaned recently in here. But where was she now? As I walked in there, by the far side of the bed, on the floor, someone laid motionless.

"Mom!" I cried out before even thinking. Running to her side, I knelt down, putting a hand to her face. She was so cold. No! I wouldn't accept that she was...I just wanted to believe this was just an innocent happening, but I knew that someone did this to her. But why? I put my ear to her chest. I felt a tiny pulse when I felt along her neck.

"Hey Mom, I need to talk to you..." Charsi has such great timing! She came bouncing into the room. When she saw me, she staggered back a little. She looked at me, then at mom.

"What have you done?!" she cried. Of course she would blame me.

"I didn't do this!" I responded angrily. "I found her like this!" Charsi did not seem to believe me. "How do I know you didn't do this?" she asked.

"Why would I?"

"You tried to kill me!" Charsi pointed accusingly at me.

I guess I deserved that.

"Charsi, I'm sorry about what happened. We need to get help for Mom right now. I need you to believe me, I didn't do this to her," I pleaded. She appeared skeptical, but she agreed and said she would call an ambulance.

I sat on the floor next to my mother. Nothing physically looked wrong with her. I felt her head for any bumps, maybe she hit her head. I didn't feel anything. Her skin on her face felt cold, so did her hands. What was wrong with her?

It took a few moments for Charsi to return to the room; she looked tired all of a sudden.

"I called them, they're on their way." She sat on the bed looking sadly at me. Now what was going through her mind?

"Do you hate me?" She finally asked. That was a question I had a hard time answering. I know I said I hated her, but I'm not sure that is the case. She just bothers me a lot. "I don't hate you. You just anger me sometimes," I told her.

"Why? What did I do?" She asked innocently, as if not really knowing. Did I really have to answer that?

"It's just that I'm not sure if you respect me," I told her. "You've gone out of your way before to make me look dumb and sometimes, that is the way I really feel," I explained.

"You're not dumb Hope. You've been doing great in your classes. You did better than me last semester," she admitted.

"Why did you make it sound like my effort was nothing then?" I asked her.

"Look, Mom and Dad are used to me getting the higher grades. I know that I am good at school, you are good at finding friends," she confessed.

"Excuse me? You have always had more friends than me. You're more popular, you're smarter, and you're more respected. People always have shown hatred towards me Charsi. It hurts. It hurts so much," I admitted to her. I got up and walked toward the door.

"Wait Hope!" Charsi begged. "I'm sorry, I know you have found friends now and you're happy. I shouldn't have been jealous," she continued to confess.

I stood at the door; I couldn't look at her. "Why would you feel that way? Am I supposed to be the one who is friendless and sad all of the time? Am I supposed to be alone? I always hear the laughter at my expense. Ever since those kids pushed me off the cliff, I felt the hatred burn me. I don't want to it anymore... I don't want to feel the pain anymore," I confided to her.

"Wait a minute, what are you talking about?" Charsi didn't know about that incident.

"Please tell me Hope," she pleaded. Why did she care to know?

"It happened a long time ago." I said. "It was at this park outside of Fallen Ridge. I was pushed off a cliff," I confided in her.

"But if you were pushed off a cliff, then you would be..." her eyes widened; now she understood. "It's true...you're....not human, are you?" She hesitantly asked.

I didn't respond. I walked out of the room.

163

At the hospital, I stood at the bed where my mother now lay.

"Mom," I felt shaken, "I'm sorry. You risked your life to save me, but I wonder if it was worth it. I don't know what I am. I know that this has happened because of me. I met my real father, Mom. He wants me to join him and become a god. I am so confused. Maybe if I go with him, I will find my purpose for living, but I can't be sure that humans will be safe if I do. I can't trust my father, but I can't trust myself either. I am not going to stay around and hurt you or anyone else. I am endangering everyone I come in contact with. I'm sorry, but I have to leave. I don't know where I'm going, but you and Charsi will be safe from me," I expressed being grief stricken. I couldn't stand seeing her lie there. I couldn't cry. My emotions were so buried by now that nothing would come out. I should find Charsi and say goodbye.

Actually, I had no idea where to find Charsi. She left to get some food. She called James who most likely believed I caused all of this. I looked for her downstairs in the café. Strange how I was here months ago with a bunch of monsters roaming the hallways instead of people. I didn't find Charsi anywhere. I hurried back to the room. But he was there, standing by the bedside. It was Xander. It suddenly came to me, he did this! He admitted that he hated her for taking me away.

"Get away from her!" I yelled. He turned toward me, trying to appear innocent.

"Hope, I am so sorry. This is unexpected," he said making an attempt to sound sympathetic. Now, in the light, I saw him clearly. His hair was a silver hue, his eyes were ice blue. He looked rather young, but I felt that he was old as time itself.

"What do you want? Can't you just leave me alone?! I'm tired of all of this!" I blurted out.

"You just assume I have done something to cause this? If I had done anything to her, she would have been dead," he replied.

"You monster! Get out of here!" I demanded. Then, as my dreams became reality, I found the guns were in my hands.

"What? How did...?" Xander just laughed in a mocking manner. "You think those things can do anything? You don't even know how to properly use them. And by your surprised expression, you never expected them to come to you," he said, mocking me.

Come to me? Of course I knew that they would come to me, they did it before. But last time I saw Xander, they didn't.

"What has living in a mortal world done to you? You are so naive, you poor child. Those weapons are bonded to you. After switching with your friend, the guns now come to you, while the previous weapons you once held went to him. But don't get too attached to them, he'll want them back eventually," he said teasingly.

My eyes widen in shock. Did Xander know Damon?

"What do you know about Damon?" I demanded to know.

"Don't worry about that now. When the time comes, you will know exactly who that boy is. It seems kind of unfortunate for you. You were really getting attached to him," he seemed to warn.

"Will you just shut up?!" I aimed both guns at him now. I wasn't sure if the guns would work since I was technically in the real world. Shooting them here might be a bad idea anyways. Perhaps if I just use them as a threat, Xander would back off. But he didn't. He just shook his head. He gave that un-calming smile again. "Believe me, you will learn more. But don't worry. You will understand everything you need when that time comes. Now put the guns away. Stop embarrassing yourself," he said to deflate my confidence.

Now I really did want to shoot him. Xander moved towards me. I don't know why, but I instinctively moved back a step. "You see, you aren't going to shoot me," he said taunting me. My hands started trembling. I tried to get them to stop.

"My, this is disappointing. Don't be this way when we meet again," he mocked.

"What do you think you're doing?" Another voice came from behind me.

James came into the room with Charsi, a nurse following behind them.

When I looked back to Xander, he was gone.

"I'm not dealing with you!" James went on ranting. "Get out of here!" He demanded.

The nurse looked somewhat confused. "Sir, is she related to you?" she asked.

"No! She is not part of this family!" He said, denying me.

"Dad, how could you say that?!" Charsi cut in. "This is Hope and we need to help her," she said in my defense.

"You've seen what she's done! She's not human! She is a demon!" He shouted.

I glanced back to the nurse who looked frightened now. I tried to talk to James about what has been going on, it was only fair.

"Hold on, let me explain…" I tried.

"No!" He cut me off. "I don't want you to explain anything!"

"Dad, please stop!" Charsi pleaded.

"It's alright Charsi," I said. "I don't have to explain myself anymore! Maybe I am a demon… Maybe that is why people have always feared me…" I aimed the guns towards the three of them. They looked so scared. Good! I felt their fear; I wanted to feel their fear. I wanted to feel the darkness inside of me.

"Get out of my way!" My voice suddenly sounded so deep and frightening. Quickly I moved my aim, pulling the trigger on Michael, the gun in my right hand. The bullet struck the light fixture on the ceiling, sending part of it swinging downward. James and Charsi were able to duck down before they were hit. The light missed them, but hit the nurse directly in the head. She flew backward into the door. I looked down at James and Charsi. They were actually lying at my feet. How ironic. With Gabriel in my left hand, I pointed the barrel down at them. They looked up at me so fearfully. I could easily end their lives, but….I couldn't do it. I was not a monster…I was not like my father. Lowering the guns, I ran out of the room towards the stairs, then down to the first floor, exiting out the side door. Now I was standing there alone. I blindly walked through the parking structure. I had no idea what I was anymore. I became a soulless being…

Chapter Nineteen:
Aria

The air felt so cold it burned my skin. It began snowing as I ran to my car. I drove here with Charsi, but I would leave alone. I knew I could not go home. I was homeless! But maybe I didn't want to go home!

The car was freezing; I blasted the heat for a few minutes before driving out onto the main road. Where could I go? I wanted to tell Damon what happened. Especially after what Xander said about us. Xander must have been spying on us the whole time this nightmare went on. Then, I thought about Aria. *Was she working with Xander?* That made sense. So now I had two psychos to worry about.

When I arrived at Damon's house, it was after eleven at night. I felt bad ringing the door bell this late. Maybe I could throw stones at Damon's bedroom window like he did to me, but I didn't know which window was his. Instead of going through the anguish of trying to find his room with several errors that could wake someone else up, I just used the knocker on the door. I thought at first that no one would come. I did it a few more times and waited again. I did not know what to do. I had to talk to Damon, I had to! As I thought of these things, someone opened the door. The dark haired man stood tall, very statuesque. It was Damon's father; I remembered him from last time.

"It's a bit late to knock on someone's door. What do you need?" He asked with a rough voice.

"I'm sorry. Is Damon here?"

He seemed annoyed with a frustrated look on his face.

"No. He isn't. He's gone," he said sharply.

"Do you know where he is?" I asked.

"If I knew where he was, I'd go drag his lazy ass back here," he said.

After what Damon and I have been through, I felt like I should stand up for him.

"Hey, listen." My voice sounded confident for a change. "I don't know what happened between you two, but I know Damon cares a lot about his future. He's trying to find out who he is and what makes him happy. Those two things aren't that easy, you know?"

The man's expression stayed indifferent.

"You're just kids. Of course you don't know what you want. Damon won't listen to me. He knows what all of this is about. He thinks because I'm not his biological father, he doesn't have to listen to me!" He took in a few short breaths. "Maybe he'll listen to you. You're name is Hope, right?" he asked. I nodded.

"Yeah, my wife told me you came over a while ago. After you talked to Damon, he came back to apologize to me," he said and turned away. I suddenly felt fear from him.

"Uh, you should go now!" He said suddenly. He shut the door before I could say another word. Did he fear me too? I didn't even do anything!

Now what? In the back of my mind, I knew my answers were at the church. I wondered though if my acts made me too evil to enter a church. The parking lot was empty when I arrived at St. Mary Catholic Church. The church was most likely locked. Still, I tried the door. I pounded the knocker into the wood door and waited for someone to come. No one did. I trod through the snow back to my car when the doors opened. I turned to look; no one was there. I held my purse tightly as I rushed inside. The doors just shut behind me by themselves. Did I really want to come inside? This was not normal, but then again, what in the past seven months has been normal?

I looked up the aisles of pews to the altar. There were two candles on the altar; they were lit. There were prayer candles around the room that were lit as well. At this time of night, all of them should be extinguished. I walked down the aisle finding myself in peace. It was strange to feel that way after what just happened. Now I stood before the altar, looking up at the crucifix. It hurt so much…I felt this overwhelming judgment upon me. If God wants to strike me down, He should do it already! But nothing changed. I still stood there. I turned to walk back up the center aisle. Now I headed upstairs. I didn't know where I was heading or why. Upstairs were those rooms I saw before. The one to the right was open. I recalled that being the room the priest ran into the other day.

It was a simple room. I walked inside and closed the door. There was one single bed with a sheet and a nightstand with a lamp on it next to the bed. Inside the drawer was a Bible. That was obvious. I didn't know if I should touch it, it might burn my hand. I lay down on the bed, putting my purse on the nightstand. I wondered if I would really be able to fall asleep. The bed was comfortable and sleep finally found me.

The glaring sun woke me. I took my cell phone out of my mahogany leather purse. It was about nine-thirty. I took my purse and walked out into the hall. Instantly, I heard people downstairs and an organ playing. I felt nervous as I walked down the stairs. There were a lot of people here. They gathered in a line, using the holy water by the door and making the sign of the cross. I had no idea what day it was now. I guess Sunday, that would make sense. Inside, people were gathered in the pews. I'd never attended a Catholic Mass before. I just sat in the back. I didn't bother doing the water and cross thing since I didn't really know how to do it. It was interesting to watch the congregation perform their usual church routine. This was much different than the church I attended. Belonging to a non-denomination church, I could compare a live band to an organ player, a priest instead of pastor, and a confession booth to a table with coffee and cookies.

The priest performing the ceremony was not Father Daniel, but the man I saw speaking with him yesterday. Sitting next to me was this woman with her kids. She had four kids with her. The kids did not seem interested in prayer, worshipping or church itself. They just looked bored. Wasn't there Sunday school or something?

The Mass went on and I had to admit, this was not a religious experience at all. The hymns were so morbid sounding and the passage from the Bible the priest read really was more of him saying the words in chant and the congregation followed with a response. At the end, I wondered if God ever showed up. I heard the priest say Amen and people piled out of the place quicker than they came in. That was disappointing. I always felt excited and moved after a sermon at my church, but I felt nothing here. Maybe Kiara is right, Catholics do zap the life out of praising and worshipping God. But that was just one group, not every church is like this.

Mass was soon over, I just waited for everyone to leave. The people there seemed to leave in a hurry. At my church, people stayed after and talked to one another or talked to the pastor. I watched two boys in robes come out and extinguish the candles on the altar. Some people were kneeling at the altar in prayer. The priest walked into the confessional booth. I wondered if he could help me.

I didn't know exactly how to do this. When I walked down towards the people praying, one woman stopped to stare at me. She looked me up and down, gritting her teeth in disgust before continuing to pray. I guess I was under-dressed in jeans and a sweater, but what gave her the right to judge?

Someone came out of one of the doors of the booth. No one else took advantage of the moment so I walked over and pulled open the door. Now I sat on a bench, a grated window was to my right. I saw the priest's face; it appeared so mysterious, covered in shadows.

"Um, I'm sorry, I'm not sure how this works," I admitted.

"Well, usually, one begins by saying, 'Forgive me Father for I have sinned,' then say what you need to." He seemed nice enough. Hopefully he won't freak out after I talk to him.

"Alright..." I repeated those words and tried to think about what I could confess....what was I thinking? I had a lot to confess. "Well, I have caused problems for my family. This woman I met, it all began with her."

"What began?" he asked.

"I began seeing things...having nightmares..."

"What did you see in these nightmares?"

"People are getting attacked by monsters or they are on fire. I fought these monsters and weird things happened to me. I hurt my sister, threw her into a wall..."

"The Lord forgives you," he spoke so casually. Was he even listening?

"No! He shouldn't! I'm doing terrible things and thinking about terrible things! Something is wrong with my mom, and my family thinks I'm some demon..." the priest still remained quiet. "Am I going to Hell?" I asked in desolation.

"Go and pray?" he told me. What was I thinking? The priest didn't have any answers, but maybe praying was the best thing for me right now.

I stepped out of the booth as an elderly lady entered. I felt so out of place. I walked over to the front of the altar and landed hard on my knees on the small bench. There in the presence of everyone around me and God, I began to pray.

After praying for a while, I felt more at peace. I haven't spent this much time in prayer before. I looked over at the confessional. A child who appeared to be eight or nine came out. She came over by me, knelt and began praying. It amazed me how a child so young had a relationship with God. What happened to me? I always went to church with my family from the time I was young. As I child, I always prayed with my family before dinner and before going to sleep. Would God really forgive me? As I studied the area, I saw a woman walk into the room. She looked familiar, her red hair, fair skin, wearing a white dress. Father Daniel showed up beside her as they walked toward the altar.

"Hope," he called to me, "I want you to meet a dear friend of mine."

I couldn't believe it at first. It was Aria!

"You!" I stood up with an accusing rage. "You started this all! You tell him that I'm not crazy, and tell him about what you said about the fallen angels, and about the dreams, tell him everything!" I demanded of her.

The woman's eyes got wide, full of confusion and fear. "I-I'm sorry?" Her voice sounded different, it was not dark and eerie like before. Her voice sounded lighter, more wholesome.

"Hope, you misunderstand," the priest informed me. "This is my friend Aria. She is a member of the church and we have discussed many times about how to improve things here," he said.

"But...she is the one that I tried to tell you about the first time I came to this church. It first happened that night on campus..." I explained. Neither of them seemed to know what I was talking about. "I'm not crazy!" I shrieked. The woman that looked at me earlier looked up at me.

"Shhh!" She made the harsh sound. I wanted to smack her. This was none of her business!

Aria still looked lost in the matter. "Hope, I'm sorry, but we have never met before," she said.

171

"Stop! I'm tired of people messing with me!" I shouted at her. By now others who still were in the room looked in our direction. I didn't care. I was going to find out the truth.

"Let's go upstairs to talk," Father Daniel suggested.

It didn't make sense at all! How could this be Aria? I met Aria before, but she was different then.

"Please, you need to listen to me," Aria said in a loud whisper, but I paid no attention. I was tired of her lies. "You are under the impression we have met before. Honestly, this is the first time I've seen you. Whoever this person was that told you they were me, they have deceived you," she explained.

"I don't know what's real anymore," I said. My voice sounded shallow.

"Hope, what did this person say, what did they tell you?" she asked.

"It doesn't matter..."

"I think it does." She said to me. "We need to talk upstairs about this now," she stated. Her voice was very direct. I didn't trust her and I didn't know Father Daniel that well either. But I also realized that no one else could help me, so I agreed to talk with them.

We sat in the office. Father Daniel sat across from Aria and I.

"Hope," the priest spoke calmly. "Explain from the beginning. How did all this start?"

I didn't know if they would believe me. "I saw Aria last summer after class. She talked about 'a quest to find myself.' I started feeling awkward so I tried to leave. But when I tried to, she called out, 'don't make this hard.' Then the place changed and I was in this nightmare world. I found my way off the campus and I found this castle," I told them.

Aria did not speak for a moment.

"I've heard that before, 'a quest to find yourself.' It was said to me too at one time," she said breaking the silence.

I kept talking, telling my story, wondering if they believed me.

"I met this guy and he told me stuff I didn't believe at first. But now my mom is in the hospital and my family thinks I am a monster," I continued. I thought about Charsi and how she tried to stand up for me. Why did she do that? She was the one who I almost killed. "I asked you about demons Father because I saw

172

these monsters in the other world. I thought it was Aria who told me about these angels she called 'righteous angels' who had offspring, but you said they were fallen angels," I reminded him.

"I think someone definitely deceived you," Aria said. "The term this person used, 'righteous angels,' what did they say about them?"

"They were thrown out of heaven because they wanted to protect the humans from God's wrath, or something like that," I recalled.

"Um, I am very open to the idea of angels and fallen angels," Father Daniel spoke slowly. "However, the only righteous angels are the ones who stayed on God's side. Remember what I said about the fallen angels and the Nephilim?" He reminded me.

"Yeah, I know, I'm just confused...I...."

"For some reason, this person you thought was Aria wanted to make you believe something that isn't real. That person was not Aria. This is Aria. I've known her for years now," he said.

"So, you two believe me?" I wondered.

"Of course we believe you, as long as you believe us," Father Daniel said. "You can trust me and Aria," he said, assuredly.

I nodded to him, but right now, I didn't feel I could trust anyone. Once I was outside the office I headed toward the stairs.

"Hope," Aria called to me. I turned to her. I guess I could at least listen to her.

"I wondered if we could talk more about all of this. There are things that I can't say in front of Father Daniel," she told me.

So the secrets continue. "Why not? What's wrong?" I asked.

"Father Daniel is human. He is open-minded to angels and fallen angels and even their offspring, but...he won't understand everything," she said cautiously.

"What do you mean?" I asked.

"I need to find out whom the other person is, the one that looks like me. Someone is masquerading around as me," she said, admitting to her suspicions.

"The only other person who I met was this man named Xander...I guess he's my real father..." Aria's eyes widened, her face whiter than ever. She took my hand and practically pulled my arm off as we went down the stairs.

We were outside now heading for a navy blue four door. I didn't know the type of car. She pushed a button on her clicker.

"Get in," she insisted.

"What about my car?" I asked, knowing I couldn't just leave it in the church parking lot.

"Um…" she looked around nervously. "Yeah, go ahead. You can just follow me to my house," she instructed me.

I barely knew Aria. Should I be doing this? I really must be desperate for answers.

I followed closely to Aria as she drove. She moved pretty fast. I usually don't drive so recklessly. I remembered the white ranch home. I pulled up by the curb and parked. Aria was parked in her driveway. She had not gotten out of her car yet. I walked over to the driver's side; the window was down. Her head was in her hands, she began breathing heavily.

"Are you all right?" I asked.

She lifted her head now breathing normally.

Kiara told me she believed Aria had a split personality, now I know it's because there are two different people claiming to be her.

"I know this girl, Kiara…" Aria's eyes focused on me when I spoke the name. "She told me she knows you," I finished telling her.

"Oh, now she knows me! Well that's a relief! And here I thought I was a stranger to her," Aria laughed sarcastically.

"I'm sorry, I don't understand," I said trying to follow her train of thought.

"Did she tell you what a witch I am?" She asked hastily. Where did that come from? I must have brought up a sore issue.

"I'm sorry. I didn't mean to say anything wrong," I apologized.

"Oh no, it's not your fault. She's the one who doesn't want to work things out," she said.

"I thought she was looking for you because she believed you were giving her the visions," I told her.

"Me?" Aria gave a heavy sigh. "She always has to find something to blame me for," she griped.

"So what's going on between you and her?" I risked pursuing the topic.

"Kiara lived with me from the time she was twelve until she was sixteen. She seemed thankful at first that I took her in, but as years went on, she became distant. Kiara lost her mother when she was young. My friend, Rein," she explained.

"I didn't know this until I met Kiara as a teenager. She actually broke into my house, tried to steal from me. She thought she was clever, but I watched her the whole time and she didn't even know," Aria proceeded to tell me.

Kiara really didn't have any morals. I guess I shouldn't be that surprised.

"When I found out that her mother was Rein, I became curious. It was strange how God brought her to me. As I learned more about her, I found out she'd been through a lot of foster homes. I adopted her and everything was fine. But then….this sounds weird, but she got into spell books, trying to find a way to bring her mother back. I tried to lead her to God and the church, but she didn't want anything to do with it. She said her previous guardians did the same and she was sick of it. So I let her go on her own. There wasn't much more I could do for her," Aria explained in detail.

It hit me hard, this woman seemed to care a lot for Kiara and she acted like this woman treated her like dirt.

"You really aren't the same Aria I met before," I assured myself. "I'm sorry, I'm just so lost. I still don't understand why Kiara is mad at you?" I asked suddenly. Aria sighed deeply.

"I'm not sure. I thought she trusted me. I don't know why it has to be this way now," she said.

"I've met this guy Lyell. She works with him at the club. He took me to your house because I needed to talk to you. You weren't home though," I told her.

"It worries me that she's with him. I'm afraid she's getting too close to him. I can't say exactly why, but I can't trust him. It's not his race, I've already told Kiara that. He's not showing his true colors," she said with suspicion.

"You can stay here, if you want," she told me. Her invitation surprised me.

I didn't know if I should intrude, but I had nowhere else to go.

"Okay," I answered. I suddenly felt ashamed. I was accepting hand-outs.

175

As we walked through the front door, I took in the interior of the house. There was a clash of colors. It appeared to be an old home. The front door led into the living room. The wallpaper was faded and I couldn't help but notice the bright orange couch and a matching chair. A tiny lamp sat on a circular table next to the couch by the wall. On the opposite side, she had a television set on top of another medium size table. A few pictures hung on the walls, looked like some famous artwork. I didn't know the artists of any of them. What good was that art humanities class I took?

Aria let me sleep in the guest room. She gave me towels and soap for a shower, which I really needed about now. I stood in the shower letting the warm water fall on me. All of the memories came to me. I felt I needed to apologize to Aria for the way I acted earlier. After that, I talked more with her. I tried once again to tell her how sorry I was for the way I acted.

"Don't apologize," she said. "I don't blame you for getting upset. You thought I was trying to hurt you. It's not your fault, you have been used from the beginning," she said nonchalantly.

"There is just one other thing I need to ask," I said. "I had an interesting discussion with Father Daniel about the fallen angels. Do you know anything about Nephilim or whatever they're called?"

Aria sat on a bright orange couch.

"They are descendants of the Watchers, a group of angels God told to watch over the human race. But they fell subject to temptation of the human women. And they had children with them," she told me.

"Okay, so these Watchers were fallen angels?" I asked to be sure I understood.

"They were fallen after the monstrosities they created. There were these giants and that is why the Flood came, to destroy their offspring," she said.

"I was told the fallen angels were the ones who rebelled against God and went with Satan or something," I said.

"Uh, yeah. I'm not sure if they were the ones who had the offspring. There are some details left out. I've found documents on this topic besides the Bible, but it is hard to discern what is real and what may be fabricated," she told me.

"What about this Xander...he's my fa..." I began.

176

Aria got up suddenly during my sentence and walked out of the room. I followed her into her kitchen. It was this small kitchen with a gas stove. It looked just as worn as the living room. Aria stood very still, looking out of the window over the sink.

"I'm sorry," I began. "We don't have to talk about him," I suggested.

Aria finally broke down in tears. She fell into a fetal position on the floor.

I knelt down beside her. I wasn't sure what to do.

"I'm sorry! I'm sorry...please don't...." I tried to comfort her.

"No...." she breathed deeply. "I'm sorry....I'm sorry for Kiara too. I....didn't know...

"It was interesting that you went to that church for someone to pray for you. I did same thing. I was only eighteen at the time," she began to explain. She gave a heavy sigh. "I was very scared," Aria admitted. "My father was abusive and I had no knowledge of God's love," she said in tears.

"I understand," I confided. "My mother wrote about my real father in her journal. I learned what a monster he was," I told her.

"What is your mother's name?" Aria seemed to become more interested.

"Amira," I said.

"I guess I've been running for too long," her voice became hollow. She turned to me now. "I'm sorry. I didn't mean to freak out like that, but Xander is..." she began.

"I know he's my father," I said.

"Yes. And Amira is your mother. Yeah, I know who she is," she confirmed.

I didn't expect her to know about my father, let alone my mother. "How do you know her?" I asked.

"She was one of the women Xander took as a mate," she said.

"What does that mean?" I asked.

"The other woman he took was my friend Rein," she said. She went on not answering my question. "Xander is...a descendant from the giants. I am descended from them as well," she told me.

Xander looked like a giant himself when I first saw him. Aria was almost as tall as he was. I thought of her as this Amazon when I first met her.

"How tall are you, Aria?" I asked.

She got up to her feet and took a tissue from on top of the refrigerator. She didn't even have to reach for it. Wiping her eyes, she kept her eyes away from me. "I'm about six foot nine, almost seven feet. How tall are you?"

I haven't been measured for some time. "I don't really know. The last time I was told was for my physical before going to college. I'm not nearly as tall as you. The last time I was measured, I was five foot...eight," I told her.

"Kiara is about the same height. See, we're taller than normal people," she said.

"I've always been taller than other girls. Now that I think of it, back in school, Kiara and I were a couple of the taller girls in the class," I recalled.

"Your height is considered above the norm. My height is unheard of," Aria said.

"But, there's one thing I don't get. Didn't the Flood get rid of the offspring?" I speculated.

"It is said that there were two forms of offspring. One of the breeds was monsters and the other was giant men," she told me.

"Aria, how do we know that this is true? I mean, it was so long ago. How do we know what we are?" I asked.

"You...just know," she said. "Look, don't analyze every little detail." The sharpness of her voice was a little startling. "It doesn't matter. You've seen all of those things and you should just know," she affirmed.

I couldn't believe this. I should just know? That wasn't good enough! The story of fallen angels and offspring was preposterous enough. Now I'm supposed to believe that I'm a descendant of them? I wasn't sure now if I should stay with Aria; I wasn't sure if I could trust her at all, but I didn't have much of a choice.

On Sunday, Aria invited me back to church. Father Daniel was doing a talk about the fallen angels. Hopefully, I would learn more about them. I guess he was nervous because many people avoid this topic. I didn't have anything nice to wear to church, so Aria let me borrow a light blue blouse and a white skirt. (She told me that they used to be Kiara's, which was kind of unsettling.) She sat next to me on the wooden pews in the same white dress she wore to last Sunday's mass.

After the congregation sang some morbid hymns, Father Daniel stood at the altar and told the congregation that he was reading from the book of Genesis. He recited the same verse he told me, about the sons of God lusting after the daughters of man. The congregation kept their eyes on the altar where the priest spoke. After ten minutes into the talk, there were some who began to fidget and look around the room. They couldn't have been bored; they looked uncomfortable.

They had communion. Aria told me I didn't have to do it. But I wanted to try it. When it was our row's turn, Aria got up with the other people and I followed along with her. The other priest whom I saw the other day talking with Father Daniel did the giving of bread. Aria told me his name was Father Paul. Father Daniel stood to the side of the altar holding the goblet of wine. The priest either put the bread directly on the person's tongue or in their cupped hands. I chose the hands. I smiled at Father Daniel before I took a sip of wine. However, he looked so serious.

I saw Aria praying before the altar. I didn't know where to go so I just joined her. I tried to pray, but I couldn't. Too many people were around. I looked up at the crucifix. I was fine for a moment, but then this feeling overtook me. I felt a little dizzy,I think I drank the wine too fast. I looked up at the crucifix. This strange feeling took over. It was the same feeling I felt the first time I came to this church.

"Aria..." I whispered. She didn't hear me; she stayed in her prayer. It suddenly became dark, I looked up at the crucifix, but I didn't see blood. It was burning this time. I had to get out of this place! I got up and ran, but my legs gave out and I felt myself hit the floor. I felt intense pain from my head, like a migraine. I put my hands on my head, it hurt so much. I think I cried out.

"Hope?" I heard Aria call to me, but I couldn't respond. My hands began to hurt too. I looked at my palms, I saw blood spouting out. What is happening to me?

"Hope! You're bleeding all over!" She cried out. I tried to look at Aria, but all I saw was blood. I heard voices of shock and dismay around me. Then...there was nothing. Everything was quiet. The murmurs of the people in the church started.

"What is going on?" "What's wrong with her?" "Her hair is full of blood!"

Aria ran towards me.

"Hope! No!"

Oh God, don't you freak out too! My thoughts raced. The elder priest, Father Paul suddenly cried out, "She has experienced the wounds of Christ! It is a sign of God!" The whole congregation became even more enthralled in my situation.

"Hope...." Aria went on. "I'm so sorry...." she whispered.

"What is happening to me?" I asked.

Aria pushed gently on my back.

"We need to get out of here!" She exclaimed.

I walked ahead of her up the aisle to the exit. People stood around watching me as blood ran off my hair and my hands, dripping a trail as I walked. As we came close to the door, a loud thunderous crash came through the roof of the church. A winged creature fell onto the altar, cracking it. The church's steeple fell down beside it, then it felt a need to crush the steeple's cross. The people screamed as they ran for the door. Aria grabbed my arm tightly, trying to move me towards the exit.

"No." I spoke calmly. "I have to do something." I pushed past her running through the people to the altar.

"No Hope! You have to get out of here!" Aria called.

Why? I wondered. I had the ability to stop this thing. I stopped abruptly in front of the fallen angel. It appeared just like the others I've seen, torn and filthy wings that were once white, decaying skin, and massive arms and legs. It towered above me, making me feel inferior in size.

Father Paul actually felt brave enough to run up to the beast, holding up a fancy looking cross. I stood there, watching him as if he lost his mind.

"The power of Christ compels you!" He cried out. The creature smirked at him, and smacked the man with one massive hand. The priest flew back into one of the stain windows. I saw blood drip from the shards. Aria ran over to the window. She turned to me with this blank stare.

"He's dead," her tone sounded empty.

I turned back to the fallen being. It took the crucifix off the wall, twisting the bronze. It came closer to me now. As he swung the object down on me, I reacted by jumping away from it barely grazing my head. As I landed, the guns came to me. Squeezing both triggers, the bullets shot out at the beast. Shooting the monster made him falter back somewhat, but didn't stop it. The monstrosity rushed at me, trying to knock me down. I avoided the attack, jumping over to the pew in the second row. Letting out a furious cry, it raised its gigantic arm and swung knocking me through the rows of pews to the back of the room.

I sprang quickly to my feet. The balcony where the organ played was right above me. I jumped up to the ledge and pulled myself over before the beast came at me again. The organ player was long gone by now. In fact, I was relieved that everyone was now out of the church. Looking down at the fallen angel, I aimed both guns at its head and fired repeatedly. Finally it fell backward to the floor, but it was only down for a moment. It rose to its feet, breathing heavily, and I felt its extreme heated anger. It cried out again with an ear-piercing shriek. It didn't really affect me; I didn't have to cover my ears this time. In response, I leaped off the balcony, making contact with my foot to its head. It flew backward, straight into the shattered altar.

Aria ran to me. "I can't believe you just did that!" she exclaimed.

"I know. I really am getting stronger," I replied.

The beast was not done yet. In a great rage, it stormed toward us. Aria tore the skirt of her dress then ran to meet the fiend. She didn't even need weapons. I watched open mouthed as she fought hand to hand with that thing! She blocked its punches then kicked it hard into the wall. I saw her take something from a sheath around her thigh and drove it into the creature's flesh. It burned away in front of our eyes.

Aria stood there a moment before turning to face me. I saw the plain silver dagger she held. I wondered why she would take that into the church. Maybe she expected to get attacked? I knew by now that these creatures didn't bleed so I didn't expect to see blood on the weapon. She re-sheathed the dagger. Then she walked over and harshly took me by the arm. She was really strong. She pulled me out of the church where people gathered scared out of their mind. As we moved, I heard thunder. The sound was almost deafening. I looked to see the scenery changed. The church changed from crumbled to like it was before the attack. Everyone around us calmly walked back into the church.

"What just happened?" I asked. Aria didn't speak. We stood in front of her car now. "Aria?" I pressed.

Aria stared gravely at me. "We need to leave," she said firmly.

"Can I clean up first?" I asked, but she already was in her car starting the vehicle.

What was going on? Was she mad at me? As I stood there, I was hesitant to get in. I was covered in blood, it would stain the seats.

"Get in!" she yelled.

I numbly followed her command.

Minutes later, she pulled into her driveway, threw the gear into park and got out. What is she doing? I got out of the car and I realized I just left my purse at the church!

Forgetting that now, I walked over to a white picket fence. Her backyard was beautiful. I looked at it before entering through the white painted gate. There was a greenhouse full of flowers. A stone path led from the white gate to the back porch. Aria sat on one of her lawn chairs beside her house. She sat there, looking up at the sky. I wondered why she had a lawn chair out. It wasn't that type of weather yet.

"Aria?" I said. She looked at me.

"It sucks doesn't it? To be this offspring," she fussed.

"Aria, what you did was amazing. I'm just not sure what happened after all that," I said.

She sat up looking straight ahead. "They don't know. None of those people will ever know," she said.

"But they saw the fallen angel." I protested. "They have to know now," I told her.

"No. They will forget everything," she said.

"But that priest! Father Paul…he got killed!" I reminded her.

"Yes, but no one will know that the fallen angel did it. They will believe it was an accident."

I couldn't accept this. "Are they that blind?! How the hell can't they figure it out?" I asked.

Aria narrowed her eyes, "They aren't supposed to know! Don't you get it? We are the Nephilim, we are the damned! Only we can see such acts," she informed me.

This was just a gigantic headache. Why did everyone have to act like this?

I felt so enraged that I might have reacted by burning everything down around me.

"I want a straight answer!" I demanded.

"Go clean yourself up!" She demanded with a wave of the hand. Feeling more confused than ever, I slowly walked towards the back door.

"I'll explain all of it," she said with a calm voice.

I went inside and stood in her kitchen. She most likely wouldn't want me to walk across her carpeting like this. The cushion of the passenger seat in Aria's car was soaked with blood, but she didn't seem to care at all.

I turned on the faucets and let the water run. I wondered what Aria was thinking right now. She came into the house now. I washed my hands off then put my head under the running water. As I did that, I felt her hands rake through my hair helping to remove the blood. I hated the feeling of the sticky substance. It terrified me when I contemplated if it was my blood or someone else's. What am I saying, of course the blood was mine! But when I felt the pain, it wasn't just mine, but the pain of many others. I couldn't really explain it.

"It will be all right," she spoke softly. "I won't let him hurt you or Kiara, not this time..." she said. I watched all the blood swirling down the drain.

"Don't feel bad, Hope. I should have explained things better," she said turning off the water then I felt a towel and her hands groping my head.

"I can get it," I said taking the towel. I stood up straight now looking at Aria.

"I'm sorry. I wish I understood more of what is going on. I wish I could explain it to my family so they won't be mad at me anymore," I told her.

"Your human family will never understand what you have suffered through," she said sympathetically.

"I'm sorry, I yelled at you back at the church," I apologized.

She shook her head. "No, you have a right to show your anger. I'm angry too," she said.

I removed the towel from my head. Aria gave a questionable look. "Hold on, I don't think we got it all," she said. She turned the faucet back on, lightly pushing my head under the water and began vigorously rubbing my head. I grunted as she rubbed my scalp. She stopped abruptly; I heard her gasp. I straightened up.

"What is it?" I asked.

She ran her fingers through the tips of my hair. "Hope, this red in your hair isn't blood. This is part of your hair!" she gasped.

Aria seemed so shaken by all of this. "I...I can't believe this!" Raising her voice she swore.

"Xander...you bastard! I hate you!" She finished by kicking the cupboard door under the sink. She glanced down at the floor. She really held this hatred for him, not that I blame her.

"What do you know about him?" I had to ask this question even if it did upset her.

She sighed. "It's because of the ritual. Xander believes he can become God and have his own angel warriors. You know how God has Michael and Gabriel?"

I thought about those names, they were labeled on the guns.

"He wanted you and Kiara to be his warriors. And somehow, this Hell is being created for only beings like us to see it, but everything will go back to normal and no one will know any of it," she explained.

That was really messed up, but it gave me insight into other events that happened. Somehow through this madness, something finally clicked. Now I understood how I saw everyone dead on campus the first night, even that instructor was dead. Then everything was fine the next week.

"Um, the night I first met you, or that person pretending to be you, that is when I first saw the Hell world. Everything on campus, not just the people, but all life itself was dead," I revealed to her.

"Yeah..." She nodded. "That must have been a shock," she agreed.

"Well, what really got me was finding all of these people with burnt skin. Even the teacher from my class was affected. I found him dead that night, but the next day everything was fine. It was like nothing ever happened," I told her.

Aria nodded to my every word. "But if those people were still alive, why isn't the priest still alive? You said he was actually dead," I reminded her.

Aria looked thoughtful. "You know, you've seen a lot of chaos and things that don't make sense. If you try to find logic in what is illogical, you're going to lose your mind," she told me.

Didn't she realize that I'd already lost my mind?

"How did Kiara's mother die?" I managed to ask.

Aria didn't speak

"You don't want to tell me?" I asked further.

"A demon killed her," she finally answered.

"A demon?" I questioned.

Aria looked away, "I need to see Kiara," she said abruptly changing subjects again.

Aria walked past me to the living room. "You can use the dryer in the upstairs bathroom to dry your hair. Then we can go," she said.

Aria really wanted to see Kiara. I wanted to see her again too. I needed some answers and I wasn't going to leave without them.

Chapter Twenty:
The Gateway

Aria and I arrived at Fantasy Nights around seven o'clock. The big dance crowds weren't there yet, but people still gathered there for food and drinks. I still needed to ask more questions. I hadn't even told anyone about seeing Kiara's mother or who I believed was her mother. I wondered what Aria would say about that. I guess it didn't matter right now. She didn't answer me about Rein's death. It was probably too painful. I probably shouldn't pry.

They were not checking for ID at the door this early; we just walked in. Security seemed to be lacking in this place. There was rock music playing, but it wasn't too loud. You could actually have a conversation without screaming at each other.

It seemed like Aria had been here before. She walked straight to the bar. The blonde lady was there again. She wore her blonde curls up today.

"Hi..." I greeted her.

"Janet! Where's Kiara?!" Aria demanded. She wasn't messing around. The woman sort of looked worried then just smiled.

"Aria, I haven't seen ya in a while, how are things going?" Janet asked her.

"I'm fine," Aria spoke sternly. She looked really annoyed now.

"I'll tell Kiara you're here," Janet responded. She left and went to the back. I sat down on the stool next to Aria. She looked nervous.

"Are you all right?" I asked.

"I just am not sure what to say to her. I want us to be on good terms. I don't want to tell her how to live, but I still feel I should give her advice now and again. I see her throwing away her life here and it just makes me sad. I know she has been through a lot, but so have I, so have you. I mean the same thing is happening to all of us," she babbled on.

It took some time, but soon we saw Kiara walking towards us.

"Aria? Now you decide to come?" Kiara spat out. Damon walked up behind her. He noticed my hair right away. "Whoa, you dyed your hair?" He asked me.

I didn't know where to start on that one. "I'll explain later," I told him.

Aria stood up, I noticed how she was quite a bit taller than Kiara and I. She even had some good height over Damon. She did say she was just under seven feet tall.

"Why are you here?" Kiara shot the question at Aria.

"The more important question is how long will it take for me to pull you out of here?" Aria challenged.

"I'm not afraid of you!" Kiara blasted back at her.

"No sweetie, I'm not the one you need to fear. You have made some powerful enemies," Aria warned her.

"Why didn't you come here before?" Kiara asked. Aria was silent.

"You could have come here many times, and you didn't!" Kiara continued.

"You could have come home," Aria reminded her.

"She has a point there," Damon said.

"Shut up!" Kiara whispered harshly to him.

"You're right," Aria said. "I wanted to come, but I don't like to come to these places by myself," she told Kiara.

"That's no excuse! I already know why you didn't come here. That stupid church brainwashed you, telling you this place is evil," Kiara accused.

"You don't know anything about that church. You've indicated before that you don't want to know anything about faith or God. I'm fine with that. This is a different matter," Aria stated.

"No! It's the same thing! I don't want to know about that church! They're a bunch of hypocrites!" Kiara further accused.

They were just yelling at each other in front of other people. A few others looked our way when they first started arguing, but soon turned away. Just listening to them was painful enough. I couldn't stand it anymore. I couldn't stand the fighting. I couldn't stand not knowing why all these things were happening.

"It doesn't matter! We're here now! Let's just get to the point already!" I shouted at them. Kiara looked at me, surprised by my outrage.

"Well, you can start anytime," Kiara said.

"I met Aria--*this* Aria--for the first time a few days ago. The woman Damon and I talked to before was not Aria," I told them. They both looked at Aria and she nodded.

"It's true. Hope thought I was someone else. It was unfortunate that it was someone she was not happy with. I got a lot of anguish from her," she said, smiling at me, I sort of returned a half smile back.

"So who did we talk to?" Damon asked.

"That part I am not sure about. I guess we'll have to find out," I answered.

Kiara still looked dissatisfied. "Well, now that Aria finally got her ass here, maybe we can figure out some stuff," Kiara resolved.

"Yes we can," I agreed. "Everything is falling apart for me. My mom is in the hospital and I don't know what is wrong with her," I told them.

"Are you serious?" Damon inquired. "What happened?"

"I don't know. I found her on the floor in her room. She seems to be in a coma. She had a faint heartbeat. My sister called the ambulance...my father or who I thought was my father hates me and thinks I'm some demon..." I told them.

"We all have our problems, Hope!" Kiara spoke hotly. "What makes you think yours are any worse than anyone else's?" She asked forcefully.

"How dare you say such a thing! What is wrong with you?" Aria said glaring at her.

"What is wrong with you?!" Kiara shouted back. Listening to their arguing just gave me this terrible headache.

"Can you guys please stop?" I pleaded. I held my head down in my hands now. A second later, I felt someone's hand gently touch the side of my head. I looked up to see Aria. Her mannerisms she showed was like a mother. I guess she kind of was Kiara's mother for a while, but Kiara probably doesn't want to see it that way.

"You're right, Hope. Arguing like this made Kiara leave in the first place," Aria said turning to Kiara. "I want us to get along, but you've lost trust in me," she said.

"You've never trusted me!" Kiara retorted. "You always spied on me when I was younger and wouldn't let me do anything I wanted!" Aria put her hands on her hips in a firm pose. "How long are you going to act in this childish charade? I trusted you when I let you into my home. I trusted you to be responsible and make your own decisions. Yes, I influenced them, but if I didn't, you wouldn't have had any direction in your life," Aria tried to explain.

How long were they going to go on like this? I thought to myself.

"Well, let's get this over with," Kiara said as she stomped past everyone. She took us to the usual spot upstairs. Lyell was there too, which seemed to upset Aria.

"I don't think it is necessary for you to be here Lyell," Aria told him. "I just need to talk to Kiara and her friends about some things," she told him.

"Excuse me," Kiara snapped. "He can be here too. The issues we discuss don't have to be affected by your racist attitude."

"Kiara! You don't seriously believe I am racist? I am not saying anything against Lyell, it's just the discussion does not really involve him," Aria clarified.

"Well, it does now," Kiara responded. "Go ahead and sit down Lyell." Lyell, who looked confused, reluctantly sat down again in his chair.

"Fine. Let me start by asking you Kiara what is it you have been experiencing?" Aria asked.

"Well, Aria, I have visions just as Hope and Damon do. You probably have visions too, right?" Kiara inquired.

"No. The visions are not happening to me because it is not me he wants," Aria replied.

"He?" Damon asked.

"Never mind," Kiara rolled her eyes. "She is just babbling. Do you know what happened to her?" She asked pointing to me. I assumed she meant my hair. It was odd. Nothing like this happened to either Kiara or Damon.

"It is his fault!" Aria spoke harshly.

"Who's?" Kiara asked.

"Xander," I told her.

"Who's Xander?" Damon asked.

"He's my real father," I said.

"What are you talking about?" Kiara asked, sounding seemly aggravated.

"He is who I've been trying to warn you about," Aria said.

"So, he's her father, so what?! What does that have to do with anything?" Kiara asked angrily.

"Because he's also y...never mind. Is there something you want to say to me Kiara?" she asked.

189

"Just tell her what you wanted to," Damon urged. "Stop holding your childish grudges against her and just tell her!" he demanded.

"Fine," Kiara spoke harshly. "Aria, you knew my mother. You know that she was killed and who killed her. Why won't you tell me?" she questioned.

"Because you don't need to know who he is. And you will spend all of your time   searching for someone you don't know and have no idea of his power," Aria warned her.

Aria wasn't going to tell Kiara anything. Hiding things from Kiara would just anger her more and I really didn't want to see how furious she could get.

"I will tell you more when you've shown me that you're mature enough to handle that information," Aria told her.

Kiara got up, in her rage she cried out. A long sword appeared in her hand. She jumped at Aria. Aria did not have to move. She raised a hand, creating a force that pushed Kiara back into the couch. She laid there for a second. Damon looked at me then Aria.

Aria now stood up. "I have nothing to hide from you, Kiara! Yes, I know who killed your mom and I won't say, but I admit to that. I don't want you getting involved in something you can't handle!" Kiara moved slowly to her feet, and looked wickedly at Aria.

"I am not a child! I am going to find out the truth on my own! I don't need you!" Kiara blasted at Aria. She finished by kicking over the coffee table. "I'm stronger than you think!" Kiara yelled. She finished her tantrum by stomping out the door and slammed it behind her.

We were all quiet for a moment. I wanted to learn the truth too, but I wasn't going to act to act like that. I was tired of Kiara's rage. What was with her attitude problem? I got up and went to the door.

"Are you going after her?" Damon asked.

"What do you think?" I answered. I opened the door and raced downstairs.

I saw Kiara on the upper level walking out of the side exit. I ran up the stairs to the balcony, past a few guys playing pool.
One of the guys stood right in my path, "Hey girl, where ya going?" He pestered me.

This was not the time! "Get away from me!" I felt that dark energy flow inside me. I pulled the pool stick out of his grip, then smacked him across the face, pushing him backwards into the table. He looked so stunned, so did everyone else around us.

Where did that come from? I handed his stick back to him, "I... I'm sorry..." I spoke then fled towards the exit. As I ran from the scene I wondered what came over me. It was just like before.

As I ran through the exit, I stopped there on the balcony. Kiara sat on the bottom step, smoking a cigarette. It was snowing again, even though it was the first day of Spring. As I was about to walk down the steps, someone else walked over to her. He looked kind of suspicious with that black hood he wore. I knelt down, hiding behind part of the wall. I don't know how well I was hidden, but he didn't seem to notice me.

"I don't mean to impose, but are you Kiara?" He asked her. Even through the howling wind, I heard his voice clearly even from where I stood. Kiara didn't move.

"Who is asking?" Kiara spoke with a snobbish tone. She always gave this tough attitude. Who does she think she is? She thinks she's so bad! Maybe she should watch her words.

"I'll take that as a yes. Here, this belongs to you," I heard him say. It looked like a book from where I stood on the top landing. Even in the darkness, I could see quite well. I liked having keen sight and hearing. They must be the good qualities of these 'special' gifts. I could see this pained look on her face.

"Where did you get this?"

"I've had that for a while," the man said. "It does belong to you, right?" he asked.

"So, who are you?" Kiara asked.

"Just a friend. There is something of particular interest on the last page. You should take a look," he said being shrouded beneath the black hood.

"What is it?" she asked.

"When you read it, you'll understand. But don't look at it yet. Wait until you are in a sacred place," he said cautiously.

Kiara nodded to him. The man turned and walked down the alley into the falling snow until he vanished.

The steps were slippery. I forgot my coat with my gloves back inside so I was gripping the icy metal with a bare hand. It was weird, the cold really did not affect me like it has in the past. I was down a few steps before Kiara noticed I was there. She spun around to see me there.

"Kiara," I spoke softly.

"Are you on her side or mine?" she asked.

"Her?"

"Aria," she spoke the name with disgust.

"I'm not picking a side. I don't understand what happened between you two," I replied. Kiara suddenly spit on the ground. That was attractive. She held tightly onto the book. "My mom was killed in front of my eyes when I was young. I saw her get ripped apart by this monster," Kiara finally opened up.

"Maybe it's best if you don't know of whatever killed her," I said looking at the book she held. I didn't recognize it at first, then I saw the child's drawing on the cover. That...that was the book her mother gave me at the hospital. Or the spirit of her mother.

Kiara spit on the ground again.

"Are you alright?" I asked.

"I'm fine, I just needed to get rid of the excess saliva," she said.

"Maybe if you didn't smoke..." I let roll of my tongue.

"It's not really that bad," she insisted. "We all die someday. This way I know what will be the cause," she said casually.

"You shouldn't think that way," I said to her, but didn't take my eyes off the journal. I don't think she noticed or cared. "I'm sorry Kiara, Aria told me about your mother." I remember Lyell telling me not to mention her mother, but I felt a need to tell her this. "There is something else I need to tell you. I know this sounds crazy, but I've met your mother," I said the last part very fast.

"What?!" Kiara did not seem to believe me. "That's impossible!" she yelled.

"I saw her one day in my room and again at the hospital. She showed me that journal, I've read it," I told her. Kiara's face was expressionless, she stared at me for a moment.

"You liar! How dare you mock me!" she exploded.

"No! No, I'm not mocking you. You're holding her journal right now. She gave it to me, and somehow that guy you were talking to got it," I explained.

192

"I'm going to find my mother's killer," she whispered.

She pushed me aside to go up the stairs. I watched her disappear through the door. There wasn't a time through all of this mess that I hadn't been confused. I didn't even want to deal with it anymore!

When I came back to the lounge, I found Lyell was gone, only Damon and Aria were there.

"I talked to Kiara. She said her mother was killed by some monster. She is really intent on avenging her mother. Did she come up here to get Lyell?" I asked them.

"No," Damon answered. "He just left."

"Aria," I began, "Some guy went to Kiara, and he had her mother's journal.

Aria gasped, "What? Who was it? What did he look like?" She asked frantically.

"I couldn't see his face. He wore this cloak or something." I told her.

Aria sprang out her seat. "This is not good," she said and began pacing.

Aria knew something we didn't. I couldn't understand why she was trying so hard to keep us from knowing.

"Aria, stop this!" I tried. "Just tell us the truth! You think we can't handle it?" I demanded to know.

Aria stood still now.

"Kiara is going to spend every waking moment trying to find him now. Do you have any idea how much trouble she's getting into? He wants her to find him. She's the one the dagger stabbed, she's more powerful than you," Aria told me. She started pacing again.

"What is she talking about?" Damon asked me.

Like I know. "Aria, tell us what's going on!" I tried again.

Aria sat down again and began sobbing, "No….no…."

I couldn't take this. If she lost control, what chance did the rest of us have? I didn't get it. I saw her fight in combat with a demon, and she's lived for quite some time. She is this superior being and she's acting like a helpless domesticated female.

"I don't get it!" I shouted. "Do you know who that guy was?" I asked.

"Xander," she spoke softly. "It had to be him."

"My father? He killed Kiara's mother? Why didn't you just say that?" I asked being annoyed.

"He is too powerful. He killed Rein, and he almost killed Amira. You would react the same way as Kiara. He wants you to find him," she revealed.

"We can stop him, right? You took out that demon at the church. Why can't you do the same for Xander?" I asked being hopeful.

"That was just a fallen angel. Xander has greater powers, he's almost like God," she said.

"Just a fallen angel? Give yourself some credit!" I exclaimed. "Why do you say he has greater powers? I don't think he's much of anything. He's hidden himself from us and then just shows up to me only, then to Kiara, and he's hiding his true self from her too," I told her.

"That is it though. He knows you and Kiara are strong enough to stop him. He is stronger than either of you by yourselves, but not when you two are together," she explained.

"But if the ritual was not done right, why....?" I realized that while we talked here, Kiara and Lyell were heading off somewhere together. "We need to find out what Kiara and Lyell are doing." I said.

Aria got up slowly.

"Yeah, let's go," Aria spoke calmly again. One minute she is hysterical, the next she is collected and reasonable.

We left the club; Aria said she was looking for Lyell's truck. She knew it quite well apparently. "Over there." I heard her say. She pointed across the parking lot. A black truck was just pulling out onto the road.

Aria rushed us to her car. I sat in the front and Damon was in the back. Everyone was quiet as she started the car and drove. Aria had her lights on, staying a few car lengths away from the truck. Lyell seemed to be a good driver, using his turning signals at appropriate times. He didn't turn around curbs too fast either.

Soon, we were on a dirt road, now Aria turned off the head lights to stay inconspicuous.

"Can you see?" Damon wondered.

"Yeah," she nodded.

The area was heavily wooded, we moved on for a few miles. The truck pulled to the side of the road now. Aria pulled over as well. We were maybe five car lengths back, hopefully, they wouldn't see us. She turned the car off. We watched as Lyell got out first. He looked around the area. He looked right in our direction, but didn't see us. He turned back to his truck. Now Kiara got out. She carried a bag with her as she walked off the road through the trees. Lyell stood there for a moment still looking around. Then he followed in the same direction as Kiara.

"It's safe now," Aria said. She got out and Damon and I followed. She still acted very strange. Why were we being so secretive? Let's just go talk to them.

I tried to be quiet as possible, but the sound of loose twigs and snow crunched under my feet. It was the same for the others so it didn't seem to matter. There was a clearing in the woods, where the two were standing. Kiara set three candles on the ground making a triangle. Lyell lit the candles for her then stood to the side. Kiara stood inside the triangle, then opened the book. This is when she chanted a familiar verse:

"Enter a place that reveals another reality. Life is reborn. God becomes the Devil. The Devil becomes God."

The flames of the candles became blue, engulfing the candles, flowing onto the snow, melting the ground to form a triangular shape. A portal formed behind her giving off an eerie green light. I remembered that light the first night on campus. It gleamed over those bodies to the fountain. The fountain was where I first read that verse.

I thought we waited too long. "Aria, shouldn't we stop her?" I asked.

She didn't move. "Both of you read that spell before entering the castle, right?" she asked. What was this? More talk? We had to stop this!

"Aria," I tried to be firm. "We really should do something."

"The Sanctuary of Fallen Angels...it is really the gates to Hell. The first Nephilim are trapped in Hell, but other demons travel between both worlds," Aria whispered.

She acted like she didn't hear me. She just ran right out there in the open. Lyell ran right in front of her path.

"Aria?" Kiara began, mocking "You are so pathetic! You really think you can stop me?" She gave this high pitched laughter as if she reached the point of insanity.

"Why, Kiara? Why are you constantly looking for your own destruction?" Aria asked.

"I'm finding out the truth for myself!" Kiara confirmed.

"Kiara, wait!" I said cutting in. "I want to learn the truth too, but do you really want to do it this way?" I asked.

Her eyes focused on me, "What the hell are you doing here?" She looked from me to Damon, "You too? Just leave me alone!" she demanded.

"Why Kiara?" I asked. "Why are you doing this?"

"You chose her side Hope! You chose the side of God, too!" She spat out.

I was so sick of people criticizing me for my faith. I didn't say a thing to her about hers. Most Christians would tell her being a Wiccan was worshipping Satan. I never said anything like that. I accepted her for who she is.

"I don't care about sides!" I told her. "What is your problem with God anyways?" I demanded.

"In God's eyes, we are damned. We are Nephilim and we don't get a chance! I'm not going to stand for it! I'm going to destroy God!" she shouted.

She had lost her mind. But I also knew that she was lying about not having a chance. We all have a chance to repent. She just chose not to. She rebels against God because she wants to do things her way.

Kiara turned to Damon. "Will you come with me?" She changed her voice into a sweet tone.

I wondered if he would. I looked over at him. Damon shook his head.

"I'm sorry...not that I chose the side of God or anything, but this is way too messed up!" he shouted.

"Fine! Lyell, deal with them!" she commanded. With that Kiara walked into the gleaming light of the portal.

"Don't you guys want to follow her?" Damon asked. At that moment, Lyell walked right in front of us, blocking our path. His opposing figure was intimidating enough, but then he suddenly changed. He suddenly grew even taller with wings coming out of his back. He leaped off the ground, hovering above us.

"What the…?!" Damon's voice cracked.

"Oh my God! He's… one, too!" I exclaimed.

Aria looked unaffected by this. "I should have known. See, Kiara has kept secrets from me too," she sighed.

"Do we really have to fight him?" Damon asked. For once, he didn't sound that confident.

"We just need to just get past him," Aria said.

I turned to Damon, the blades that were once mine appeared in his hands. I looked at my hands to see the guns, and then up at the giant. All that mattered to me was getting to Kiara, but Lyell would be our toughest opponent yet.

Chapter Twenty-One:
Hell is Revealed

The giant flew down at us, landing hard trying to stomp us into the ground. We scattered away like ants.

"Attack his feet!" Aria yelled. Damon rushed toward the giant. "Hope, aim for his torso or head, if you can hit it!" She yelled to me. I nodded. I tried to concentrate, but I was too concerned about Damon getting stepped on. *He really shouldn't try to tackle a ten foot giant.* Lyell flew up before Damon could hit him. Then the flying giant swooped down at Aria. She moved out of the way in time. She ran sideways alongside where the giant flew.

My heart was pounding as I shot at him, hitting him in the chest, but he didn't seem to be affected. Now the giant landed hard shaking the ground. He stood there in front of Aria. She faced him, unwavering. It seemed that she would not lose her ground. I've seen her fight that other monster. But I wasn't prepared for her next actions. Before my eyes, she changed. She suddenly grew cotton white wings. Her hair was no longer red; it became white. Wind drew up from behind her as he raised her arms, as the wind blew. Damon and I stood aside while this happened.

"Go to Hell!" She shouted as she threw a hard kick into Lyell sending him backwards to the ground. At that moment, Damon took advantage to strike him while he was down. With a few swipes, Damon cut into its flesh at the neck. I knew I could hit his head now. I aimed both guns directly at its face and shot them both at once. The blasts were intense enough to blow his head off!

I looked down at it now, a lifeless body. The wind died down and Aria returned to her other form. She came over to me and put her hand on me.

"Good job. You are using your abilities with greater strength. You too, Damon," she complimented. We stood there staring at the fallen giant.

"Is that it?" Damon asked. "I thought it would be harder."

The body turned to dust before our eyes. When I first began fighting these monsters, I could actually feel their pain when I either stabbed or shot them. But now, I felt nothing. I didn't even feel relieved that the monster was gone. Maybe I had lost my emotions.

"You know," Aria broke my thoughts, "Kiara is not a bad person. She is just lost. She's hurt...just like a child. She really has no idea what will come from her actions," Aria explained to us.

"So, we're going through that portal thing then?" Damon asked. Aria nodded.

"Well, I guess we should thank you," I said.

"It is not necessary. You have done more than enough for me," Aria said.

"What do you mean?" I wondered.

She smiled. "Going after Kiara was very brave. Even with my experience, I am a bit...afraid of her," she revealed.

"Why?" Damon wondered. "It's not like she is really that juvenile. She just puts on that act of being tough," he said. She didn't answer, but glanced over at the portal. It appeared to get smaller.

"We need to enter that portal before it closes," Aria stated.

"Is it going to close with us inside?!" I asked.

"Don't worry about that," she said.

"Is any of this freaking you out?" Damon asked me.

I thought about everything I've been through in the past months. "It can't be any worse than what we've already seen, right?" I said.

"Don't be so sure," Aria responded.

We entered into the light of the gateway into this unknown dimension. On the other side, the answers began to come. The place...the place it all began, stood before us.

"It's the castle," I said, feeling a little numb.

"This is the Gateway," Aria responded.

"The Gateway?" Damon asked.

Aria took a few steps and looked up at the massive structure. "The Gateway into Hell..." she further explained.

The entrance looked like how I remembered it from before, the Gothic structure with towers reaching towards a darkened sky. I couldn't get over how eerie it looked. The sky looked red mixed with gray clouds. The forbidding oak door stood tall above us. Aria put a hand on the door, pushing it open. There were still more questions I had to ask and didn't know when I would get a chance if I didn't ask now.

"Those words Kiara said before the portal opened, I remember those words. From the beginning of this chaos, I saw those words on the cement rim of the fountain on my school campus. What does that passage mean?" I asked.

"I'll tell you in a moment," Aria said. We walked into the foyer. The statues of armor still lined the walls and a red carpeted stairway led up to another large door.

"I remember this room," I said."

"Yeah, it looks familiar," Damon said.

"Of course, you've been here before. And to answer your question Hope, the passage is sacred to the fallen angels. This is their world. The Devil is God to them and God is the Devil," she said as a matter of fact.

"Unfortunately, the fallen angels are not the only ones that think that way," I said.

"I have not been here in a long time," Aria went on.

"What do you mean?" Damon asked her.

Aria looked annoyed. "This is not the time! We have to move!" she said as she aggressively walked across the floor to the next room.

Damon looked at me. "Uh, I'm still having issues with trusting her," he whispered.

"Aria? She does seem to be full of surprises," I agreed.

Although we felt this way, we knew we had no other choice but to trust in her.

"I found this shack outside the castle, just storage stuff in there," Damon told me. "I actually crawled through a hole in the back into the place. I believe I was in the basement and I walked through darkness, bumping into things on my way to the stairs leading up to the first floor. I found a room with pictures hanging and other stuff like vases and plates. The room with ancient weapons hanging on the walls and stuff is where I found the guns. They were the only weapons I could use. Everything else was too old and fell apart when I tried to use it," he explained.

"Wow! Really?" I asked.

"I don't remember much after fighting those vampire chicks in the halls...I found a large room with huge metal tables...and I found a spiral staircase," he said.

"Hold on," I said. I didn't meant to be rude by cutting in, but the mention of the large room returned a vision to me. "You saw this very large…enormous room. There were rows of tables," I asked. I thought Damon didn't see that room by the discussion we had months ago.

Aria paused from her steady walking. She looked fearfully at me. "Where was this room?" she asked.

I remembered just randomly going to rooms. I really couldn't recall the exact location of the room.

"I…I'm not sure. It was really large and these tables were metal and…just ugly. I can't imagine whatever used them," I said with a shiver.

Aria turned away from us. "The Nephilim…," she whispered. "And they were beds, not tables. Those giants were sent here and for some reason. This is where they lived. I still don't know why they were allowed to live in this castle instead of suffering in Hell," she said.

"Are any of them still here?" Damon asked sounding a little nervous.

"No. I don't believe they would be," Aria said shaking her head."

I suddenly remembered what Father Daniel told me at the church. He said he's seen Hell. I didn't ask too much about it to him. Maybe Aria knew what he meant.

"Do you know about the experience Father Daniel had with Hell?" I really blurted out that question. Aria turned to me surprised.

"Hope, how do you know….? He actually told you?" she asked.

"Whoa, what is all this?" Damon became curious.

I wasn't sure if Aria was upset that I knew about that. "He told me briefly. Um…was I not supposed to know that?" I asked.

Aria turned away and began walking, faster this time. I tried to keep pace with her.

"Aria…wait!" I called to her.

"We are wasting too much time with idle chit-chat," she said with disgust. "You don't need to know more about a place of eternal torment!" She exclaimed.

"She just asked if she should know about it," Damon intervened. "If we shouldn't know about it, then just tell us that," he said.

"Fine! You don't need to know about that!" Aria shouted at us.

She quickened her pace even more; Damon and I were running now to keep up with her. There was a familiar staircase and then a hall, then a larger room, the ball room, and another staircase.

"We're almost there," she said. "You two found this place before, you have no idea how close to the gateway you were," she warned us.

Upstairs and to the right, as I recalled, there was a wooden door. Aria tried to open it, but the door wouldn't budge. In a cry of aggravation, Aria kicked the door open. Damon looked at me with that fearful look again. Now Aria was in the room, we followed to find ourselves in the circular tower.

"We've been here before?" Damon asked.

Several large crates were stacked on top of each other in the far corner of the room.

"Oh, those are what you climbed up on, Damon?" I asked him.

"Yeah. There they are. Someone likes to move stuff on us," he said.

"The Nephilim use those as chairs. It gives you an idea of how large they are," Aria said bluntly.

I thought it was interesting how those creatures are known as Nephilim, but we are too. It was hard to believe I was related to such creatures.

"Are we waiting for something?" Damon asked. "We're just standing here," he said impatiently.

Aria looked really disturbed. "How could Kiara get through here, but we can't!" she said in frustration.

"Maybe he can help," Damon said pointing at a cloaked figure. The figure just showed up suddenly, floating inches off the ground. The white cloak it wore completely covered its face and body. It stood taller than all three of us.

"All will pay for their sins!" It spoke in a shallow voice.

"Let me speak with him," Aria said, carefully approached the strange being.

"I need to get to the gate," she spoke bravely.

"You are foolish to come here, Nephilim," it said. It was upsetting how I couldn't see a face. Maybe I didn't want to. He or it looked at me, then at Damon.

"So, you two decided to come back? I thought I gave you a fair warning to stay away from this place. Was letting you escape a mistake?" It said to us.

"Letting us escape?" Damon became boastful. "I'm the one that shot you! It didn't take more than one shot to get rid of you!" Damon arrogantly stated. Why did he choose now to act cocky?

The being just laughed in an eerie, hollow tone. "My, how arrogant we are. Arrogance is one of the deadly sins. I shall take note of that act," it said.

"Damon, please let me take care of this!" Aria snapped. She looked up at the being; it was disturbing that its height was even taller than her.

"I am sorry for this intrusion. I am Aria..."

"I know," the being answered. "I know Damon and Hope too... or I should say Angel Cry," it said.

Now I was deeply disturbed. What kind of name was that anyways? Is my father really that demented? Aria now looked lost in what to say next.

"Your father is Xander," the being said. What really got me was that he said that to Aria, not me.

"Wow, that Xander guy got around didn't he?" Damon smirked.

"You know him," Aria spoke solemnly. "You know that he believes he is higher than other Nephilim. He helped birth two offspring into the world on the same day and time to perform a sacred ritual for them to become gods, his two archangels," she stated.

"I know you are here looking for the other girl. She demanded to be let into the gateway," the cloaked being said.

"Kiara?" I let out a sudden outburst. "Why did you let her in?" I asked in my rage.

"She wants to know the truth, if there is a Hell. So I gave her the option to find out," the being said.

"But Kiara is still young," Aria stated. "She won't completely understand."

"I suppose I need to let you three in too," the being stated.

"Please," Aria spoke earnestly.

The tension built up now. I looked at Damon who stared at the figure in front of us. I think he was afraid, but he tried hard to cover up his emotions.

"The Nephilim twins will meet their fate. Nothing can stop it," the cloaked figure spoke.

Twins? I learned that Kiara was my half-sister. I really didn't consider us twins, we didn't come from the same mother. I guess the ritual bonded us so now we were considered twins.

"I know," Aria sighed deeply. "It's all right."

Wait! I didn't say it was all right! No one ever asked me what I wanted! They didn't ask Kiara either. That was probably the greatest reason why she was so angry all the time. No one asked either of us our permission for any of this! I couldn't take it! What the hell am I expected to do?!

While I had these thoughts, I didn't notice at first that the floor underneath our feet slowly began to disappear. We just seemed to float in this black void that overtook all of us. Now, all three of us were surrounded in darkness. Somehow I could still see Aria and Damon.

"The world is spiraling downward. Soon there really won't be a God anymore. We slip more and more into eternal darkness every passing day," Aria's grave words really upset me. Why would she say that?! God will always be there to those who seek Him.

"Where the hell are we?" Damon pounded. There was complete silence. This place was dead, no signs of life anywhere.

"So, that was the gate keeper or something?" Damon continued with the questions.

"You could call him that," Aria responded.

"I thought Jesus would be the one guarding the gate to Hell. Doesn't he give judgment?" His voice mocked.

"You sound sort of sour about that," Aria noted.

"Hey, I don't have a problem with Jesus. I just don't know why he has to be brought up all the time," Damon retorted.

"You're the one who brought Him up," I stated harshly. "And what's wrong about discussing Him anyways?"

"Well for one thing," Damon began. "People don't discuss it because of all the arguing it starts. You know, Christians profess Jesus is God and that is the only truth and everyone else is wrong. Other religions have a right to express themselves too, but they are told they are sinners who are going to Hell," he spit out these accusations so sternly. I felt like I was back in a religious discussion that I couldn't win. The same feeling came over me when I talked to Kiara. I hoped Damon would be more understanding.

"So, I take it that you don't believe in God either," I inferred.

"I believe in God. I'm not an atheist. I just see truth in all religions. Unlike Kiara, I'm not mad at God for anything. I'm not crazy; I don't want to destroy God--that would destroy life. But there are things I do that the church believes is evil. For example, that little séance we did," he reminded me.

I recalled how my sister and James, my stepfather acted when they found out. It did seem like the church was so cut-throat about those types of things. *They really should be more accepting of people. How are we supposed to share the love of God when we're judging everyone like that?*

"You know what?" I said. "You're right. There are too many judgmental people out there. I've been judged unfairly too. It's sad that people are treated that way. I was even judged by my own family. But...I don't believe that is how God wants us to be. I think that people, even Christians are guilty of being judgmental."

"How about this," Damon tried. "Let's put aside religious beliefs and just hold onto faith to get through this," he suggested. That had to have been the most gallant thing he's said yet. I nodded to him.

"So what now?"I asked. "Kiara is not here."

Suddenly Kiara appeared. She jumped towards Aria, kicking her to the ground. Aria laid on her back looking up at her. "How dare you follow me here!" Kiara rebuked her.

Aria jumped up to her feet. "How dare YOU come here!" Aria shouted at her. "Do you even realize what destroying God means?" she asked.

"Yeah, it means freedom! Freedom from everything!" Kiara cried.

"It means not existing! It means death!" Aria corrected.

"Fine! Then I'll die!" Kiara burst.

I was so tired of this girl that I couldn't see straight. "Will you grow up?!" I yelled. "You are just acting like a hurt child!"

Kiara looked at me, her sharp glare gave me a chill, but I did not back down, not this time! She walked over to me; her expression was more of hurt than anger. Her next sudden movement was slapping me across the face. It had such force that I felt a pinch of pain in my neck. She shouldn't have done that. I'm not as nice as I used to be.

"You wanna fight, you little witch?" I screamed. She harshly grabbed my shirt as if she intending on tossing me somewhere.

"Kiara! Stop this!" Aria warned. "Doing all of this will not bring your mom back!" Kiara let go of me, looking at Aria with hurt eyes. I saw them exactly as a child would look after being hurt.

"Shut up! You don't understand anything! YOU BITCH!" Kiara took her swords and once again tried to attack Aria. Aria moved away using this inhuman speed. She made a strong wind just by swinging her hand. The gust of wind knocked Kiara backwards to the ground.

"Kiara, you know that won't work. I just took down your friend Lyell, a much more powerful being," Aria warned her.

"Didn't we all take him down?" Damon whispered to me.

Kiara got up and ran away from us.

"Where is she going?" I wondered out loud.

"What do we do?" Damon looked frustrated now. I looked over at Aria who looked like she would cry. "I...I don't know what to do!" She breathed hard. "She doesn't know what she's doing. She won't be able to handle what's here," she explained.

I looked over at Kiara. She looked like she was so far away.

"Kiara stop, please!" Aria cried out as she started running towards Kiara. They both looked so far away, they actually looked smaller.

"I won't let you do this!" I heard Aria's voice echo.

"You can't stop me!" Kiara cried out in rage. "You are not my mother!"

"No! Your mother is dead!" Aria shouted. I heard the sound echoing of someone being slapped. I ran towards them now.

"Hey, wait!" Damon cried out. "Don't leave me alone in here!"

Aria was on her side. I looked over at Kiara again. This enormous gate stood before us. She was trying to open this gate! There was a tremendous screech as she pulled the handle. How she could move it was so far beyond me.

"She's going to do it," Aria said hopelessly.

"No! She can't go in there alone!" I said this feeling myself being pulled to Kiara. It was too much to comprehend. I couldn't describe it. I suddenly couldn't be without her. "I won't let her!" I cried out.

I ran toward Kiara. I saw this gigantic gate. Kiara had it open and she entered. I ran in after her just before it closed.

I heard the closing of the gigantic metal gate. I suddenly felt terrified. It was beyond darkness. I didn't think this kind of darkness existed. Then I heard crying and moaning. It grew more and more, becoming more intensified. I couldn't breathe. I recalled the air in the one cavern, I could barely breathe there. But now it was greatly increased. All at once, I saw the fiery blaze explode all around me. I looked around, there were cells; like jail cells and people were in there. There were these gigantic monsters...they tore the people apart. It happened over and over again, there wasn't any blood coming off these people. But they cried out in immense pain. In the distance, I saw a burning cross. There were many more like it appearing in a row. Then, I found myself by a pit of fire, people were down there too! Noting was left of them, just their skeletons. Their bony hands reached out, trying to escape, but they could barely move. There were monsters everywhere! They were taking joy in hurting these people! I couldn't take it! I just felt this hopelessness overcome me. I didn't even try to escape this time. I fell to my knees just feeling so weak.

Kiara...where are you?

Suddenly, I saw her. She stood by the furnace, looking down with this terror stricken face. I wanted to go to her, but I was too scared to move. In this total darkness except for fire, there was no comfort. But something made me turn my attention away from this pain to see a white light from the other direction. It was the only true light that came through this place. I had the strength to get to my feet. I ran to Kiara and grabbed her hand. There wasn't any resistance. I ran towards the light, not paying any attention to anything else. The light outlined the gate leading us out. I ran with

207

Kiara through gate, and then I pushed as hard as I could to close it. It was almost impossible to move, but it suddenly got easier. I noticed that Kiara was pushing the door closed too. Once it was shut, we fell to the ground I was shaking so badly. I could sense that Kiara felt the same way. There was only silence now. Suddenly Kiara started screaming.

"What...what is going on?! Those people...all those people..." Aria walked over to her and knelt down beside her.

"Kiara, it's all right. Your mom is not in Hell," she said to assure her.

Is that why she wanted to come here? To free her mom? No, I knew Kiara's mom was not in Hell because I saw her spirit in my house and at the hospital. But why did I see her at all? I really prayed she wasn't in that place I just saw. It was true. It hurt...no, it was worse than pain. I just wanted to die. Why did I see it? Was it a warning?

"Hope." I heard Damon's voice. I couldn't look at him. "Hope, what did you see?" He asked desperately. I felt his hand on my shoulder. It felt so warm, full of life.

As we all gathered there, another presence came.

"Look at this. This is one of those irreplaceable moments." I heard a deep voice speak.

"Xander?" Aria spoke with disgust. "What do you want? You realize you are trespassing onto sacred grounds?" she questioned him.

"Well, so are you," he responded rather cordially.

"I can't believe you were let in here. What did you do?!"

"I didn't do anything," he said sounding joyful. "I guess its part of God's plan."

"Don't you dare mention God! You should be in there with the rest of the misshapen monsters!" Aria cried out.

"Oh yes, I should be with them and all of you are so innocent. Of course all of our kind are destined to go there. But I think my daughters have suffered enough," Xander said mockingly.

He moved towards Kiara who seemed to be stuck in a daze. "Were you glad to get your mother's journal back?" he asked.

She suddenly snapped out of the numbness. I didn't quite understand why that spell was in her mother's journal or why she would use it. *Or perhaps Xander put it there?*

"You gave the book to Kiara," I concluded.

"My, you are bright," Xander mocked.

"What do you want from us?" Aria's voice shook a little when she spoke. "Are you still trying to get us on your side? Making us believe God is just a tyrant?"

"God is a tyrant!" Xander cried out. "You should know why we are here. Kiara understands. Isn't that right? God let your mother die and then tossed her into Hell. There is so much enjoyment that God receives from suffering," he spat out his lies.

"That is crap!" I yelled. "You don't know God! Everyone keeps saying how God wants suffering…how Christians want suffering… it's all wrong!" I shouted.

"Yes, you can believe that," Xander went on. "But where is your God now?" He finally asked.

That question, that repeated question. It finally clicked. "He's here," I said. "He's always been here." That was my answer. Xander laughed at me, of course.

"How gullible can you be? Kiara gets it," he turned to her again. "So I guess she will have to convince you. Tell your dear sister the truth. Both my daughters deserve at least that," he tried to persuade her.

"I am not your daughter!" I shouted in my greatest rage yet. It just hurt all over. I really thought that nothing would stop me from attacking him. I knew what Aria said, but I couldn't let him talk like that. He just mocked us over and over.

"My…Father…?" Kiara asked faintly.

Before our eyes, Xander changed, scales covered his body, his eyes turned black, his arms and legs looked thick as tree trunks.

"What is that?!" Damon cried out.

The fear I felt back in that horrid place beyond the gateway returned. He…it looked just like the creatures in that place. I turned my eyes over at Kiara. Suddenly two swords were in her hands. Charging at him, she pushed him to the ground in a rage. Raising her arms, the long blades appeared. "YOU KILLED MY MOM! IT'S YOUR FAULT!" She yelled staggering above him.

"Kiara! Don't!" Aria warned. Xander,or what was now Xander looked up at Kiara, showing his enormous teeth.

"Kiara, why do you look so scared?" The voice coming from this beast was beyond terrifying. It was painful to my ears to hear it.

"You have waited for revenge yet you are too afraid to take it?" Xander derided.

Amazingly, Kiara didn't back down. "I'M NOT SCARED!" she cried. "I'LL KILL YOU!" She spoke with strong words, but she looked like she would pass out.

Xander snickered crudely. "Oh, will you? You can barely stand," he teased. With a smirk, Xander kicked out at her legs, making her collapse. Now he stood, towering over her.

I looked at Aria. She just stood there! What's wrong with her?! Was she really that afraid of him? Kiara still spoke while lying on the ground. "My life has always been one nightmare after another...your fault..." Kiara's words became faint.

"What the hell is Kiara doing?" Damon wondered aloud. "Why is she acting that way?"

Suddenly, Xander did a full kick to Kiara's head. She didn't move.

"How sad, I thought you were the strong one," Xander vehemently stated. He now turned his eyes to me once again. He seemed to really enjoy this little game of his. "I hope you can put up a better fight," he jabbed at me.

I was sick of everything. All I wanted was peace. If killing Xander was the way, then that was fine with me. I guess I've had more of a violent side then I realized.

"So Angel Cry," Xander began.

"My name is Hope!" I yelled at him.

"You still don't realize who you are. Your given name is Angel Cry and Kiara's given name is Blood Child. You were to be as powerful as the Archangels Michael and Gabriel. Even though your mother disturbed the ritual, both you and Kiara can still succeed in becoming one ultimate power. Of course you also had to be of age. This day is the birth of you and your sister. Both of you are old enough to handle the change," Xander explained.

"So, we are supposed to be twins? Then why does she have a different mother than me?" I asked.

"It's part of the ritual, Aria spoke quietly. "Two women needed to give birth at the same time. I had to witness that terrible event. I only wished that I was as brave as your mother, Hope. I never should have let you and Kiara go through all of that," she said.

I realized that Damon was no longer standing beside me. He took advantage of the heated discussion to help Kiara. Xander suddenly noticed as well.

"Get away from her! You're not worthy of touching her!" He yelled warning Damon. Rushing at Damon, Xander took him by his shirt and flung him the opposite direction. I watched as Damon rolled over multiple times.

"Stupid boy! How dare you!" Xander fumed.

"You should know that Damon is just as strong as Kiara and me. He's survived the nightmares too," I told him.

Damon moved to his feet steadily. "You think I'm weak?" he asked.

"You? No. That's the problem," Xander said flatly.

I didn't understand any of this. What was Xander not telling us?

"Oh, I guess you stuck around just so you can get your weapons back? You don't really care about either of my daughters. You want them to die," he charged Damon.

"What are you talking about?" Damon looked as lost as I was. At this point I didn't care.

"Stop messing with everyone's head," Aria cautioned him.

Aria knew what was happening. I understood Kiara's frustration with her. Aria was keeping too many secrets.

"Aria, now would probably be the time to tell us what we don't know," I suggested to her.

She shook her head, which really ticked me off. "Tell us! I'm sick of all this!" I demanded.

"Forget it Hope!" Damon spoke with great irritation. "She's not gonna tell us anything. He's not gonna tell us anything..." He pointed at Xander. "And God doesn't give a damn!" He cursed.

"Don't say that!" Aria cried. "I can't tell you everything, not yet. You won't be able to understand it anyways," she stated.

"No," I said sternly. "That's it. I'm so tired. I don't care anymore. I just don't care. You and Xander figure out your issue, but I'm done!" I blasted.

I ended that remark by just walking away.

"Alright, alright! Yes, Xander is my father, and he's yours and Kiara's father too. I was born way before you two and I knew what your fate was. I told him I didn't want anything to do with it. But I didn't have a choice, he threatened me! And yes, he pretended to be me last summer. He did it so he could safely watch you and he wanted to get Kiara away from me. I'm the reason for your problems, it's all me!" Aria cried out.

I stopped walking. Xander was the one who masqueraded as her last year. I thought so. But why? Did Aria know what he was doing the whole time? Why didn't she say anything? Now, turning to Xander, I spoke.

"We won't do it! Whatever it is you want from us, we won't do it!" I yelled.

"Of course you will, how else will you stop me?" He said with an evil grin.

He disappeared suddenly, and we were back in the tower now.

"The guy just ran away," Damon ridiculed, "He must be scared or something," he joked.

Kiara finally woke up.

"Good morning," Damon greeted.

"W-what happened?" She asked looking around. "Where's Xander?"

"He's gone," Aria sighed. "I'm so sorry."

Kiara gave a sudden scream of frustration. I couldn't blame her. She ran to the tower door, flinging it open.

"Kiara, wait!" I ran after her. I followed her down the stairs to the ballroom. "Kiara, hold on," I called. She turned focusing me.

"What do you want? Leave me alone already!" She yelled at me.

"We are not finished," I told her. "We have to stop Xander."

"What do you think I'm doing?" she asked in an aggravated tone.

"You can't do it alone," I said. She walked away. This was so stupid. Did she really want to do everything on her own?

She stopped in the next hallway. As I approached her, her hardened expression changed to sorrow. She actually started to cry.

"Mom...do you hate me?" she sobbed. I never saw Kiara like this. She was showing emotion like a normal person. "I can't stand this! I thought she was in Hell because God sent her there. That is what Lyell told me. That's why I came here. I thought I would find God and I could demand my mom back," she cried.

212

"I know you are angry with God. It's all right. I have to admit that I am mad at God too. I wish people didn't have to suffer. But you know I believe that it was God who got us out of that place. I saw this light and without it, I wouldn't have known where to run," I revealed to her.

"I didn't see a light; all I saw was darkness. Why wouldn't God help me?" She asked me.

"He did! And He is still with us whether you want to see Him or not," I told her.

"Or Her," Kiara imposed the possibility of God being female.

I couldn't help but smile, "Whatever. You have your beliefs too," I said.

"Don't you think I'm going to Hell for those thoughts?" she asked.

"It is not for me to judge. I already told you I don't like the idea of Hell, but I know that it exists. God never created Hell for humans," I told her.

"I was so young when I saw my mom die. I watched as she was beaten...and I did nothing," Kiara revealed to me in tears.

"You were just a child," I reminded her.

"I could have done something! Try to stop him...," she said sounding dissatisfied.

"Well, we can stop him now!" I assured her.

Kiara looked at me.

"You are braver than I gave you credit for. I'm sorry for the way I treated you, I am sorry for how I treated everyone...it hurt, I can't get that day out of my mind. And since then, terrible things happened to me. I went from foster home to foster home with people who did not know me, but tried to control me. I went to church with these people and I was told I was a sinner and going to Hell. I don't believe anyone should go there. You saw those people... What did they do to deserve it?" She blurted out.

"You know, I sometimes wondered if Hell was just a state of mind, but we just actually saw it..." I told her, trying to make sense of it.

"Just stop!" Kiara pleaded, shouting. "I don't want to discuss it anymore!"

"I don't know what else to say!" I said feeling frustrated.

She turned away. "Don't say anything," she sobbed. Finally, Damon and Aria showed up. Strange, Kiara's demeanor changed. Turning to Damon, she embraced him.

From where I stood, their expressions were one of contentment.

"I'm glad to see your human side again," Damon told her.

It struck me hard, seeing them together. They had dated at one time. Did they still have feelings for each other? I really liked Damon. But I never told him. That's just like me!

"We need to go!" Aria shouted to us.

She rushed past all of us. I really didn't want anything to do with her. But Kiara followed after her alongside Damon. I guess I couldn't stay here.

At full speed, all four of us ran down the flight of stairs that led into the atrium. We were almost at the door when this darkness engulfed us.

"Oh, not now!"I heard Aria whine.

"What the hell is this?" That was Damon's voice. I couldn't see anyone!

"Damon! Hope! Can you hear me?" That was Kiara.

"Don't stop moving forward!" Was that Aria again?

I listened to it even though I felt lost in this dark cloud. The door opened, I don't know who opened it and we all got through. As I turned back to the doorway, I saw a woman with dark hair. I've seen her before, my room, the hospital…

Kiara saw her too, "…Mom…." Now she started running back towards the door.

"No Kiara!" The woman cried. "Go! Go!"

Kiara was suddenly stopped by Aria who held her tight. There was a blinding light, and the castle was gone. Kiara who struggled in Aria's grip just fell to her knees. "Mom!" She gave a final cry and threw her head to the ground, sobbing. Aria tried to comfort her.

"NO! GO AWAY! JUST GO AWAY!" Kiara screamed.

"NO!" Aria's sharp voice broke through Kiara's ranting. "No more running! You keep pushing me away, but I'm the one who cares about you! Your mother is gone, Kiara! Nothing will change that!"

Kiara kept sobbing, pounding her fists into the ground.

"She saved us," Aria whispered. "I love you Rein. Goodbye." I thought I heard Aria cry a little too.

Chapter Twenty Two:
Eternal Battle

I felt the chill of the wind; I had no idea where we were now. As my vision returned from that light, I saw my house across the street. Everyone else was with me too.

"How did we get here?" I asked out loud.

A car pulled into the driveway, James' car. Of all the people I had to see right now...

He got out; he didn't notice all of us standing there. It was Aria who first began walking towards him. The rest of us just sort of followed.

As we approached the driveway, I saw James at the passenger door. Opening it, I saw my mother climb out. She looked so drained, like the essence of her life got pulled out of her. He held her arm, leading her to the door.

"Excuse me," Aria called to him. James looked over at us for the first time. He looked shocked, not expecting company. He studied all of us, then he looked directly at me.

"W-what do you want? Look, my wife was just released from the hospital..." he stuttered as he spoke

"I'm sorry," Aria told him. "We don't mean to intrude, but your family is in danger."

That's putting it mildly.

"And I'm supposed to trust you?" James made an outburst. "You and your demon friends?" He asked indignantly.

"Demon friends?" Damon whispered the question. "What the hell is he talking about?"

"When I went to see my mom at the hospital, he and my sister Charsi were there too," I began explaining. "He...called me a demon," I said.

"That's stupid!" Kiara spat out. I never expected her to stand up for me.

"Leave or I'm calling the police!" James finished. After that threat, he took my mother into the house. It hurt to see my mother like this. She barely looked alive.

"Call the police?" Damon questioned. "Yeah, and tell them to bring the National Guard with a tank to take care of the monster on our backs!" he spat out.

With everything that happened to us already, that was enough to drive anyone into madness. But now we were all being treated like criminals. Everyone has always hated me! It started with those kids pushing me off the cliff, and the ostracizing never stopped. Xander started all of this because of that ritual. If he tried to hurt my mom and sister...there are no words strong enough for me to come up with. I was just so furious. I wanted to show my family that I wasn't a monster, but I wasn't sure if it were possible now. Not after what I've done.

"He won't touch them," I felt the inside of me burn. "I'll do whatever it takes to stop him!" I cried out.

"You're not alone in this," Kiara spoke.

I turned to her, "You're not mad at me?" I asked.

"No! I'm mad at him!" she said dramatically. She didn't say his name, but I knew she meant Xander. I think 'mad' was an understatement.

We raced through the front door. As we barged into the living room, I saw my mom laying on the couch, James knelt beside by her. They sensed the disturbance of us entering. He turned his attention to us. He looked on guard now.

"Why won't you just leave my family alone?" he begged.

I ignored him, moving over to see my mother. Her eyes looked up with a blank stare. As we stood around, James suddenly got thrown back into the wall by an invisible force. My mom snapped out of her trance and sat up.

"James! What in the world?" she cried. Suddenly Xander appeared by her. He looked human again. Well as 'human' as he could appear. He towered over everyone, even Aria. He had to be over seven feet tall, I realized.

"Hello Amira. My, it's been a long time," Xander said in an eerie tone. By the look of terror on my mother's face, I would say she prayed that she would never see him again. I didn't think I could be anymore enraged by this guy until now.

"If you touch her, I'll kill you!" I screamed. My voice was so sharp it could cut him.

The edges of his mouth curved up into this nasty grin. "Oh, I'm not going to hurt your dear mother. Why would I hurt someone I deeply love?" He asked pretending to be concerned.

"Love?!" I barely choked out the word.

In that loathing moment, Charsi came bouncing down the stairs. That girl has awful timing.

"W-what's going on?" She asked looking around fearfully.

James finally moved. He raced at Xander, a really stupid move to charge a demon. And he acted like he knew so much about them. Xander turned around, grabbed James by his arms and flung him to the other side of the room. I heard a crack and I hoped his neck didn't break.

"Xander..., my mom tried to sound forceful. "You know God will strike you down if you continue this," she warned him.

"He cares nothing about you humans. When will you understand?" Xander said with a wicked laugh.

"Hope?!" My younger sister seemed happy to see me. She ran to me. "What's happening? I'm so scared," Charsi cried.

I kept my eyes on Xander. I felt almost helpless. I wanted to stop him, but nothing we did seemed to work. That is when I realized that I did not just feel my rage, I felt Kiara's too.

"Why do you want them?" I asked. "They don't care about me," I said this knowing James' reaction to me earlier.

"What?" Charsi spoke. "Hope, don't say that!"

I was not sure if that was really the case, but maybe Xander would leave them alone if he saw no emotional connection between us.

"Yes, well maybe because they think you are not being a good Christian, staying out all night, doing séances, spending time with boys...," Xander said. His gaze went to my younger sister, "Right Charsi?" She shook her head.

"How do you know me?" Charsi asked in a trembling voice.

"I've been watching you, all of you," he said looking around the room. "See, after you took Angel Cry away from me, Amira, I had to find a way to get her back. I chose to impersonate Aria to gain Hope's trust and my spy Lyell did a good job keeping Kiara in check," Xander explained.

I looked at Kiara who turned pale. "Lyell...." She spoke distantly.

"Oh yes, you know Lyell. He worked at the club. He was a good friend of yours Kiara?" He asked knowingly.

I still don't know why I started feeling Kiara's emotions, but by now they were really intense. She thought of Lyell as more than just a friend. He took care of her.

"Oh did Lyell ever get his cards back?" Xander smiled gleefully, really enjoying the dismay he caused.

"The cards?" I asked.

Xander swiftly moved in on Charsi, drawing a dagger from under his cloak, he held the blade to her neck. Looking at Charsi, she didn't know how to respond to his attack. She stood there, frozen in fear.

"Charsi, you silly girl," Xander hummed. "You thought your sister actually was a Satanist because you found those cards in her bag? My how the church screws up its people," he taunted her. The tarot cards. They belonged to Lyell. He put them in my bag then.

"You tried everything to separate me from my family," I concluded.

"Yes, and it worked!" Xander sounded like he was bragging.

I tried to remain in control. On the inside, my mind raced with all sorts of thoughts. I was mad at Charsi before and even tried to kill her myself, but I really didn't mean to do all that. Would Xander leave her alone if he thought I didn't care? Would he leave everyone else alone too?"

"I…I don't care about her," I said attempting to sound convincing.

"So you don't care if I slash her?"

My mother suddenly got up. She tried to rush at Xander. I didn't expect that.

"Oh please Amira, don't insult me!" Xander chided her. Another force pushed her backward into a lamp, knocking it over. It crashed on the floor. The light flickered, then the room was dark.

"I guess I could have killed you by now, Amira. But I think you're daughter is mad enough now," he said.

"You tried to kill her!" I screamed at Xander. "Of course I am mad!" I yelled.

"Oh no, if I wanted to kill her, she would be dead. I just put her in a coma for a while. Just to get your attention," he said tortuously.

Kiara shook her head. "You are sad! Let's end this already!" She exclaimed.

"No, that's what he wants," I said starting to understand. We couldn't become these creatures he wanted us to change into. We couldn't give him that power over us. I knew we couldn't get enraged; we couldn't lose control. "I'm not losing control." I thought if we acted indifferent to what Xander did, he wouldn't involve anyone else.

"Kiara are you mad?" I gave her a cunning smile. I think she understood where I was going.

"No. I'm not mad at all," she answered. Inside, I wish I could just tear him apart!

"Not her then?" Xander asked the strange question. "Okay," he agreed.

Xander smiled and tossed Charsi aside. Moving at inhuman speed, Xander rushed past Kiara and I towards Damon. Damon didn't even see it coming. Grabbing his arm, Xander threw our friend into the wall, almost hitting the television set. He laid there next to James who still was out. Damon was still conscious, however. In the next second, Xander was practically on top of the boy with the dagger, driving the blade into his chest. Damon gasped and I saw Xander lean down, whispering something to him before withdrawing the dagger. I cannot fully describe the painful feeling inside of me and it was intensified by Kiara's feeling too. Both of us felt strongly toward Damon and Xander knew that.

"All of you are pathetic!" Xander shouted, then looked at Aria. "I know your emotions, Aria. You're afraid. You've always been a frightened little girl!" He mocked her.

I looked at Aria; she kept her head down not even looking at him. How could she let him have that power over her?

Xander looked at Kiara and I. "We will see who is stronger!" Xander challenged. He took his dramatic leave. He was always running away!

"Get back here you coward!" Kiara shouted. She started running after him. I followed her outside. Xander stood there waiting for us.

I suddenly felt myself drawn to Kiara. Our souls combined and we acted as one being.

"You see Hope. We are connected." I suddenly heard Kiara's thoughts. *"Remember I said that I saw you and Damon at the hospital? I've seen you guys other times too. When you were fighting those monsters, did you feel me there?"*

Now that I thought of it, I always felt another presence with me during the battles I faced. I looked at our opponent. It was Kiara and I against this false god who called himself our father. I prayed that we would still have free will and not lose control.

"We still have free will," Kiara's mind spoke to me. *"We need to end this, finally…just end it,"* her thoughts said to me.

We finally joined together. We entered each other's thoughts and finally, I understood Kiara's every feeling and beliefs as she understood mine.

"Now you probably understand why I am this way," Kiara sent her thoughts to my mind.

"And now you understand that I'm not the person you thought I was" my thoughts responded to her.

"You are in pain too," her mind spoke. *"I'm sorry I didn't understand that,"* her thoughts said.

Kiara and I joined fully. We had wings that were pure white. We stood side by side in battle. I held the swords that found me at the sanctuary. The weapons I had from the beginning of all this. Kiara held her swords; we were ready.

Xander's appearance changed before our eyes. He became the beast we saw at the gateway. This time, he had wings, battered and torn, the whiteness had faded.

I was afraid, but I knew I was not alone. I had Kiara, and there was a part of me that still had my faith. Was God with us now? I wasn't sure when all this began happening to me. But now, I felt stronger than I ever have before in my life. If God is here and if He cares, we will win this fight. My thoughts went to Kiara.

"We can stop him…together," my thoughts said to her.

We looked up at this creature, our father. It felt strange to address him as such. But we needed to understand this. Finally, we sprang into the air. We followed in pursuit. As we flew higher, darkness engulfed us.

"I can't see!" My thoughts raced.

"I can still see," Kiara's thoughts said. This time, she took my hand, guiding me.

We dove down at him, slashing at him with our blades. He cried out from pain. Blood poured out from his wounds. I was amazed. He was the first monster I fought that bled. What did that mean? In return, he rushed at us, knocking us backwards toward the ground. We didn't fall too far. We were right back in his face, slashing him some more. I still couldn't see, but I still knew where our enemy was thanks to Kiara. She slashed at his side, trying to avoid his massive arms. He cried out again; his cries sounded victorious each time we hit him. I didn't understand this, but at the time I didn't really care. He was going down!

"I wonder if we are wearing him down," my thoughts dwindled.

"Looks like it," Kiara's thoughts responded. *"Just keep striking until he falls!"* Her thoughts yelled out.

Our blades stuck him; we flew in circles and in opposite directions from each other throwing off our opponent. He appeared disoriented, wavering about trying to grab us. Xander looked sort of foolish. Do they become dumber when they get bigger?

Suddenly, he rushed at us again, making us fall farther downward.

"Let's try attacking him from behind," Kiara's thoughts suggested to me.

Swooping upward and around his back seemed to be a task in itself. He saw the attack before we did it. He turned around so he still faced us. Once again, he raised his arms creating a whirl wind that engulfed us. It threw us back, making us feel dizzy and nauseous. Then, we felt a jolt as each gigantic arm smacked us hard enough for us to fall straight to the ground.

"This is not working!" my thoughts cried out. I felt so frustrated. *"He just keeps throwing us toward the ground,"* my thoughts said to Kiara.

"Maybe we need to stay down here so he'll come to us," Kiara's thoughts suggested. We both stood now, waiting for him. No one was around; everything was silent. It was as if we were the only beings on this Earth. Xander landed in front of us.

"What's wrong, girls? Are you too weak to stop me?" he taunted us.

I was already angry enough. He didn't need to aggravate me further. Kiara sent out another feeling. She just studied him calmly.

"Kiara, what are we doing?" I asked her with my thoughts.

"We can't just tire ourselves out. We need to weaken him using as little effort as possible," her thoughts relayed to me.

Well, yeah I got that, but how were we supposed to do that?

Xander went to grab Kiara, but when he did, he cried out in pain, wincing back. I looked to see her arms glowing red. Both of her arms were in the same glow and I noticed that mine were too.

"No more! It's over!" Kiara's thoughts stated furiously. We followed our instincts, charging at Xander, pushing him to the ground. Readying our weapons, we attacked his wings, shredding them. He looked mortal without them. With our next movements, we took our blades and ran him through. He looked intently at us, then collapsed. He was still alive--he breathed in a hard gasp of air.

"Finally, I waited to see your power. You defeated me as I knew you would. You are strong enough now," he said attempting to pacify us with that statement.

Our emotions were of great loathing. We stared coldly at him.

"Actually, we kicked your ass and now we can begin to live our lives normally again!" Kiara spoke hotly.

"Normal is far from what we are. You want to live a normal life in a world that doesn't accept you? You think you've won? You just proved to humans that you are monsters. No one will ever trust you. You're offspring of the Nephilim, of the fallen angels, and you will spend eternity in Hell!" Xander still taunted us.

"No, I won't see that place again!" Kiara shouted. Her feelings were strongest on that thought.

"You're wrong," I told Xander. "We still have a choice. We can't give into darkness just because of the bad experiences we have. We always want to blame someone else instead of fixing the problem. You're plan almost worked. I was mad at God. And after seeing all those people in that place…" I almost began to cry, but I made my emotions harden. "I guess I've finally grown up and I understand that it's my choice to be happy or sad. We always have a choice," I stated.

Xander exploded in laughter as his body began to burn and the wind blew his ashes away.

"It is not done yet!" He called out. Those were the words he spoke before he faded away.

"Is he really gone?" I wondered.

"Yeah, I think so," Kiara answered.

When Kiara and I defeated Xander, the feeling of gloom in the environment faded away. We were in the mortal world again. After entering my house, I looked around at the ones I called my family. James woke up and looked around the room.

"What happened?" He asked out loud.

"Hope, Kiara…"Aria began.

"You don't need to tell us anything anymore," I said to her. "We found out everything ourselves," I said coldly. I couldn't help but be a little annoyed. She could have saved us a lot of trouble by just telling us what we needed to know earlier.

"I couldn't tell you," she answered anyways. "I know you and Kiara are angry but…" she tried to say.

"Hope and I defeated Xander," Kiara spoke quietly. "I don't need to deal with anything else now," she said.

I looked down at Damon, just laying there. He couldn't be dead…he couldn't. Kiara sat beside his body, putting her head on his shoulder.

"Damon…" she whispered. "I'm sorry. This wasn't supposed to happen, not like this." She put her hand on his chest where he was stabbed.

It was just wrong. We had a victory, but also a defeat. I couldn't let Damon die! Not after everything we'd survived. I sat on the other side of Damon, across from Kiara. I touched his wound, right beside Kiara's hand. We just sat there. I didn't know exactly what we were doing. This light came from our hands, a small spark grew into a glowing light and engulfed the gash. As the light grew, the wound became smaller until it was completely healed. Damon began breathing again. He was alive! Now he opened his eyes and looked around cautiously.

"Whoa, I have two chicks on me!" He exclaimed. Kiara and I rolled our eyes and grinned. Only Damon would make a joking comment even after nearly losing his life. Kiara looked over at me.

"Listen to him, thinking he's a lady's man," she said. We both laughed.

By Aria's surprised look, I guess she didn't expect this.

"You two can heal others?" She questioned. "Not even Xander, with his great power, could heal."

I couldn't believe after all this, she still thought of him in awe.

"Aria," I said, "Xander is gone. You don't have to be afraid anymore."

She didn't say anything, she just had this blank stare on her face. I don't think we'll ever know what is really going on with her.

My attention turned to my family. I wasn't quite sure I could call them that again. "Who? What....what's going on?" James seemed disoriented. "Who or what was that thing in here and how can you people just have these weird powers?" He asked being disoriented.

I stood now, regarding James with confidence for a change.

"You believe I am a demon, you believe my friends are demons...but we aren't. We didn't choose to be born this way. I have free choice and I am not a monster," I told him.

I felt the sudden urge to say everything I felt.

"You know what? It hurt what you said at the hospital!" I lashed out at James.

"How could you just say those things? Then we show up to help and you threaten to call the police?"

"James?" My mother spoke harshly. "You really think Hope is some demonic creature?" She stood up off the couch. "I thought you understood! I thought you accepted who I am and who Hope is! If you can't get over this phobia about demons and monsters living under your bed, then you're not the man I thought you were!" She blasted at him.

That was interesting? Does James have fear of demons being around him? I wondered.

He gave a heavy sigh. "I'm sorry Amira."

"Don't say sorry to me! Say it to Hope, your daughter!" She demanded.

He turned to me, but I didn't want his apology if it would be forced.

"I'm sorry," he finally spoke. "You are my daughter and I should have tried to help you," he apologized.

Was that it? I've been in agony for a long time! He had no idea! I chose not to say anything.

"I...was scared. I grew up in the church, the idea of demons and Hell is so terrifying to me. I really don't like the idea," James admitted.

At that moment, I felt closer to him than ever before. He had the same thoughts I did. I never knew that was how he felt.

"I'm always too cautious, looking over my back," he finished.

"Yeah, and I'm sorry too Hope," Charsi said. Her apology actually sounded genuine. "I was mad at you for how you attacked me, but...I guess I deserved it," she finished turning her head away from me.

"Oh Hope! My Hope! You are so strong!" Mom said as she walked over to me hugging and kissing me. She looked at Damon and Kiara.

"Thank you for being true friends to Hope. I felt just so awful that I couldn't do anything for her," Mom said to them.

"I don't know how much of a friend I've been to her," Kiara whispered. "Or to anyone," she ended the sentence before walking towards the door.

"Kiara?" Aria called. But she didn't respond. She opened the front door and was gone.

"I should thank you too," my mom said to Aria.

Aria's eyes saddened, her mouth was a straight line.

"No, you shouldn't," she looked past everyone. "Excuse me."

She said as she walked past us to the door. I guess she was once again going after Kiara. She really did feel like she was that girl's mother.

Chapter Twenty Three:
True Understanding

Weeks passed; I tried to catch up with my studies. I wanted to just drop my classes, but Charsi wouldn't let me.

"Don't give up, you're almost done!" She kept saying.

My life was normal again with my family. I liked it that way. It was amusing when the change in my hair grabbed attention. Charsi was the first to realize my hair looked different. They assumed I dyed it and I won't correct them. Nothing more was said about the events for the past several months. I think they just wanted to walk away from it all.

Some weeks past, it was mid April and finals week soon approached. The trees were filled with new buds and the snow quickly melted away by the warm sun. It was on Sunday that I went to St. Mary's with Damon and Aria. Damon actually walked into the church! Kiara wasn't there. I thought after what she saw, she would think differently about God and the church. Maybe, she wasn't ready yet.

Now that the elder priest was gone, Father Daniel had the main responsibility, which meant he finally could make his dream of changing the church for the better come true. His talk was about prayer and speaking in tongues. I remembered how he prayed for me in tongues that one day. It is said that people can be healed by prayer. When Kiara and I healed Damon, I prayed as hard as I could. Kiara prayed too, I heard her thoughts. Suddenly, I really missed her.

As we left, Aria made an interesting comment.

"Remember Father Paul, the priest that got killed here?" She asked me in whisper.

I nodded.

"He never worked for God, he was in the church for money," she told me.

"What do you mean?" I wondered.

"Not everyone in the church is saved," she said. I recalled that Father Daniel said the same thing. "Maybe now that he's gone, people can come here and receive the real gospel," she revealed.

At first, it struck me hard how cold Aria sounded. But maybe she was also sick of the jabs Christians got because of those who only claimed to walk in the Word, who didn't.

The next week passed in a blur. I walked along the sidewalk on campus, feeling the relief after I finished my last final. How I survived everything, I really don't know. This is why I always believed in God. There had to have been a higher power involved helping me through everything. I approached the middle of the campus to see a familiar face sitting by the fountain. It was Kiara. Why was she here? I walked towards her feeling excited, and somewhat nervous.

"Kiara?" I asked. .

She looked up at me. I noticed she held her mother's journal.

"Oh, hello," she said and not much else.

"How are you?" I asked.

"Fine," she assured.

"What have you been doing?" I tried to make conversation.

"Nothing," she said.

Her casual tone towards me was unsettling.

"Kiara!" I tried to get more of a response from her.

She focused more on the journal than me. Her facial expression was emotionless; her eyes casually drawn to what she was reading. When I got closer to see the page she read from, she abruptly slammed the book shut.

"I'm not working at the club anymore," she said. Her voice was indifferent.

"Oh, what happened?" I asked being interested.

Her eyes narrowed into a peculiar glance.

"Lyell! Hello?!" She reminded me.

Why was she being like this? I can't read her mind...oh, I guess I can now... but I really didn't want to. She can still speak to me like a normal person.

"Are you mad at us for what happened to Lyell?" I cautiously asked her.

"No, don't think that," she said suddenly. "I was mad you guys killed him. But I didn't know he was on *his* side," she said meaning Xander when she said '*his*.' "I just feel betrayed now," she said.

"I didn't know who or what he was. I knew he had powers and he told me I had powers too. But I...thought he cared about me," she opened up telling me.

I wavered on my feet, wondering what I could say.

"Are you living with Aria, again?" I tried to change the subject. She was quiet now.

"Aria isn't around right now. She left without a word," she explained.

"Aria was a bit strange," I admitted.

"He abused her!" Kiara spat out. "That was why she was afraid of him," she told me.

I figured that Xander did hurt Aria; he hurt a lot of women.

"Forget him Kiara. He's gone now. We're free!" I rejoiced.

Kiara jumped suddenly to her feet with a rush of energy.

"I don't know why I'm hanging around this place anyway!" She blurted out moving away from me. I felt her hurt feelings. She really didn't want to see or deal with anyone she knew. She didn't want to even see Fallen Ridge anymore. I had to say that I was sick of this small backwater town too.

"Hold on!" I tried. "Don't just fade away on me. You're not alone anymore. We know who we are and we're together..." I pleaded with her.

"I don't know why I'm alive," she said numbly.

"What? Why would you say that?" I asked.

"All those people...down there. I hear those crying souls still. I can't get them out of my head. And my mother...she was at the castle, so she's suffering too," she cried.

"No, just because she was at the castle, doesn't mean she's in Hell," I explained.

"Then where is she?!" Kiara asked me. I really didn't know what to say.

"Come on, I don't have all the answers! Some things need to be left to faith," I told her.

"I don't have any faith left..." she spoke softly.

"You know that isn't true. I've told you before, I'm here. You can rely on someone else for a change," I assured her.

Suddenly, she suddenly embraced me. I never knew what to expect next with this girl. The bond I felt between us made me feel stronger, I didn't want that feeling to go away.

"You are the one who is strong," she whispered. "I wanted to give up. You kept me going. Goodbye…" she said. Her voice choked. She pulled away. I watched her walk through the grass towards the street. In a few moments, she was completely out of sight. The overwhelming emotion pushed down on me. I just sat on the side of the fountain wondering if I'd ever see her again. Tears welled up in my eyes. This time I didn't even care if others saw me. As I sat there, an elderly lady walked with a basket of roses. She stopped in front of me.

"Here dear, this will make you feel better," she said as she handed it to me by the long stem. She moved on after that. I really believed that the world was still good. The whole world hadn't gone completely to Hell yet. There were still good people out there.

There was something I still needed to do, something that would finally calm my soul. I walked all the way to the outskirts of town, to that park I went to in my childhood. I made my way up the steep hill. I stared down the side of the cliff. It appeared to be higher than I remember. Below me, waves crashed into the large rocks by the shore. It was so long ago that I was pushed off this cliff, but that memory would always burn inside my mind.

I stayed still for a moment, as if waiting for something to happen. The wind howled and I thought I heard something else, too. It was faint at first. The sound grew louder, there were kids appearing around me. I looked at them and realized they were just that…kids. I was so much bigger than them. The children began chanting,

"Die witch! Die witch!"

But I would not die! Not now! Not like this! The blades I had used so many times before came to my hands. One by one, I cut all of the little demons down. One could be as foolish as to call them just children, but to me, they weren't. I made sure each of them would perish. I would not see this horrid memory again!

The children were gone. Someone else was there. I shook my head in loss of words.

"No! What the hell is this?!" I shrieked.

Xander was here. He showed that sinister smile.

"Angel Cry, you are the worthy one," he said confidently.

"No!" I swung the blade at him, but it went through him as if he were just an image.

"Ah yes, this must be a frightening scene for you. This is where it all began, the pain. You fell off this cliff...and you lived. You knew you were different," he said.

"Why?! Why are you still here?!" I demanded to know.

His pathetic grin just infuriated me.

"Don't think it's just you, I plan to see my other daughter too. But you are the real special one. After seeing what happened at the Gateway, I knew you were the stronger one. Those visions you saw. They are the future you and your sister will make.

"What? No. I don't want that to happen!" I exclaimed.

Xander laughed, mocking me again. I was so sick of him!

"Of course you do. You want the wretched humans to suffer. You are the offspring of the fallen angels. You are the same as them. But you need a leader. I am the god that created my archangels, Angel Cry and Blood Child," he said proudly.

"Stop calling us those weird names! Her name is Kiara and my name is Hope!" I cried out.

"No, not anymore. Not ever again will you be known by those mundane names. I am so proud of you, my daughter," he said. His words made me cringe.

"Just go away! Go away!" I kept screaming.

I closed my eyes. I didn't want to see him.

The disturbance left. I dared to open my eyes; he actually was gone. I stood on the edge of the cliff. This overwhelming feeling took over my body. I suddenly fell backwards. It felt like I was floating downward. Something caught me. I felt a radiant presence from all around me. I felt peace as the angelic being held me. I finally felt...peace.

I woke up in my bed. All around me was silence. I knew that everything was fine now. It is said that everyone is put on this Earth for a purpose, and I am going to learn mine.

Biblical References

These are some examples of scripture that back up issues discussed in the story. There are many more verses which relate to the topics, but I chose ones I felt had a particular significance.

The Nephilim

"And it came to pass, when men began to multiply on the face of the Earth, and daughters were born unto them, that the sons of God saw the daughters of men that they were fair; and they took them wives of all which they chose." (Genesis 6:1-2 King James Version)

"There were giants on the earth in those days, and also afterward, when the sons of God came in to the daughters of men and they bore children to them." (Genesis 6:4 KJV)

"Indeed his bedstead was an iron bedstead...Nine cubits is its length (approximately 13ft.)" (Deuteronomy 3:11 KJV)

"And it came to pass when the children of men had multiplied that in those days were born unto them beautiful and comely daughters. And the angels, the children of the heaven, saw and lusted after them....And all took unto themselves wives...and the women became pregnant, and they bare great giants...the giants devoured mankind...devoured one another's flesh and drank blood." (Book of Enoch)

Speaking in Tongues

"For as yet he was fallen upon none of them; only they were baptized in the name of Lord Jesus. Then laid they their hands on them and they received the Holy Ghost." (Acts 8:16-17 KJV)

Demons

"…Immediately there met him out of the tombs a man with an unclean spirit who had his dwelling among the tombs, and no man could bind him, not with chains." (Mark 5:2-3 KJV)

"And always night and day, he was in the mountains and in the tombs, crying and cutting himself with stones. But when he saw Jesus afar off, he ran and worshipped him,
And cried with a loud voice, and said, What have I to do with thee, Jesus, thou Son of the most high God? I adjure thee by God, that thou torment me not.
For he said unto him, come out of the man, thou unclean spirit.
And he asked him, "What is thy name?" And he answered, "My name is Legion: for we are many." (Mark 5:5-9 KJV)

"Now there was there nigh unto the mountains a great herd of swine feeding.
And all the devils besought him, saying, send us into the swine, that we may enter into them.
And forthwith Jesus gave them leave. And the unclean spirits went out and entered into the swine: and the herd ran violently down a steep place into the sea." (Mark: 5:11-13 KJV)

Hell
"They shall go down to the bars of the pit." (Job 17:16, KJV)

"And the devil that deceived them was cast into the lake of fire and brimstone, where the beasts and false prophets are, and shall be tormented day and night for ever and ever." (Revelations 20:10 KJV)

"And whosoever was not found written in the book of life was cast into the lake of fire." (Revelations 20:15 KJV)

www.ingramcontent.com/pod-product-compliance
Lightning Source LLC
Chambersburg PA
CBHW072232170626
46813CB00003B/1185